SANTA'S MOST ELIGIBLE

The Marry Me Series

SANTA'S MOST ELIGIBLE

Vivi Barnes
Julia Silverwood
Amy Christine Parker

Published by Infinity House Creative

Library of Congress Control Number: 2025916538

Cover Design and Artwork: Books and Moods

ISBN (paperback): 979-8-9890150-3-0

Also by the Authors

Books by Vivi Barnes

Olivia Twisted

Olivia Decoded

Paper or Plastic

Books by Julia Silverwood

The Ninth Realm (Coming Soon)

Books by Amy Christine Parker

Gated

Astray

Flight 171

You're Dead to Me

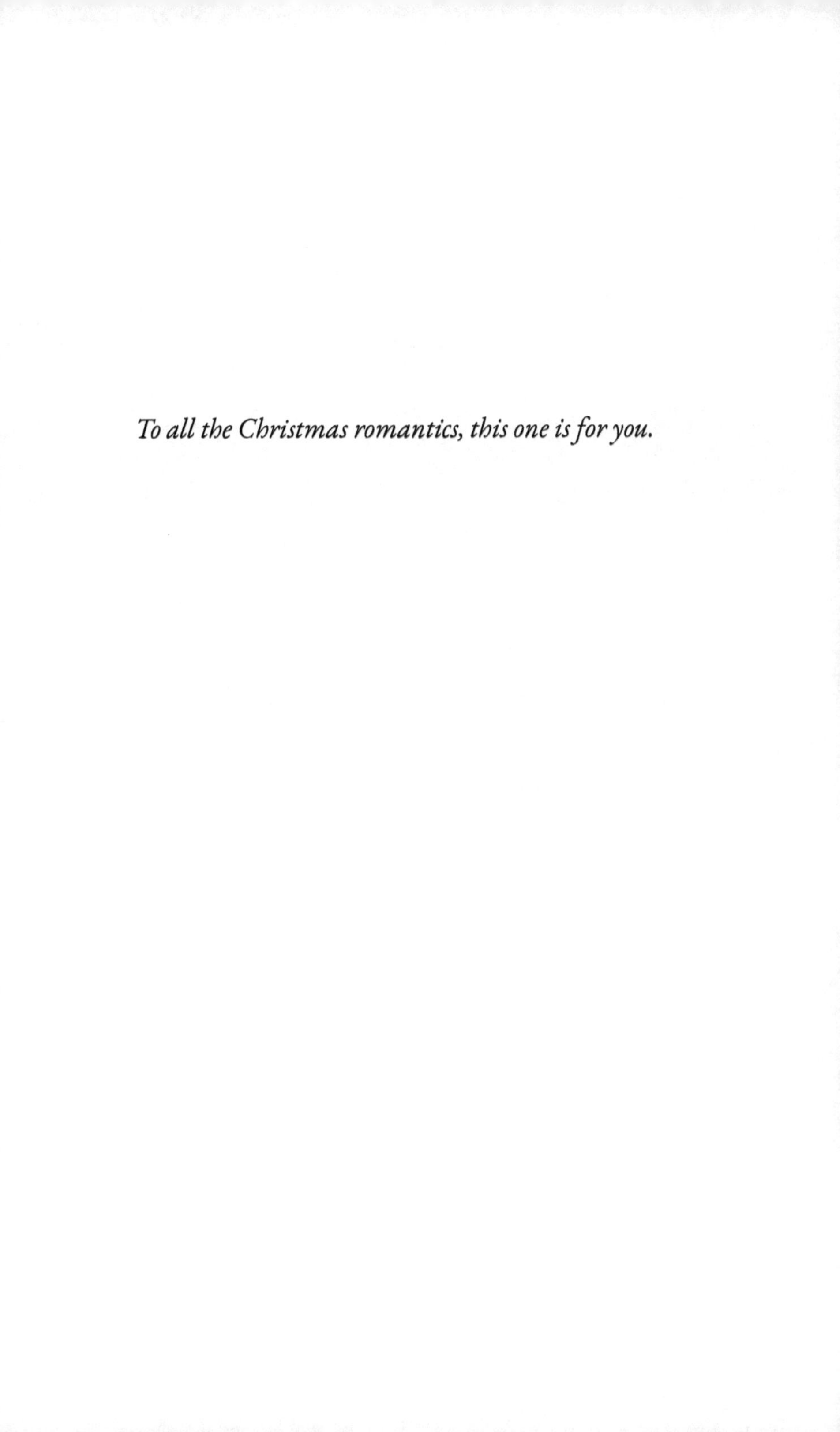

To all the Christmas romantics, this one is for you.

CHAPTER 1
The Invitation
EVIE

"Surprise!"

Still breathless from running to get here, I push my disheveled blonde hair out of my face and stare at my book club friends sitting in our usual corner booth at Chili's, trying to make sense of what I'm seeing. They're each wearing a reindeer headpiece. Candice's has a nose that's actually blinking, Melody's is slightly crooked, and Stacy's is so glittery one needs sunglasses to deal with its brightness.

An actual fake Christmas tree that looks like it was borrowed from Charlie Brown sits in the center of the table.

Stacy snaps a photo of me, a wild grin on her face.

"What's happening?" I glance around the restaurant to gauge how big of a scene we're making. But it's eleven on a Saturday morning so thankfully the place is dead. "I must have gotten confused about this month's book pick."

"Nope." Candice holds up her copy of *First Chapter Love.* "We'll get to book club in a minute, but first, we have something to tell you."

My confusion shifts into wariness. It's October, not even close to my birthday, and even I, the lover of all things Christmas, haven't started thinking about the holiday. What are they up to? I clench the strap of my purse, not liking where this is going.

"Surprise!" they chorus.

"Surprise?" Frowning, I sink into my chair. "Did I miss something because I was late? I have a great excuse this time."

"Were you making out with a random hot guy?" Stacy asks, eyebrows raised.

"Oh!" Candice leans forward. "Was it your principal?"

"Gross! No, I like my job very much, thank you." Ever since my recent breakup, they've been encouraging me to have a fling and get back into the saddle again. *Not happening.* "I was helping paint the set for my school's fall play. I even have evidence."

I point to my T-shirt and jeans where remnants of my efforts linger. The three stare at me, unimpressed.

"At least you weren't slaving over report cards or mopping up kid throw-up," Candice says with a sigh. "Listen. It's actually what our surprise is about."

"Making out with random guys?" I laugh as I pull out my book.

"Kind of?" Stacy's nose wrinkles and my laugh dies.

"Please tell me this isn't about Sir Cheats A Lot," I say, trying to lighten the mood, but really my heart rate kicks up a notch, and not in a good, swoony way. "Because I thought we agreed to never speak of him again."

"Absolutely not." Melody shakes her head.

"Never!" Candice exclaims fiercely.

"Mr. Two-Timer is dead to us," Stacy says. "Metaphorically of course, but if we were in a rom-com, we'd totally have buried his body by now. What we're trying to say is we feel it's time for you to explore other options."

"Oh, crap." I groan. "This is an intervention, isn't it? Nope. I'm starting book club."

My hand slaps START on the big red timer in the center of the table. Our rule is when the timer starts, it signals book club has begun. For one hour, we are only allowed to eat, drink, talk about our book pick of the month, and most importantly, have fun.

No kid talk, ex talk, or job talk. Definitely no cheating-ex-boyfriend talk.

Six months ago the four of us formed the Hopeless Romantic Book Club as a way to escape our daily lives. We were at the library, waiting in line and talking about how life sometimes likes to kick you in the ass and the only way we'd get through each day was to escape in a rom-com.

Candice lost her six-figure dream job and now works at Tacos Are Us to pay the bills while she hunts the job market. Candice's two kids, whom she loves with her soul, drive her to hide in the shower just for five minutes of peace. Melody runs a full-time design company that has her phone blowing up all hours of the night. The woman truly is sleep deprived.

And then there's me. Teacher whose boyfriend cheated on her because apparently, she gave too much attention to the kids and not enough to him so he had to find love elsewhere to meet his needs.

Scumbag.

So on that fateful day in the library when Melody suggested we form our own group, we were all in. This club would be our safe place where we'd complain about our lives and then for one hour we'd escape it and live in our monthly rom-com book pick's world where happily-ever-afters exist.

And cheaters do not.

"Nope. Book club has not started." Stacy taps the timer off, smiling gleefully at me.

"If this is about me dating again, I'm not ready," I finally admit, staring at the drooping Christmas tree on the table. "In fact, I don't think I'll ever be ready."

That ache, sunken in my chest, is still very real. Not the need for Ted—I'm totally over his sorry ass. It's the fact that I wasn't enough for him. And deep down, I don't know if I'll ever be enough for anyone.

"We have a surprise for you." Melody gently places her hand on my arm. "We know you love Christmas, and we thought you...um...needed something to cheer you up."

"Really?" I squeeze Melody's hand. "That's sweet. For a moment there I thought you all were going to try to convince me that I should date." I laugh and take a big breath. The three women give each other side glances.

"You sure this is a good idea?" Candice asks the other two.

"It's a brilliant idea," Stacy says firmly.

My stomach drops. "What's a brilliant idea?"

"Merry Christmas, Evie!" Melody beams and passes me a gift wrapped in snowy-white paper and a big scarlet bow.

"Thank you?" I say.

The three smile at me like the Grinch who just stole all of Whoville's presents as I hesitantly unwrap it. A velvet Santa-red box falls onto my lap. Inside is an ivory envelope. The edges are trimmed with gold filigree, and it's sealed with a wax imprint.

"What is this?" I ask as I break the seal. "It's super fancy."

"Read it," Melody says, and her eyes shine bright. In fact, it's the first time I can remember when she hasn't looked exhausted.

Stacy rubs her hands together. "I can't wait."

"Right?" Candice clasps her hands. "I couldn't sleep last night."

"Now you've got me really curious what this is." I unfold the letter and begin to read. "Dear Evie Winters. The snow is falling, the fire is crackling, and love is in the air. Thank you for applying to the reality show, *Santa's Most Eligible*. We were thrilled with your entry."

I stop and gape at my friends. "What are they talking about? I never entered a reality show."

"Just keep reading." Candice waves for me to continue. "This is so exciting."

"Fine," I agree and smile back at them. This must be some sort of joke or game to cheer me up, and since it's obviously making them happy, I'll just go along with it. They sure put a lot of effort into it, after all.

"This Christmas, we formally invite you to be part of something magical—*Santa's Most Eligible*. This is a once-in-a-lifetime chance for you to experience romance and potentially find your happily-ever-after with handsome hotel millionaire, Noah Frost."

Candice squeals like she's one of her kids. Quickly, she covers her mouth, face reddening. Wow. They really are into this.

I continue, "You have been chosen to be among a select group of women to join Noah at his luxurious Vermont ski resort. There you'll enjoy cozy dates, snowy adventures, and festive parties. The real prize? True love—and maybe a dazzling engagement ring under the Christmas tree. We can't wait to see you next month in Vermont where you'll get to vie for one of the most eligible bachelors in the country. Warmest wishes, Santa's helpers and residents of Everpine."

I set the letter on the table. Candice snatches it up and presses a hand over her heart, sighing.

"Wow," I say. "You ladies are even more creative than I thought. Is this an escape game we're going to play?"

"Oh, no," Stacy says and nods to the letter. "That's the real deal. You got invited to be on a TV show."

My brain stutters. "I don't understand. I never applied."

"We applied for you, Evie," Melody admits. "We thought this was the perfect way for you to get out and have some fun. All you do is work after...you know."

My mouth falls open. "This is real?"

"I saw an ad saying they were seeking applications," Stacy explains. "We thought you'd be perfect."

"I'm not going to talk about how you signed me up for something without my permission. The real issue is I don't want to date and I definitely don't want to date on national TV."

"Don't think of it as dating," Candice says. "Think about it as *revenge*."

Not going to lie, that catches my attention. "How?" I ask.

"Mr. Oopsie Dupesie is now dating one of your coworkers, right?" she presses. "And not being too subtle at that."

I try to block out the memory of walking into Misty's classroom and finding them practically sprawled on her desk.

"The guy is a piece of work," I grumble.

"Imagine him watching you on TV, capturing the heart of one of the most sought-after bachelors looking all sexy and glamorous in this," Stacy says and passes me another gift. "He will lose his damn mind watching it unfold on TV."

"That does sound tempting." I can't help but take the bait and open the next gift. A red sequin dress glitters back at me from inside. "This is beautiful but definitely too much."

"No, it's perfect." Melody wraps her arm around me. "We want this for you. You deserve it."

"I love the idea," I tell them. "And it was so kind of you to do this for me, but I can't leave my students and I'm terrible at pretending I like someone when I don't."

"I checked the dates of the filming." Candice opens the calendar on her phone. "Part of it is during your fall break, and besides, when have you ever taken a day off from work?"

Never. "Still, the fine print says it's a four-week commitment."

"Before you say no," Stacy holds up a finger as she pulls out her tablet, "there's one more person you should listen to."

She taps her tablet and a video plays. A guy, wearing a flannel shirt and jeans, appears on the screen, standing in front of a stunning ski lodge with a smile that challenges my skepticism. He has swooping brown hair, warm blue eyes, and sculpted cheekbones.

Damn, he's hot.

"Hi, Evie. First of all, thank you for signing up for this adventure. When my neighbors approached me with this idea, I was skeptical, but after talking to the production team running the event, I'm feeling hopeful. As you can see behind me," he turns and waves to the lodge, "I've been blessed with an incredible life, an amazing family, and the best friends a person could ask for. Except, I'm missing one thing—the love of my life. I'm going to be straight with you. I'm not here for a holiday fling. I'm here to find my person. The one I can share my future with and build a life with."

The camera switches to show him strolling through a quaint mountain village with paned-window shops and cobblestone streets.

"The best part is I don't have to do this alone," he tells the camera. "My hometown is going to help me along the way. They've watched me grow up and know me better than sometimes I think I know myself." He chuckles at this. "I can't wait to meet you and to see if we have a connection as magical as Christmas itself. See you soon at the lodge."

The camera pans out to reveal a bunch of people whom I'm assuming are from the town surrounding Noah. He flashes another dashing smile and the video fades as holiday music plays in the background. Stacy sets the tablet down and all three of my friends lean in.

"So what do you think now after meeting the bachelor?" Melody asks.

"He does seem like a nice guy," I admit, feeling my defenses falling.

"Nice?" Alex snorts. "More like hot. Definitely a ten."

Or maybe a fifteen. "Still, if he's so good-looking, why isn't he already married?"

"Who cares?" Candice throws up her hands. "None of us are expecting you to actually marry the guy. This is your chance to have some fun and live a little before you're tied down. Trust me. I love my kids, but they're a lot."

"And imagine Captain Can't Keep His Pants On when he sees you on the show," Alex adds. "He'll be so jealous."

I take the tablet and freeze the video frame on Noah Frost's face, grinning back at me. He seems like a nice guy and the thought of taking an actual vacation sounds like heaven. They're right. Snowy adventures and festive parties do sound pretty amazing. How bad can it be?

"You know what?" A devious smile plays on my lips. "I'm going to do it. I'm going to go on the show, have fun, and let that scumbag know what he missed out on."

"That's the spirit!" Melody says.

The three cheer and Stacy calls the server over for a round of drinks. The tight cord wrapped around my heart loosens. For the first time since Ted's betrayal, a spark of hope flutters in my chest. This experience is exactly what I need to help me move on and start living again. And maybe this little adventure will set me on the path to start believing in love again.

CHAPTER 2

A Novel Beginning
ALEX

The loneliest moments of my life have always begun with "and they lived happily ever after." Okay, maybe not those *actual* words but more poetic equivalents. The second my fingers type "the end" on one of my books I get this overwhelming sense of sadness. My characters' stories are told. Their futures secured. Up to this point, I've spent months with them inhabiting my head, keeping me company whether I'm awake or asleep. And okay, yeah, they're still there, but fading already, arm in arm into a haze of romantic bliss. Not for the first time, I swallow the envy I feel. That sort of happiness has always been so elusive for me. Maybe that's why I'm so obsessed with writing about it.

I attach the finished draft of my latest novel to an email addressed to my editor and sighing, press send. The little *whoosh* sound punctuates the sense of abandonment I feel. It's ridiculous and I know it. I've just completed my ninth book. That's a big accomplishment. I should feel elated.

And yet.

I close my laptop and get up from my favorite writing spot near the window. It has a sweeping view of the lake behind my cozy North Carolina cabin and the mountains beyond. It's nearly dusk and the sky is deepening to a midnight blue. The trees are ablaze with color, all fiery oranges, reds, and yellows. I gather my fluffy cardigan closer to my chest and shiver. It'll be cold out there, but that won't stop me. My end-of-book ritual is mandatory. I'm convinced it's part of the magic making my books successful—a talismanic rite that I have to observe. I started it with the first book that made the *Times* and now I'm afraid to deviate—like a baseball player who always wears the same lucky pair of socks.

Besides, I've always thought having a ritual is important for writers—ever since I saw the movie *Misery* and watched Paul Sheldon smoke a single cigarette and pour himself a glass of champagne from an elegant silver tray. Of course, some people would argue that for him, the ritual was anything but lucky since right after it, he got into a car accident and ended up in the clutches of Anne Wilkes, but then again, he also escaped her and went on to be an even bigger success—so who's to say his ritual wasn't partially responsible?

I throw on some workout gear and head outside to the dock where my kayak is waiting. I prepped it a few hours ago when I knew I was close to finishing. Seconds later, I'm out on the water, rowing briskly across the lake, my heart pumping hard, my breath coming fast. I've got my end-of-book playlist going, a Taylor Swift-palooza I hope will knock me out of my funk. When I reach the center of the lake, I take out my bottle of bourbon and a plastic tumbler, then pour myself a drink.

"To me," I say, my voice echoing over the water. I lift the tumbler to the dusk-deepening sky and drain it.

My cell phone starts vibrating in my jacket pocket. Shaking my head, I dig it out. I don't need to check the caller ID to know who it is. "You have notes already?"

My editor, Owen, laughs. "Of course, but that's not why I'm calling and you know it."

I put the phone on speaker and pour myself another measure of bourbon. "I'm celebrating, I'm celebrating. I swear."

"Yeah, let me guess: on your sad little kayak with your sad little bottle of bourbon? Honey, that isn't celebrating, and don't you dare argue because you know I'm right. Finishing a book—especially one with high expectations and a tight deadline—is cause for a party. A *real* one. Not some drunken twilight workout sesh."

I fight a smile because he knows me far too well and it's sort of comforting. "I don't know. The squirrels around here are pretty rowdy. We're about to get *turnt*." I emphasize the last word, purposefully hamming it up.

He groans. "Um, no ma'am. You aren't deflecting with forest humor. Now get your booty back to shore pronto. Don't make me come out there after you."

Wait. *What?*

I glance back at the cabin in time to see Owen jogging across the grass to the dock. He's here?

Good grief.

I tug at my stringy ponytail and make a face. I'm not presentable for any kind of human company—especially not my meticulously neat and fashionable editor. Not by a longshot. The last few days before I turn in a book are *intense*. I'm lucky if I remember to eat, let alone shower on the regular. This is so not good.

"What the hell are you doing here?" I ask, hiding my face in my hands even though I'm far enough from shore that he can't get a good look at me or the little zit patches dotting my forehead and cheeks. Writing is stressful business. "Email is my preferred mode of communication, man."

"Oh please, stop." He waves his hands dismissively. "I don't care about the condition you're in." He strides out to the end of the dock putting his hands on his hips and yelling across the water at me instead of into his phone. "Because you're going to row over here, go inside, take a long-ass shower, and scrub all the things."

He squints at me from his spot on the dock, his forehead puckering above his thick black glasses as he gives me a once over. "Twice, possibly *thrice,* and then we are going out to dinner. Someplace fancy...and hip. If there is such a thing in this town."

"Can't we just order pizza?" I whine, downing the rest of the bourbon in one go. I need to be thoroughly buzzed if I'm getting through this.

"Alexandra Ryan!" Owen's voice booms over the lake. "I will not take no for an answer." He taps his foot impatiently.

I pick up my oar and reluctantly start the row back to the dock, cursing softly the whole way.

An hour later, we are tucked into a booth at a farm-to-table restaurant in nearby Asheville that's a solid compromise between my need for uncomplicated cuisine and Owen's obsession with Instagrammable eateries.

"See? Isn't this so much better?" Owen grins as the waiter serves us our appetizers: roasted Brussels sprouts with bacon for me and an endive salad with artfully arranged sections of orange on top and a sprinkling of walnuts for him.

I tip my Cosmo in his direction. "It's not terrible," I say, my buzz making me more amenable. "But I still don't know why you're here."

"To celebrate this new book with you," Owen says between sips of hard cider, his eyes carefully avoiding mine.

I give him a look. "Truth."

He leans back in his chair, makes a show of running one hand across his navy wool pant leg like he's brushing off imaginary food crumbs. "It's just I know sometimes you get a little sad after you finish a book, and I didn't want you to be alone."

His eyes seek out mine, but I can't quite get myself to meet his gaze.

"And?" I prompt.

He takes a deep breath. "And I just think maybe getting around people more is something you should do."

I give a little laugh. "I'm around people. I see people all the time. I'm here with you right now, aren't I?"

"I'm not talking about me or your retired neighbor, Linda," he says, and then when I open my mouth to argue, "Or your writers' group. I'm talking people of the opposite sex— who aren't your editor and gay." He raises an eyebrow.

Heat flushes my face.

He reaches out and gently pats my hand with his. "When's the last time you've been on a date?"

Owen's been my editor for eight years and somewhere along the line he's become my best friend. And maybe this little speech of his is still crossing the line, but it's coming from a good place. After my last book, I sort of slipped into a funk... okay, not a funk so much as a prolonged depression. I went all-out hermit, sticking close to my house, only venturing outside when I had to for author events and industry stuff. I ended up in counseling and for a while I wasn't sure I could write another novel. Who was I to write about love when I have had so little experience with it? Owen and his partner ended up staying with me on and off from June to early July until I was some semblance of my old self, just in time to throw myself into writing my latest book. Now he's worried history will repeat itself.

"I'm fine," I tell him, but it's hard trying to make it not sound like a lie.

"You can't keep hiding in the work, Alex," he says softly. "Sooner or later, you have to put yourself out there. Stop writing about the perfect guy and go find him."

"Okay, okay," I say, a lump forming in my throat.

"Good, no time like the present," he says, grabbing my phone off the table. "Let's take a little tour of your dating apps and see who's out there."

I groan and drop my head in my hands. "No one. I've looked."

Owen ignores me. "This guy seems promising. Adventure guide. Local. Very ruggedly handsome." He whistles.

I peek out from between my fingers as he turns the phone to show me.

"No! I went out on a date with him last fall. He's got hair on his neck...and ears."

"Hair is shaveable."

"Not that much hair."

Owen laughs and I can't stop from joining in. We spend the next few minutes scoping out at least a dozen guys. "I don't know. None of them seem right," I say.

"Who would seem right?" Owen asks.

I shrug. "Handsome, but in a wholesome kind of way, like boy next door—but sexy. Athletic, but not psycho "on the grind" about it. Smart. And a reader, of course.

I push my food around my plate with my fork. "Ideally, I'd

like someone who comes from a big family since I don't. Someone fun. Outgoing since I'm not. Creative but also logical. Opinionated but not a douche."

"Wait,' Owen says suddenly. "I think I've found him."

I make a face. "Sure you have."

What I've basically described is a romance novel guy—someone who doesn't exist in real life, the kind I write about all the time.

"No, seriously," Owen says. "He owns a ski resort in upstate New York—took it over from his dad. The whole family still lives out there even though they own hotels literally all over the world. And he's into sci-fi. Ted Crouch—isn't he one of your author faves?"

I nod. "Yeah, but—"

"Handsome. Wholesome. He's it." Owen turns my phone so I can see the screen.

The burst of laughter that erupts from me is so loud I startle the couple eating dinner at the table next to ours. "A guy from a reality dating show?"

"*Santa's Most Eligible*, yeah," Owen says. "He's cute!"

I stare at the photograph on the screen. The man is definitely easy on the eyes. Dark hair. Gray-blue eyes. The kind of chiseled jawline that makes me itch to trace it with my finger. A nice smile. Some intangible quality that does something to my stomach. Undeniably hot.

"He's on a reality show," I say.

"So?"

"So, a guy who looks like him is on those shows for one of two reasons: he's trying to get famous and break into acting or he's a total player looking to kiss as many girls as possible."

"No. Read his little bio thing. You're wrong. He's really looking for a partner. There are interviews with people from his town in here. And his parents. Seriously. He's straight out of a Hallmark movie." He keeps scrolling. "The show films soon and airs in December. And they've got an application here for contestants." He sets the phone down. "Alex, you have to do this."

I wrinkle my nose at him. "I most certainly do not."

Owen makes a frustrated noise deep in his throat. "Come on. Take a risk for once. Be the main character in your own romantic adventure. Don't you ever wonder what that would be like?"

All the time, but I'm not admitting it.

"Just think it over," he says. "The application window doesn't close until tomorrow night. Please."

I promise I will—but only because he won't stop begging all through the rest of the meal and into dessert. I have no intention of applying for some silly dating show.

But later, when Owen is fast asleep in the guest room and I'm neck deep in a bubble bath nursing the beginnings of a hangover, I pull up the *Santa's Most Eligible* ad we saw on the dating site again.

Noah Frost.

Jesus, even his name is perfect for the show—like something out of a Christmas novel. I shake my head and stare at his face for a full second, then two more. He *is* cute.

And Owen wasn't wrong to worry. The sadness is working its way into my bones again like the October evening chill, settling in for a spell. I am lonely. I've been lonely for a long time. Somewhere along the way I stopped dreaming about a romance for myself and started pouring it all into my books. And that's not okay. Admitting it feels good, like the first step back to finding out who I am outside of my stories.

I pull up the application, take a deep breath, and fill in my name.

I can always chicken out later, I think, if they ask me to be on the show.

I hit send. Weirdly, a little thrill of desire runs through me. I want them to invite me, I realize.

If they ask me to be a contestant I'm going to say yes.

CHAPTER 3

Introducing Sophie Hicks

SOPHIE

The ambiance of this location couldn't be any more perfect. A soft glow crests the snow as the lake behind the lodge glitters with the rising sun, and the crisp air is scented with fresh pine trees. I close my eyes, and for just a moment imagine vacationing here, watching the sun ascend over the distant mountains, relaxing on the porch of the lodge with a hot chocolate in hand, far away from bleak reality.

"Sophie Vaughn!" a harsh voice cuts in over my headset, making my heart jump. "Get your ass over here!"

"Reality calls," I mutter. I glance back at Drew, the second unit's director of photography, who is trying his best not to laugh as he sets up his camera to grab some morning shots. He's one of the few people who doesn't end up with ulcers whenever our producer is around.

"Why is Mack even here?" I ask him. "She's not supposed to come up from LA until tomorrow."

He shrugs. "Maybe she's giving you that promotion you've been asking for."

"And maybe this lake will dry up tomorrow." I sigh and jog

along the lamplit snowy path toward the lodge, stepping around the ladder where a guy is adding the finishing touches: a sprig of mistletoe to each of the overhead hanging lamps. We want to ensure our cast have any and every opportunity to kiss.

I pull the heavy oak doors and step into the warmly lit lodge. We didn't have to do too much to make the interior presentable. Even the lengths of cables stretching across the lobby and bustle of camera assistants running around don't diminish the warmth of the lodge. Its natural cozy, welcoming charm and homey yet elegant appeal was one of the reasons the network dished out the money to make this show.

The other was Noah Frost himself. Standing by the check-in desk, looking as handsome as if he's just stepped out of a magazine, Noah would make any girl's heart flip. I'd spoken with him a few times when I arrived, and he's actually really nice. Gentlemanly, the kind of guy who opens doors and pulls out chairs for you. Who spends his time volunteering in the community whenever he's not helping his family run the lodge. In my opinion, he's even a little naïve, which you'd have to be to agree to be on this show. I grimace, thinking of some of the girls the casting agents chose to be here. They'll eat that guy for breakfast.

The guy he's talking to, on the other hand...

Jake Logan, host extraordinaire, looks over at me as if on cue. I'd be lying if I said my stupid heart doesn't race when his gaze meets mine. His eyes twinkle as they take in my light brown hair pulled into a loose bun, comfortable sneakers, wrinkled baggy slacks that I've worn two days in a row, and a faded Metallica T-shirt that belonged to my older brother who passed away three years ago. I scowl at him.

Once Jake told me I was the most beautiful woman he'd ever met.

He was twenty-three, playing the seventeen-year-old lead role on *Paradise*, a short-lived teen drama six years ago. I was twenty-two and in my first post-college job as a production assistant. I fell hard for the charming, confident guy who said all the right things but did all the wrong. We dated for six months until he got famous and became America's heartbreaker. The heartbroken being me, who he dumped via text because I wasn't ready for a relationship. I let my anger out on a tell-all podcast with an influencer, which I regretted as soon as I did it. Jake's reputation as the good boy of Hollywood was tarnished, and it took extra finessing by his agent to do damage control. I hated him, and he hated me.

Fast forward to this year, I was thrilled to get the job of field producer for *Santa's Most Eligible*—the first time "assistant" wasn't in front of the title. But when Jake was announced as host for *Santa's Most Eligible,* it took everything in me—and a lot of sessions with my therapist—not to turn and run from it.

Mack is talking to the two guys but stops when she sees me. She strides over, her eyes narrowed. "What the hell, Soph. You look like shit."

Her voice is loud, causing me to blush as Jake's grin widens.

"Thanks," I say. I want to say "Same to you," but not only would that be instant career suicide, it'd be untrue. With her long black hair, angular features, dress that hugs every perfect curve, and six-inch Manolos, Mack looks like she just stepped off the runway, even though she stopped modeling to go into television production a decade ago. But for all her beauty and smarts, she's a pit viper. We all know to stay on her good side or never work in the industry again.

Mack grabs my elbow and steers me around cameras and the gaffers setting up their lighting, leading me to a quiet spot. She stops and takes a deep breath. "I have something amazing to tell you. Caitlin—our number six contestant—was in a car crash. So now we're down a contestant and no time to find another since we start rolling in three days."

She raises her eyebrows and waits as if I'm supposed to agree that a girl getting in a crash is amazing. So I nod. "That's...great?"

She rolls her eyes and taps me on the forehead. "Didn't you hear me? We're down a contestant. We need someone to fill in for her, like now, or we'll be in a shitstorm with the suits. Someone who is passably cute, and I do mean passably. Like seriously, do you ever not look like you rolled out of bed five minutes ago?"

My eyes widen. She can't mean...

"Yes!" She grins like she just gave me the biggest Christmas present. "I mean, once you clean yourself up, you'll be perfect. Really, Soph, haven't you heard of getting a facial for those pores? Or applying the slightest bit of mascara?" She slaps my cheek lightly. "Take a shower, scrub up, get some damn makeup on, and send my assistant to get appropriate clothes for you in the next town. Charge it to the network. Tomorrow I want to see you looking like you stepped out of a magazine. And not *Dog Fancy*. Got it? Great."

"Wait," I call out as she walks away. "What about my job?"

"What about it?" She turns and shrugs. "Carianne can fill in. Don't worry, you'll still get your producer pay, but not till after we stop filming. That way I know you're putting your all into it. And no one is to know who doesn't work on the show, got it? If any of the contestants find out while filming, well, let's just say we won't be working together again. Oh, and also..." She gives me a very direct look. "Remember the rules. No boyfriends, no fraternizing with the crew—unless you have a scoop you need to share with me only. And absolutely *no* flirting with the host."

"Jake?" I scoff. "Why would I do that?"

"I know you have history. Keep it that way."

"That's easy enough. We can't stand each other."

"Good. Where were you from before you moved to LA?"

"Texas."

"Oh, a hick." She purses her lips and taps her chin with one perfectly manicured finger. "Okay, you're a small-town girl from Texas. A florist. That's cute. You can keep your first name but we'll give you a different last name. Actually, what do you think about Hicks?"

"I don't—"

"Hicks for a hick. Perfect. Oh, and remember that every girl is bringing a gift for Noah, so don't forget to pick up a gift when you're in town."

Mack turns and walks away before I can tell her that I'm from Houston, one of the largest cities in the country. And a florist? Any plants that are unlucky enough to cross paths with me end up in the trash. But Mack has made up her mind. I'm a small-town florist from Texas named Sophie Hicks who is looking for love on *Santa's Most Eligible.*

What a joke.

I walk over to Noah and throw out some jazz hands, hoping I look more enthusiastic about this than I feel. "Apparently I'm going to be a contestant now."

He chuckles. "Mack told us. I'm looking forward to meeting you for the first time...again." He kisses my hand and winks at me. "Until then." He turns around and walks away, humming to himself.

I whip around to face a very amused Jake, sipping from his travel mug and grinning. "What?"

"I didn't say anything. This should be fun, watching you try to get out of the limousine without falling on your face."

"I only did that one time, and I am still not convinced you didn't push me in your eagerness to be in the spotlight."

"Says the woman who's about to get more of the spotlight than she might like." He gives me a wicked grin. "A lot more."

My stomach twists. I forgot that the host has a say in some of the shots since they are on set constantly and interact with all the contestants and the bachelor. Knowing Jake, he'll probably try to get the crew to film me eating, or blowing my nose, or anything that comes across as unattractive.

Jake blows me a kiss. "Until then," he says in a voice that sounds like Noah's. He walks away, chuckling to himself.

I grit my teeth and notice Jake left his travel mug on the desk. I recognize that mug—his mother gave it to him when he got his first acting job. Written on it is a quote by Jean-Paul Sartre: *Acting is happy agony.*

I grab it and drop it in my bag. Looks like I have the perfect gift for *Santa's Most Eligible.*

CHAPTER 4

Flurries & First Impressions

EVIE

The gift in my hand will look like it's been chewed by a bear if I don't stop clutching it like a stress ball. I pace the boarding area of the gondola station, telling myself to calm down and not think about how in just a few minutes I'll meet Noah Frost, my new boyfriend. Well, one that I'll be sharing with eleven other girls.

I'm the last of the twelve women to ride up the gondola that will take us to Everpine Lodge, and watching each of those stunning ladies head up one by one has my nerves tied tighter than a Christmas bow. It sure doesn't help that a cameraman is capturing my every moment.

"You're next," one of the show's crew members says. "Watch your step when you get inside."

I try to smile, but it probably looks like some twisted Grinch grin between my shivering and terror. I tuck my thick wrap tighter around my body and go to step inside the gondola.

And trip.

The attendant gasps but I manage to catch myself. I try to

laugh it off as I quickly settle onto the bench, but as the cameraman follows me inside, there's no doubt he captured every moment of that stumble.

The show just became very real.

"Hello!" A lady pops in and settles across from me in the gondola. Her natural curls are twisted back into a sleek bun. She's wearing jeans and a thick blue jacket that accents her dark skin. "I'm Charlotte, and I'm here to ask a few questions as we ride up to meet Noah."

She shoots me a warm smile that's disarming and calming as our gondola swoops away from the station and the cute town of Everpine, lifting into the air.

"It's nice to meet you," I say. "I'm Evie Winters, but you probably already know that."

I try a light breezy laugh. It's more of a chortle. As we zip along, I remind myself this is just a little holiday getaway where I can get in some skiing, drink heaps of hot chocolate, and sit by the fire. Oh, and make sure my ex sees me flirting with the bachelor. Nothing to stress about. Except the stunning red dress that hugs my body and shows more cleavage than I'm accustomed to is screaming at me that this is a big deal.

And is it just me or is that camera lens leering at me? Not to mention all those other women and...

Nope.

Do not think about those things!

"So, you excited to finally meet Noah?" Charlotte leans forward, eyes twinkling. She's acting like we're two friends gossiping about a cute guy.

"Absolutely." I give a big smile for the camera and especially for The Cheater. "The video of him really made me think he's a great guy."

But I know how videos and first impressions can lie.

"He is the real deal," Charlotte agrees. "Where are you from and what made you sign up to be a part of this Christmas experience?"

I tell her I'm from Florida, and a teacher looking for the right man. I don't mention the lying, conniving dirtbag. A ripping sound warns me I've finally managed to tear the paper of my gift. "It should be a fun experience."

"Well, it's more than just an experience," Charlotte says with a knowing look. "Noah is looking for a wife. He's not messing around."

I gulp at the word *wife*. Definitely not ready for that, but I don't want to get eliminated on the first night. "I'm glad to hear he's taking this seriously."

"The important thing is for you to see if you two have that spark that will last a lifetime. And it can't hurt to have a little fun while you're here too, right? This is as much of a decision on your part as it is his."

The camera continues its never-ending stare. Desperately, I try to smile but the knot in my stomach is as twisted as my wrapping paper. One wrong word could easily send me packing on the first night. I can't let that happen. I need to last a few days to ensure The Cheater sees me looking fabulous and happy without him.

"I think that's what I'm most excited about," I add as we rise over snow-dusted pines. White peaks sweep above in the distance. "Noah seems serious about this process, and I'm looking for a guy who is committed to a relationship."

This must be the right answer because Charlotte grins. "That's great to hear."

And I *am* looking for a committed man; it's just not going to be Noah or any guy until I can get my heart back on track. We're rising higher up the mountain, and this might be a chance for me to get insider information to keep me here a few extra days.

"I was curious," I begin, "Noah obviously is a catch. I'm surprised some girl hasn't snatched him up yet."

"Oh, they've tried." Charlotte gives me a knowing look. "You can be sure of that. Now don't tell anyone I told you, but his last girlfriend cheated on him. Apparently, she was just with him for the money."

My heart clenches at the thought and a small gasp escapes me. "That's terrible," I say, while a small voice in my head questions why she's telling me this.

"Nearly broke the guy." She shakes her head sadly. "I really hope he finds his soulmate on this show. Maybe it will be you?"

She's fishing, but she's not going to get anything from me. As we finish up the interview, I wonder why he chose a reality dating show. It seems like the worst place to find your partner. Still, hearing about Noah's past changes everything. I know exactly how he's feeling. Maybe I can even help him find the right woman because if anyone knows about cheaters, it's me.

The gondola crests above a ridge and Everpine Lodge comes into view, nestled between two mountains. It's a grand timber-framed building with windows spilling honey light as the sun sets. My heart skips a few beats. It's truly magical.

By the time we zip to the lodge's station, my nerves are completely fried. Up close, the lodge is even more stunning than on the internet. It's styled like a chalet with steep gable roofs, quaint balconies, and stone chimneys that spear up, smoke drifting into the cold night.

"Good luck!" Charlotte tells me when the gondola doors swish open. An attendant wearing an Everpine uniform waits for me. "I hope you have a wonderful time."

"Thank you," I say as I step, waving her goodbye. Cold

whooshes across my bare skin. I adjust my too-thin wrap over my shoulders.

Mental note: Get a warmer wrap.

The air is crisp and pine-scented as the attendant directs me down a path to the lodge's entrance. Snowflakes dance around me as I carefully walk in my heels toward the massive double doors while my camera guy trails silently after me. My stomach twists despite the beautiful twinkling fairy lights and draping garlands. Two men in crisp black hotel uniforms greet me as I walk up to the entrance and swing the doors open for me. Another cameraman is waiting for me on the other side, and I startle, nearly toppling over in my heels. One of the doormen whispers, "Smile."

Frantically, I plaster on my brightest grin and stride confidently into the grand lobby. But that's as far as my confidence lasts. Between the cameras scattered across the area, a full production crew running about, and a group of the most beautiful women I've ever seen, I'm feeling completely lost and intimidated. The vaulted ceiling is draped with garlands, a roaring fire crackles from a large hearth against one wall, and in the center of the room is a glittering Christmas tree that could hold its own in Rockefeller Center.

"You must be Evie Winters." A woman with dark brown hair and light brown skin rushes up to me. Her hair is escaping its bun and her shirt is rumpled. "I'm Carianne Riggs, newly appointed field producer."

"It's great to meet you," I say. "I brought my gift."

"Right. Just give it to Noah when you see him. You can put it under the Christmas tree and then come back here for your photos."

I hurry to set down my gift, wishing I had double-wrapped it. Just before I set the mangled package under the boughs, something smashes against my head. I cry out, mostly from shock, and look up to find a sleek brown-haired woman with plump red lips and delicate brows. She's lugging a massive gift as tall as her.

"Look what you did!" she exclaims. "You ruined my wrapping."

"I ruined it?" I touch my forehead. A small streak of blood coats my fingers where her gift cut through my skin. "More like you attacked me."

"Now Noah won't be able to get the full experience opening my present." She sets the giant gift by the tree and frantically tries to push the top flap back in place. But without tape, it just flaps open, revealing a life-sized cardboard cutout of her.

In a bikini.

"Wow, that's some gift." I press my lips together to keep from laughing.

"Don't even think about trying to copy me." Her eyes flick over me. "Not that you could. I'm Bianca, by the way."

"Evie." I hold out my hand, but her nose crinkles up like I've made a faux pas. A quick glance at my hand warns me that I've got blood on it. *Fabulous.* Quickly, I tuck it behind my back and glance around, hoping no one has started filming yet. "Well, I'm looking forward to getting to know you."

"If you last the night." She gives me a look and takes off.

I sigh. I guess I see how things are going to go. Meanwhile, blood is streaked across my own gift.

"Great," I grumble. "This is just my luck. Blood everywhere."

A guy wearing a sleek black suit with a Christmas-red tie strolls up to me from the other side of the tree. "Hey, you okay?"

I blink. "Are you..." I gulp. "Noah?"

Stop being an idiot. Of course it's Noah, I lecture myself. *You've only watched his video like twenty times.* Except in person, he's way more handsome and seems so polished and effortlessly commanding in that black jacket and red tie.

"Guilty." He shrugs, but gives me that very same melt-worthy smile that I remember from the video. Man, the dude is even hotter in real life. He's going to give the TV show plenty of great footage. "And you are?"

"Evie Winters from Florida."

"It's nice to meet you. I was walking past and heard you saying you're bleeding."

"It's not a big deal. Someone hit me with their gift."

"Hit you? That's terrible!" His eyes widen. "And you're still bleeding. Let's get you a Band-Aid before you decide to sue." He winks and chuckles.

"It's not a big deal." For some reason, my whole body feels hot and off-kilter. "I'm sure Carianne can help me. You likely have more important things to do before the show kicks off."

I try to laugh it off but then he's placing his hand lightly on my back and directing me to a side room. "Don't sweat it. I've got bandages in my office."

Once we're inside the office, I take in the map of the resort and the rows of bookshelves. He must like to read. He hurries to a large mahogany desk that overlooks the ski slopes. They're lit up like twinkle lights strung out for a holiday party, illuminating the desk in a soft glow as he rummages through it.

"Bingo!" He holds up a Band-Aid. "We'll get you fixed up in no time."

"Thanks. I suppose it wouldn't look good to be a bleeding disaster on camera."

"Something tells me the production team would love that."

He comes up to me and gently cleans the blood away with a tissue. "Once they see your Band-Aid, they'll likely make up a dramatic story about it."

He places the bandage on my forehead. Maybe it's the way his presence calms me, but as his spicy scent drifts over me, my heart kicks up a notch.

"Thank you," I say. "This is really kind of you."

"Not a problem." He steps back and tosses the wrapper into a trash can. "You excited about tonight?"

"Oh, um...yeah. I've got to be honest. My friends signed me up for this, actually." I shake my head, smiling at the memory of their surprise. "Anyway, I figured why not go have some fun, you know?"

"Yeah, fun." He rubs his chin, and his face dips as if he's disappointed. "That's important."

"Speaking of fun," I say, holding out his present. "I know we're supposed to give this out later, but I'm worried if I don't give it to you now, I'm going to destroy it."

He takes the gift, lifting his brows. "Impressive wrapping."

Oh god, it's ridiculously ugly. I should've tossed it in the trash.

"The wrapping style is meant to resemble being chewed up by a dog," I say, trying to make light of the disaster. "Oh, and the smeared blood is to show my commitment."

He laughs. It's deep and throaty and honestly, really sexy. Damn, what is my problem? I only just met the guy.

"I love it," he says. "In fact, I don't want to ruin the effect by opening it."

"Trust me. You want to get that wrapping paper into the trash ASAP."

He gently pulls back the tape like he's savoring the moment. It's kind of sweet. When he pulls out the brown leather toiletry bag with the tag "Dating Survival Kit," a wide smile lights up his eyes.

"Ah, I like how you think."

I bite my lip as he unzips the pouch. When I packed it, I had a lot of fun, but now I'm worried he might think it's cheesy. He pulls out the package of tissues labeled "After Santa's Eliminations."

"Let's hope I won't need this," he says, waving the tissues. "I hate crying."

I scrunch my nose. "Me too. Especially in public."

When he pauses, worry stretching over his face, I realize my mistake at insinuating my moment of betrayal by my ex. *Move things along, Evie*, I tell myself and say, "There's more!"

Next, he pulls out the bear spray. His eyebrows lift.

"That's meant to repel drama," I say, grinning.

"Ah, clever. I'm keeping this close to me." He pockets it in his suit jacket.

"The cue cards are lines you can use in case you get nervous and forget what to say," I explain.

He reads one, "What did the snowman tell the other one? I only have ice for you." He shakes his head, but he chuckles. "Funny."

"As you can see, I've got the best jokes," I tease. "The mints are meant for kisses, but only take them before you kiss me." Suddenly, my face burns on fire. Why did I say that? I sound desperate! "Not that you want to kiss me, of course."

He smiles warmly, which makes my whole body start sweating. *Fix this!* "And the stress ball," I quickly add. "Well, let's just hope you won't need that."

He squeezes the heart-shaped ball. "This was so thoughtful, Evie. Thank you for this."

"Of course."

There's this really awkward pause like neither of us knows what to do or say.

"I should probably go for my photos," I say, backing away. "I bet Carianne's freaking out about where I disappeared to."

He nods, and I hurry out of the room, feeling all discombobulated. What's wrong with me? I'm getting all swoony over Noah, which just proves I can't control myself with the first hot guy I see. This isn't about Noah. This is about me getting my game back.

When I step back into the lobby, Carianne finds me and her eyes practically pop out. "There you are! We're about to start and you disappeared. Wait, what happened to your head?"

"I hit my head and..."

"Shit!" Her eyes bug out and I think I see actual sweat beading on her forehead. "This is bad."

"It's fine. It's nothing to worry over."

She touches her headset. "I need makeup in the filming room ASAP. We've got an emergency."

Despite my protests, she continues talking into her headset as she escorts me to a set with a red background with garland and lights. "Yes, she's here. The last contestant has arrived so prep Mr. Jake, the host. No, I'm not in charge of him! Seriously? I'm not a babysitter. This is what happens when we're understaffed. No. Fine."

With a deep breath, she spins around and plants on a smile. "Sorry about that. We had a situation so the crew is scrambling a bit. Now let's get some photos and then you're free to mingle."

It's like I've been thrown into a washing machine at full spin. The photographer has me pose for shots. By the time I exit the media room, my stomach is growling and I'm regretting my choice of shoes.

The buffet catches my eye. It's loaded with pastries, tiny quiche shaped like Christmas trees, and platters full of holiday cookies. I snatch up a mistletoe plate and pile it high with food.

"You're seriously going to eat all that food?" a bleached-blonde woman who likely is a model asks, slipping to my side. She's wearing a black evening gown that crisscrosses over her stomach and pushes her boobs out so far it's like they're demanding to be stared at.

"Hey," I say. "I'm Evie, and yeah, everything on this plate called to me to be eaten. I didn't want to disappoint them."

The woman's thin brows lift and she laughs in a way that makes me feel like I'm a total moron. This is the problem when you're surrounded by little kids all day. You become socially inept. If I told that to my students, they'd laugh, but here, my humor is just weird.

"I'm Amber Stone, and by all means, eat up. If I ate like that I'd be so bloated when I wore my bikini."

"When were you planning on wearing your bikini, Amber?" another woman asks, joining us. She's tiny compared to Amber's towering height, with short brown hair that lightly skates her shoulders and hazel eyes that sparkle. "Is it while you're skiing or bear hunting?"

"Bear hunting?" Amber gasps. "They have bears here? Are you sure?"

"Vermont is the home to a thriving black bear population," the woman says and sips her drink as if this is normal. She turns to me, saying, "I'm Sophie Va...Hicks, fellow contestant and black bear enthusiast."

I laugh, instantly liking her. "I'm Evie Winters, third grade teacher."

"I need to talk to one of the producers about this," Amber says, pressing a hand to her chest.

"You should." Sophie nods solemnly. "Actually, you should talk to the host, Jake Logan. He's an expert on bears. Tell him I sent you."

"Good idea. Thanks."

As Amber scurries away, I roll my eyes. "She's awful. Thanks for the help."

"I can spot sharks a mile away. I haven't decided yet if it's a gift or curse." Sophie shrugs. "She's probably just starving to death, and I don't know about you, I get cranky when I'm hungry."

A server comes up with a tray full of crimson-colored drinks served in martini glasses rimmed with crushed peppermint. "Would you like a Mistletoe Martini?" he asks.

"Definitely." Sophie snatches one up.

I take one and thank her just as another woman joins us. She has glossy brown hair that's styled in soft curls and her emerald organza gown makes her look like a princess that stepped out from a romantic fairytale.

"Hey there," she says, grabbing herself a drink. "I think I could use one of these. Tonight has been harder than I expected."

"Right?" I say. "It's definitely overwhelming."

"I'm Alex Ryan," she says, sipping her drink as we introduce ourselves and I tell her I'm a teacher. "I'm a romance novelist."

"Really?" I gasp. "Romance novels are my jam. I'm part of a rom-com book club and they will die when they find out I met a real-life author. Actually, I might die before I tell them."

She chuckles. "Well, I don't know how special that really is. I mean, it sounds glamorous, and I do love my job, but I spend more time with books than real people, so this is...a lot."

"I can't imagine." I stir the cocktail pick skewered with

cranberries and scan the room. "Have either of you met Noah yet?"

"Yes. I mean no." Sophie clears her throat. "What I mean is I saw his video online. Oh, look, Jake is coming."

A guy in a red suit, trimmed with white, stands by the tree and rings a bell. I bite back a laugh at the show's attempt to make him look festive.

"Ladies," the guy says, "I'd like to officially welcome you to the home of Noah Frost and to the first ever *Santa's Most Eligible* show. My name is Jake Logan, and I'll be your host for the show. Now, I know you're not here for me."

"You got that right," Sophie mutters beside me.

"If you would all please give a warm welcome to Noah Frost, the man of the hour," Jake says and nods to his right.

And there's Noah once again striding from off to the side. He's wearing a black tux and his hair is gelled back. A candy cane is clutched in his hand. When he turns to face us, he smiles broadly.

"Hello, ladies," he says, his voice deep and rich. "Welcome to my home. I'm thrilled each of you agreed to come and spend time with me."

The girls cheer around me, but my mind pulls back the memory of his hands pressing the bandage to my face. The scent of him seems to be seared into my brain. My heart does this weird rattling—I think something is seriously wrong with me.

Get your act together, Evie!

"I'm looking forward to spending the evening with you and opening the presents you brought," Noah says.

"Here's how this will work," Jake says. "Tonight you'll get time to spend with Noah and tomorrow morning when you wake up, you'll check your stockings hanging by the fire."

He points to the massive fireplace where twelve stockings are lined up in a row.

"If you get a candy cane in your stocking," Jake says, "it means that Noah would like you to stay longer and get to know you. But if you get a lump of coal, I'm very sorry to say, it means it's time for you to go home."

"A lump of coal?" Amber gasps. "That's awful."

"Unless it means you're on the Naughty List," Bianca says seductively, winking at the camera.

"Also, if Noah ever feels you are not right for him," Jake says in a somber tone, "he'll ask you to leave."

I grimace, remembering how I told him I hadn't come here for love but that my friends signed me up and I decided to do it for fun. Looks like I'm about to be sent home.

Way to screw up your first day, Evie.

"As we count down to Christmas, Noah will eventually narrow it down to two of you," Jake says. "At that point, the people in town will have a say by voting for their favorite finalist. Their choice will weigh heavily in Noah's decision. He grew up here, and they'll be helping him find his soulmate."

We glance at one another. Surprise flickers across the group. I didn't see that coming, but I guess I shouldn't be shocked. I've heard that this small town is like one big community.

"Before we begin our holiday party, I have good news," Noah quickly adds, interrupting some of the girls whispering to each other. "I asked my staff and family to pay careful attention to each of you as you arrived, plus I may have done some sleuthing myself. Based on all our observations, I'm going to give out one candy cane now to the girl I would like to have my first private conversation with. "

The group gasps. His eyes find mine and my face burns a thousand degrees.

"Without further ado, I'd like to give this candy cane to—"

I know I don't deserve that candy cane, but still, I'd be lying if I didn't think we had a connection. I hold my breath, crossing every finger and toe hoping he calls my name.

CHAPTER 5

Run, Run, Alex

ALEX

A tense silence descends on the room. I glance over at the other contestants. All eleven of them are watching Noah with eager anticipation as a trio of cameramen circle the room like a pack of hungry polar bears, their lenses focusing on each girl's face with what feels like rabid glee.

And yeah, okay, I knew when I signed up for this experience that being recorded was part of it, but standing here now it's one thing to know this intellectually and another to experience it in real time. I can't help it; I start imagining all the people who will watch the first episode someday soon. What they'll think. What they'll say to each other about us.

Suddenly my dress is too tight, squeezing my rib cage, compressing my lungs.

What am I doing here?

I glance at the contestant closest to me—Evie I think her name is. She's biting her lip, which means she's nervous, but even so, she's got this radiant warmth about her, her red sequined dress playing beautifully off her creamy skin and golden blonde hair. She's stunning. All the girls are. Well, except for the red-haired one wearing a Christmas tree costume with jingly ornaments all over it. It's hard to tell what she looks like since only the circle of her face is visible and half of it is obscured by red-rhinestone glasses. But even she has a sort of quirky, magnetic charm.

Standing beside them all, I can feel my introvertedness increasing tenfold. I do not belong here. I know it. They all know it. I bet the producers are already regretting picking me. My fancy dress and freshly blown-out hair aren't hiding who I really am: an awkward shut-in far more comfortable writing about romance than pursuing it. This was a big mistake. Book marketing plan or no, I should not be here. This isn't going to help break out my career—it's going to torpedo it.

I fidget with the charm bracelet around my wrist, tugging at one of the little gold books dangling off it. There are eight in all, one for each of my published novels. I wore it hoping it would bolster my confidence; now it's just increasing my panic.

"Get a hold of yourself," I murmur under my breath. But my heart is apparently deaf to my plea because it's currently idling at what feels like hummingbird speed.

I glance at Noah. He's literally the physical embodiment of every leading man I write: ruggedly handsome, dark hair, eyes as blue as a crisp, cloudless winter sky. He's got the sort of arms you just know will make you feel safe when they're wrapped around you. Broad shoulders. And he owns a freaking ski lodge in the heart of Vermont, for god's sake! There's literal snow falling outside the floor-to-ceiling windows behind him.

I'd be a fool not to be attracted to him. To want to buy into the fairytale being created right in front of me.

Noah clears his throat and eyes the show's host, waiting for the signal so he can announce who he's picked for his first private conversation and hand them the first candy cane.

Okay, I can't stand one more minute of waiting to find out who it is. Because it won't be me. Not when there are literal models and beauty queens surrounding me. Very slowly, I start backing up. The lodge's front doors are to my right. And the three cameramen are currently focused on the other side of the room where the girl in the Christmas tree costume is swaying back and forth, her hands outstretched toward Noah.

"Well, come on darlin'," she coos flirtatiously. "Who is it gonna be?" Her southern accent is pure Mississippi and so sweet it makes my teeth ache. "Me, right?" she asks, giggling in the most silly, charming way. A tendril of red hair escapes her costume and curls against her cheek.

The other girls laugh.

Oh hell no. I am definitely not staying. I turn for the door and slip off my heels so they don't give me away.

Behind me I hear Noah clear his throat.

I take two steps toward the exit. Then four more.

"I'd like to have my first private conversation with..."

Almost there. So far no one's blocked my path. I reach for the door, exhaling softly in relief. I picture my cabin. My cozy bed. The covers I'm going to pull over my head when I get home until I recover from the embarrassment that is this whole experience.

"Alexandra."

I freeze at the sound of my name.

When I turn around, every person in the room is staring at me.

I clear my throat nervously. "Um, yay?" I blurt out, my nerves stealing any decent response out of me.

The show's director, Alison, yells a perfunctory "Cut!" Then she strides toward me, mouth set in a firm line.

"I was just going to get some air," I sputter as I step back into the Louboutin heels I spent my last royalty check on. They're too tight and too high, but god, are they gorgeous.

"And here I thought you were trying to escape," Alison whispers, gripping my arm firmly as she guides me back to my spot among the girls. More than half of them are whispering about me to each other. The other half just look shocked.

And then there's Noah.

He's watching me with a slightly hurt expression, the candy cane held loosely in one hand. My stomach twists. I hadn't thought about how he might feel—me leaving without a word. The only thought rattling around in my head a second ago was RUN. I wince and mouth the words "sorry" and "got nervous," hoping he'll understand. His mouth quirks up slightly and he nods. So on top of everything else, he's understanding too. Damn, this guy seems very near perfect.

Alison lets go of my arm and claps her hands. "Okay, so we're going to do a second take on that. Noah, let's just have you announce Alexandra's name one more time." She turns to me. "And Alexandra will be surprised and delighted to hear it." Her expression is intimidating.

"Absolutely." I swallow hard.

Cut to a few minutes later and Noah and I are headed outside—not through the lodge's front entrance, but the back. It opens onto a sprawling expanse of snow-covered lawn that leads to a lake and the cutest Christmas-light-covered gazebo.

A plush loveseat is set up at the center of the gazebo. It's covered in furry pillows with a large blanket thrown casually across the center. There are candles lining nearly every square inch of the gazebo's floor. A bundle of mistletoe hangs from the entry.

I duck quickly beneath it and skirt around the small coffee table in front of the loveseat. Two mugs of mulled wine sit steaming on top of it beside a plate of butter cookies in the shapes of hearts and Christmas trees. I perch on the edge of the loveseat and one of the show's crew members spends a few minutes arranging my dress so it falls perfectly around me.

It's the oddest feeling—being somewhere so romantic with a guy as handsome as Noah with nearly twenty people surrounding us, recording our every move.

Noah settles in beside me and smiles before he leans in close enough to make my heart skip. "Kinda feels like we're in a fishbowl, right?"

Carianne, one of the show's producers, clears her throat and smiles encouragingly. "Okay, I know it feels weird with all of us watching, but I promise you'll get used to it. A few more days and you'll forget we're here at all."

"I sincerely doubt that," I say softly and then shiver because despite all the candles it's freezing out here.

Noah laughs. "Actually, she's right. They've been following me around for more than a week now and it does get easier. I promise." He picks up the blanket and drapes it around my shoulders. His fingers brush briefly against my collarbone as he moves away again. A jolt of electricity travels from my chest to my toes.

"Better?" he asks.

Good grief. This man is trying to kill me.

"Absolutely," I manage to choke out, my mouth suddenly so dry I can barely speak. I pick up one of the mugs and sip at the wine. It's lovely and warm.

"So why me?" I blurt.

Noah's smile widens in the most endearing way. It makes him look almost shy. "Truth? Because I'm a fan. I've read all your books."

"After you found out I was going to be one of the contestants?" I ask.

He shakes his head. "Before." He leans toward me. "I know I'm not your typical romance reader and yeah, normally it's not my genre, but my grandma likes me to read to her sometimes since she can't see all that well and *Just Say Yes* was one of the ones she asked me to read." He runs a finger over the flame of one of the candles, averting his eyes. "I liked the way you described the town and the people. They felt so real. After we finished it, I went out and bought all your other ones." His eyes find mine again and that electric jolt I felt earlier returns times ten.

I can feel my cheeks heating up. I blow on the mug of wine and try to think of what to say in response. Annnnnd I've got nothing. The problem with real life is it's the opposite of a book. When I'm writing I have hours to come up with the flirtiest banter. I can hone and perfect it. Right now, my mind is totally blank.

Noah clears his throat. "You talk about small towns like you're from one."

"I am," I say. "In Pennsylvania. Lived there for the first seventeen years of my life."

"But you don't live in one now?" he asks.

"Actually, I do. Just outside of Asheville. I live in a little cabin on the prettiest lake. In the summer the sunsets reflecting off the water are truly stunning. I love taking my kayak out, rowing through the swirls of pinks, oranges, and reds. It's like floating in the middle of an Impressionist painting."

Talking about home has a magical effect. I start to relax a bit and lean back against the loveseat.

Noah is watching me intently, his blue eyes twinkling. "The way you describe it makes me feel like I've been there. You really are a good writer."

"Thank you," I say, shivering once again, but this time not from the cold. There is something between us. I can tell he feels it too. And yeah, Carianne was right. For a moment there, I totally forgot about the cameras. Almost on reflex my gaze travels from his eyes to his lips. What would it be like to kiss him?

"Hey there, handsome," one of the girls interrupts us then —a brunette named Bianca with glossy lips and curves that won't quit. She's leaning in the entry to the gazebo, directly under the mistletoe. She turns to me. "Mind if I steal him for a second?"

I can practically hear the cameras zooming in on my face, recording my reaction.

"You don't have to say yes," Noah whispers so softly only I can hear.

Except I do. Everyone knows how shows like this work. If I say no, I look like a selfish jerk. And besides, I need to get out of here, get some fresh air. This girl is a stark reminder that I am not the only girl Noah is trying to get to know or the one he'll ultimately decide to choose. I can't let my guard down this fast. Not if I want to keep from getting my heart broken.

"Not at all," I say brightly, avoiding Noah's gaze. "He's all yours."

I let the blanket slip from my shoulders and as gracefully as I can, start walking back to the lodge. The cameras don't bother following me. It's only once I reach the lodge's deck that I risk a glance backward...and regret it immediately.

Bianca has seated herself on Noah's lap. Her hands are in his hair and then she's pulling him to her and he's not resisting. Slowly she lowers her head to his. Their lips meet.

My stomach hollows out and my heart fills with a familiar ache. This is not going to be my fairytale ending. I can feel it.

CHAPTER 6

The First Christmas Cane

SOPHIE

To date, I've worked as either a production assistant or coordinator on three different reality shows, each one connected by a common thread: random and sometimes seriously annoying contestants, selected by design to get viewers. This one proves to be no different as I get myself ready in the room and bathroom I share with two other girls.

The lodge is big, but not big enough to allow individual rooms for each of the contestants when single rooms go to the host, executive producer, director, director of photography, any key talent, etcetera. The show managed to squeeze three twin beds in these rooms, and considering the amount of luggage some of these girls arrived with, I'm surprised anyone can even fit inside. The room is pretty nice, though. I can tell the lodge staff tried to make it special for all the girls descending upon it, with flowers and a bowl of fresh fruit on the small table in the corner.

I met one of the girls I'm rooming with last night: Evie. I could tell right away that she's actually nice, not just smile-for-the-camera nice. An elementary school teacher with a heart of gold who works hard to earn a living. She will be framed up as the good girl everyone likes and roots for. Mack will probably encourage Noah to keep her around for a while.

The other girl will also be encouraged to stay on set, but not for the same reasons. The epitome of a vixen, red hair and all, Kristin brought a framed photo of herself snuggling an adorable golden retriever puppy to Noah as his Christmas gift. Except I happen to know she doesn't have a dog. On the application, there was a place to list pets. She typed "No thanks." But of course, one of the photos Noah shared of himself prior to the show was a picture of himself with his golden retriever, so suddenly Kristin became a dog lover.

Kristin is also a pole fitness instructor who specializes in aerial inverts. I know this because within thirty seconds of asking her about her interests, I was shown no fewer than five videos of her swinging her legs around the pole while her rapt audience looked on. I'll admit, she's good. Really good. But she also knows it, and witnessing her watch her own videos and gasp in awe as she slid down the pole upside down was weird. No one could love Kristin more than Kristin loves herself.

This morning, Kristin's bags have yet to be put away. Evie and I each have a few hanging dresses and some resort-casual attire, a few pairs of shoes, and one toiletry kit. Kristin has two huge trunks in addition to about twenty dresses, ten pairs of shoes, and a huge hanging bag for the bathroom that won't allow the door to fully close. Evie is too nice to say something, but I might've yanked that ridiculous hanging bag down to the floor a couple times.

I bang on the bathroom door, where Kristin's been since she got out of bed forty-five minutes ago. "Time's up. My turn."

I get a syrupy-sweet drawled response back. "Be out in a moment, love."

"Ugh, that girl." I perch on the table across from Evie and bite into an apple from the bowl. "We have to be downstairs in thirty minutes for the Candy Cane Reveal. When are you and I supposed to get ready? Five minutes before?"

Evie sighs. "It is a little inconsiderate. Maybe we can talk to her and explain that we all need to share this space."

"Sure, and monkeys will fly out her butt." I bite my lip, hoping I didn't come across as too crass. Mack gave me strict instructions to get close to these girls better so I can report out any quirky peculiarities she can use.

But Evie giggles. "I'd pay to watch that."

Evie is definitely going to be one of my favorites.

Kristin finally emerges, her hair perfectly curled into long red waves. We were given instructions last night to go downstairs this morning with a TV-worthy "just woken up" look. In other words, just a hint of makeup, beautifully mussed hair, and pajamas to give a natural feel to the morning Candy Cane Reveal.

Kristin clearly decided that didn't apply to her, with her bright red lipstick, long and clearly fake lashes, and diamond tiara. The only thing that looks remotely morning about her is her long pink satin gown that could probably double as an evening dress, complete with the thigh-to-floor slit on the side. She does have the figure for it, slender with long legs and large, perky breasts.

Not that I'm jealous as I sit here in my blue-striped cotton PJs with my B-cup boobs and non-existent butt. Even though our production assistant, Jane, picked out a couple of nice silky pajamas for me, there's something comforting being in the ones I brought from home. Besides, I don't care whether or not

I get picked for a special date. I'm here as a favor to the show and really hope it gets me on Mack's good side for future opportunities. Not to mention, she told me that the longer I stick around, the bigger bonus I'll get. So there's that.

I join Evie in the humid bathroom and try to find myself in the steam-covered mirror. I take an arm and swipe it across the vanity, allowing some of Kristin's crap to fall to the ground so I can put my bag on a corner of the counter. "Oops."

"She's such a mess," Evie says. "Where are we supposed to put our things?" She pulls out her hand mirror to apply a little mascara. She's one of the fortunate ones who don't need much makeup to look gorgeous. Still, she frowns at her reflection, tucking a strand of blonde hair behind her ear. "Do you think my hair is okay pulled up like this? Or should I wear it down over my shoulders, like Kristin?"

"First of all, never use the words, 'like Kristin.' You'd look beautiful either way, but I think having it up gives you this sweet but sexy vibe. Here." I pull the strand from behind her ear and carefully tug a strand from the other side of her face. "This frames your face nicely."

Her face lights up. "Thanks, Sophie."

"Of course." I glance at my watch. We aren't allowed to have cell phones or smart watches, so many of us are wearing regular analog watches, which is hard to get used to. I keep wanting to tap the face of it. Mack wanted to give me a phone so I could text her, but the director talked her out of it so it could be a more authentic experience. "We better get downstairs."

"I'm so nervous," she says, grabbing my arm as we head out of the room and down the hallway. "I might just die of nerves."

"If you do, I'll make sure Kristin doesn't get her hands on any of your stuff."

We soon arrive at the top of the stairs where we are supposed to make our entrance. Carianne is there with her headset on and her clipboard in hand, clearly relishing her new role as producer since she had to step in for me. She calls out each person's name to line up. Curious, I step over to try to catch a glance at the predetermined order. I'm only able to see that Kristin is last before Carianne yanks the clipboard away.

"I just want to see what ranking we ended up with," I whisper to her, but she steps away from me.

"Okay, honey," she says loudly. "Get in line behind Alexandra. Move it, now."

And just like that, I've been effectively cut out of the production details. Grumbling, I step behind the dark-haired Alexandra, who's wearing a white spa robe over her pajamas, the belt tugged tightly around her waist. She turns and gives me a half smile.

"You okay?" she asks.

"Yeah. You?"

She nods, then shrugs. "At the moment, I'm wondering why the hell I agreed to do this," she whispers.

I grin. "Same."

She grins back. "I like your pajamas. You look like a real person. Not, you know, like..."

I follow her gaze to Kristin, who is at the end of the line and tapping her finger on her arm like she's impatient for this to move along. "I'm sharing a room with her. She's...a lot."

"She looks like a lot. I'm Alex, by the way."

"Sophie. Where are you from?"

"North Carolina. You?"

"LA," I say before remembering I'm supposed to be from Texas.

"You mean real people actually live in LA?" Alex asks in fake astonishment.

I laugh but don't have the chance to respond before Cari-anne is shushing us. She waves at the first girl in line to go down the stairs, a sweet-faced blonde named Noelle who told us last night she's from the country and not used to being around so many people. Which, of course, I already know. It's honestly strange and more than a little dishonest to be the only one who knows who each girl is already, not to mention their entire story. I shrug that thought away. None of the reality shows have a foundation in honesty, so why should this one?

Poor Noelle walks down the stairs, just to be told after a loud "CUT!" to go back upstairs due to technical issues with the camera, then down again, then up and down again because her pink bra decided to play peek-a-boo. By the time she heads down for real, I can tell her nerves are getting the best of her. She trips at the bottom of the steps and falls forward, barely managing to catch herself with her hands on the floor. I notice that the cameras haven't stopped rolling. They'll keep that clip in to frame Noelle as a clumsy, nervous girl. I feel sorry for her, but even more sorry for myself that I'm not the one calling the shots behind the cameras.

The next girl to walk downstairs, Bianca, has poise, confidence, and beauty. With her long slender legs, smooth dark hair that cascades over her shoulders, pouty red lips, and almond-shaped eyes, she's the whole package. She's also the one I've noticed all the girls have pegged as an absolute bitch to be avoided at all costs. Kristin may be a lot, but at least she's fairly nice to everyone. Bianca doesn't seem to care about nice. Even though I know as a producer I'd encourage Noah to keep her in for ratings, it's going to be hard to actually coexist with this woman.

Late night I snuck over to the production trailer to give Mack a heads-up about the muttering I heard from several girls last night as Bianca stole Noah away from Alex. She nodded but didn't seem surprised. I'm sure she's hearing it all in the control room, and whatever she doesn't hear, Carianne will fill in.

"Step forward," Carianne whispers harshly, putting her hand on my lower back and shoving me slightly.

I'm really starting to hate Carianne.

My stomach starts to turn in on itself as I get closer to the steps. What the hell am I doing here, anyway? Behind me, Evie has her eyes closed, probably counting to ten and praying that she doesn't trip and fall on her face. Which I'm pretty much expecting to do myself. Even though I questioned wearing these pajamas instead of a long satin gown like most of these other ladies, I'm grateful now as I face the staircase. I manage to make it all the way down the stairs with what I hope is a sweet smile plastered to my face. Noah is there, grinning and nodding at me. Part of me is glad he knows my situation, and the other part of me wishes I really could just be like these other girls. It'd be more fun to actually be here for the right reasons, hoping I'd get the chance to fall in love.

We mingle with each other and with Noah as the staff of the lodge bring out platters of fruit, croissants, and steaming cups of hot cocoa, complete with marshmallows. An interesting choice, since having a chocolate mustache isn't exactly sexy. Still, the people at the lodge went through all the trouble to make it, so I take a cup and sip from it. Delicious. I almost swipe my hand across my mouth to remove the whipped cream but remember that I'm supposed to appear refined. I take my napkin and dab my lips. I glance at Bob, my favorite of the camera operators who will tell me point blank if I'm acting like an idiot, but he gives me the thumbs up.

Kristin comes over to the table and picks out a plump strawberry with her red manicured nails. "Strawberries are one of the few things I'll eat on a first date," she whispers to me. "They're very sexual." She winks then wanders over to Noah, slowly sucking on the fruit as she takes his arm. As annoying as she is, I give her points for pulling Noah away from Bianca, who is left fuming over her uneaten croissant.

"Good morning, ladies!" Jake appears from nowhere, his hands clasped in front of him. He's wearing a deep red Santa-inspired suit with white trim and a million-dollar smile that will, of course, melt the hearts of millions of TV viewers. "Welcome to your very first Candy Cane Reveal!"

Everyone claps a little too enthusiastically for what is going to end up as someone's moment of rejection.

"Noah, you got to spend a little time with each of these ladies. What's your impression so far?"

Noah smiles at us. "I'm incredibly honored that each of you left your lives for a little while to come all the way to Vermont. I'm excited to show you more of my town and get to know you more."

"Unfortunately, though," Jake pipes in, "one of you will have to take Santa's sleigh home today." His eyes find mine and I scowl at him.

"Please know that if you got coal in your stocking, it's not personal," Noah adds, almost too quickly. I can tell the poor guy is nervous as he clasps his hands together, then unclasps them. "I just didn't get to know you well enough, that's all. I'm sure you are all amazing women, and I wish I had more time to get to know you."

"I know this is hard, Noah," Jake says, putting his hand on

Noah's shoulder to cut off any continued rambling. "But now it's time. Ladies, please reveal what our single Santa left in your stockings."

Most of the girls rush forward. I notice Bianca takes her time, sauntering slowly and giving Noah a shy but seductive glance. I head to the stocking personalized in glittering gold with my name, my heartbeat pounding a little harder than I would have thought. I have no idea at this point what Mack is planning. Noah knows I'm with the show, so will he ditch me right away? After all, I'm here only to fill a space as one of the twelve girls of Christmas. He doesn't have to keep me.

Taking a deep breath and trying to ignore the fact that there is a camera focused on my face, I dip a hand into the stocking. I breathe a sigh of genuine relief as my hand wraps around the smooth, hard stick. I pull out the candy cane and hold it up to the camera, grinning.

"No!"

I look around quickly to see Sarah May, one of the sweet, quieter girls, holding a lump of black coal in her hand. Noah quickly runs to her side.

"I'm so sorry," he says, wrapping his arm around her shoulders. "I'm sure you're an amazing person who deserves happiness. I wish I could've gotten to know you better."

"Cut!" Our director, Alison, heads to the center of the room. "Noah, you're supposed to walk her outside and then say these things. Not here with the other girls. And don't gush."

Noah flushes. "I'm sorry. I'm not used to having to do this."

"Well, get used to it," she replies. "You're going to have to do this ten more times."

He blanches but nods. They call "action" again and Noah

dutifully walks Sarah May to the door. The rest of us turn and give each other hugs, feeling a little subdued now that one of us has been sent away. Or at least I am. Bianca and Kristin are giggling and waving around their candy canes like they've already won Noah's heart.

We are all instructed to go change clothes for the day. I loiter around for a bit, hoping Mack comes up to ask for insights or tell me she needs me back behind the cameras, but that never happens. Jake, who is leaning against the bottom of the banister, watches as I walk toward the stairs.

"I'll be honest," he says. "I didn't expect you to last even this long."

I narrow my eyes. "You not believing in me? There's a shocker. Actually, Noah and I have had some really great conversations. He's a sweet, sensitive, sexy guy. Exactly what I'm looking for in a man."

Jake frowns at that. I move past him and head up the stairs. Putting Jake in his place felt even better than revealing the candy cane. Maybe this won't be such a bad gig after all.

CHAPTER 7

Sparks on the Snowmobile

EVIE

I am not falling for Noah.

Because that would be a first-class ticket to a broken heart. I promised myself I was here to have fun and get a break from life, which is what today is about. It's not about going on a romantic date with a guy that makes my heart flutter when I see him. Or the fact that I was chosen for the *first* date.

Cameras will be lurking, eager to capture my every mistake while The Destroyer of My Confidence is in the back of my mind, reminding me how unworthy I am.

I grip the edge of the bathroom sink and breathe in deeply. *You can do this!* I swipe red lipstick across my lips like a coat of armor and head out of the bathroom.

"There you are." Sophie perks up from where she's sitting on her bed. "We were getting worried you weren't going to reemerge."

After I got the snow gram announcing my date, I hurried upstairs to our shared room to change into warmer clothes and get my coat. Though Alexandra doesn't share a room with

Sophie and me, she joins for moral support. The three of us bonded right away and now I'm wishing we were roomies instead of having bitchy Bianca lurking around.

"You must be excited to find out what you and Noah will be doing," Alexandra says, but I don't miss that tinge of yearning in her tone.

"I am." I tug on the end of my evergreen cable sweater. "But mostly nervous. I mean, what if the date is a disaster?"

"You're going to have so much fun," Sophie says.

"You don't know that," I say as I gather up my coat and slip on my boots. "It could be something boring or awkward."

"Well, I kind of..." Sophie clears her throat. "Feel good about this."

If only I had her confidence.

"Here's the thing," I say and take a deep breath. "The night we all arrived, I met Noah before it started."

They gasp. Then I tell them about how my friends signed me up and I was only here to have fun. And how I told him that.

"Oh, wow," Alexandra says, cringing.

"That's bad, isn't it?" I ask them.

"Did the cameras catch you telling him that?" Sophie asks.

I shake my head. "Filming hadn't begun yet. Thankfully."

She nibbles on her bottom lip. "As long as the production crew doesn't know, you'll be fine. Just don't tell anyone else."

"You think they'd kick me out?" I ask.

"You think that's bad?" Alexandra laughs. "I was literally trying to sneak out when Noah called my name for the first impression rose."

"No!" both Sophie and I exclaim.

Alexandra nods, rolling her eyes. "It was utterly embarrassing. So with that in mind, I think you're going to be just fine."

She hands me my coat. "The important thing is you started your relationship on trust. You're not the only one here because of weird circumstances. On top of walking out, I signed up for this on a whim while drunk, so don't stress."

"You're right," I tell them, giving both a hug. "I know we just met but it's like we're already good friends."

We head downstairs where the women are gathered around Noah, laughing and looking like they're having the time of their lives. Cameras ring them, capturing every expression. You'd never know that Sierra had been complaining nonstop earlier or that Noelle and Bianca had gotten into a huge fight over Bianca hogging all of Noah's attention at the Candy Cane Reveal. I'm surprised Amber isn't here, but also glad because the girl seems to hate me and I can totally see her trying to ruin my day.

But all that is forgotten when Noah's eyes land on mine as I take the last flight of stairs. A smile pulls at his face, revealing a small dimple I hadn't noticed earlier. He's wearing a sleek, jet-black thermal jacket lined with dark silver accents. Beneath it, he's wearing a charcoal-gray shirt that clings to his toned muscles. Damn. He's sexy. A wave of delight swoops over me that he chose me to go on this first date.

I step near him and he lightly touches the hollow of my back. Even though I've got a sweater *and* coat on, it's like his hand burns right through all that material, and my whole body flushes.

"Okay, ladies," he tells the group. "We're going to head out, but I'll see you all tomorrow."

Amber comes out of nowhere and slips to his side, whispering in his ear while Zuri blows him a kiss and Bianca makes a playful boo sound. The cameras trail after us out the front doors, which is awkward, but also great because it reminds me this experience is fabricated.

Two snowmobiles wait for us outside in the cool afternoon. The sky is bright blue and the snow glitters under the sun.

"Snowmobiling?" I say with a wide grin.

"Is that okay?" He's looking at me with this hopeful expression like he really wants me to be happy.

"This is awesome! I've always wanted to try it out, but where I'm from, the closest thing we have is jet skiing."

"I grew up riding these so it's like second nature to me."

I step up to the machine and run my glove across the surface. "You'll have to teach me how to drive. The last thing I want is to crash your snowmobile into a tree."

"I'm a great tree-dodger." He winks at me. "Let me show you."

A gust of snow flurries stirs in my stomach as he slips to my side. I'm acutely aware of the women watching us through the glass doors while the camera crew moves in to get a better angle of us. But right now I don't care because his presence is chasing away all those things as he leans in close.

"Now sit on the sled," he says, and I settle onto the seat, a swirl of excitement rushing through me. "Place your hands on the handles like this."

His hands curl over mine as he shows me how to use the throttle. The cool air catches the scent of his aftershave. It wraps around me like a cocoon, making it hard to focus.

"The key to sledding is a combination of speed control and shifting your weight in the turns."

"That sounds complicated." I tilt my head only to find his lips are a breath away. I blink, my heart tumbling.

"We'll take it slow," he says, and his lips quirk up slightly. I don't miss the teasing in his voice as if he's talking about more than just the snowmobile. "Just keep your finger on the brake and use it whenever you need to."

"Avoid trees, shift my weight in the turns, and use the brake. Got it."

"And no running off until you've given me a chance." His eyes twinkle.

An assistant brings us our helmets, which have cameras attached to the top so the crew doesn't have to follow us the whole way. It's a bit of a relief knowing those large cameras won't be staring at me every single second of the time.

"It's hard to talk while on the sleds," Noah says as he settles on his own vehicle. "But I'll check in on you every once in a while. Thumbs up means all is good. Thumbs down means stop."

I give him two thumbs up, which makes him chuckle. He revs up his vehicle and I follow suit. Soon, we're zipping down the drive and turning onto a snowy path. He takes off slowly, obviously easing me into the experience. As we ride along the powdery trail, he points out the ski slopes along the way. My engine hums beneath me and the wind snaps at the edges of my jacket.

He picks up speed and I match it, a thrill shooting through me. A thick forest stretches before us and we slip onto the path that cuts through the thick pines. Since it's clearly marked out for us, it makes it easy to follow him. Every once in a while, he glances over his shoulder to check on me, and I give him a thumbs up.

We're dodging around a fallen log and I slow down to make sure I don't run into it. I manage to get past the obstruction and give Noah a thumbs up again. I wish I could see his face, but it's covered by the visor. He nods and takes off again. I go to speed up when my snowmobile sputters, chugging along like it's resisting the gas.

And then it just stops dead.

Frowning, I try to start it up again, but it doesn't respond. I lift up my visor to get a clearer view of where Noah is but he must have turned at the bend up head. The forest is silent other than the distant wail of his vehicle and the wind slipping between the boughs. I climb off my seat, slightly panicked that he's going to leave me out here alone. It's moments like this I wish we were allowed our phones. Another reminder of how weird this process is. I wait a few minutes before I pull my walkie-talkie to contact Carianne, the producer. She gave it to me in case of emergencies.

I'm pressing the button to make the call when I spot Noah's black form, streaking back through the forest toward me. Relief washes over me. He skids to a stop and leaps from his vehicle, pulling off his helmet in one swift motion.

"You okay?" His eyes darken as he rushes to me. "I'm so sorry. I didn't realize you weren't behind me. I feel terrible about abandoning you. Did you fall? Are you hurt?"

His hands touch the sides of my arms and his eyes sweep over me, checking to make sure I'm okay. A shiver of delight sends goosebumps over my skin.

"I'm fine. The sled just stopped suddenly. All is good."

Relief flashes over his features. "You've no idea how glad I am to hear that. Let me take a look and see what the issue is."

He bends down and inspects the snowmobile. Finally, he taps one side. "Looks like you've got a small cut in the fuel line. Small enough that the fuel leaks slowly. Probably why it didn't show up until now."

I squat next to him, inspecting the fuel line. "I don't think I ran into anything that would do that."

"It was probably an accident or oversight."

"I hope it wasn't someone trying to ruin our date," I say, standing and crossing my arms. The cold creeps through my jacket and I shiver.

Noah rises and rubs his hands up and down on my arms to help warm me up. "Regardless, I don't want this to ruin our date. Besides, now this gives me an excuse to have you ride with me."

"The sled holds two people?"

"I promise I won't bite. Well, not on the first date." He grins wickedly at me until I laugh as my heart swoops.

Oh, this boy is dangerous to my heart.

"I'd actually love that. It was fun to ride on my own but you felt so far away. Especially after I apparently ran out of gas."

"Guess you'd better keep me on a tight leash then." He settles onto his sled, patting the seat in front of him. "Come on, we'll take turns driving."

I climb in, sitting between his legs. My heart does a little somersault as our bodies connect.

"Hold on tight," he whispers low against my ear.

My breath escapes, but I pretend we're just two normal people going for a ride through the forest. We put our helmets on and then his arms wrap around me like a warm blanket. The engine roars to life, and we take off, shooting through the wintry forest. I scream, not in fear but from the thrill of it. The pines blur past us as we weave our way higher and higher up the mountain. Before I know it, the trail opens up to a viewing area. He putters the sled to a small bench that overlooks the valley. Thick fur blankets drape over it.

The moment I climb off and pull free of my helmet, a cold wind blusters across the peaks. I'm instantly missing the warmth of his body. I shiver, but he must have noticed, because he wraps his arm around me again protectively.

"I've got a surprise for you." He escorts me to the bench. "I just hope it's not too cold to enjoy it."

A small table has been set up in front of the bench with a glowing lantern, a thermos, and two mugs. My heart melts seeing this. No one has ever done anything so sweet and thoughtful for me. This day has changed my whole perspective on Noah and this experience.

"Looks like Santa's elves have been busy." I grab a blanket and tuck it around both of us. "This is so sweet, and what an incredible view. From this high up, your lodge looks so tiny."

We're situated about halfway up one of the mountains. Below, I can make out Everpine Lodge, its rooftops dusted with snow and smoke curling up from its chimneys. The sun is starting to sink below the horizon, sending streaks of pale gold across the sky. He opens the thermos and pours hot chocolate into two cups, handing me one. I take a sip, and its warmth sinks into my chilled body, relaxing me.

"I like to come up here when the pressure gets to be a little too much," he says. "There's a lot to manage. Running a company, guest complaints, toilets overflowing, roof damages, and ski lifts breaking. But when I come up here, I get my focus back. I remember why I'm running this business and why I love it so much."

"I love that perspective." I study his profile in the twilight. The sharp jaw, the straight nose, and the way his eyes drink in the sight as if it's his passion. "So tell me, Noah, what is it about your business that you love so much?"

"My family has been running the lodge for over a hundred years. We joke in our family that we learn to ski first and walk later. It's a part of who we are. I think my mom has a picture somewhere of me skiing in my diaper."

"I *need* to see that photo."

"Mom loves showing it off. I think she secretly orchestrated the whole thing to brainwash me into the business."

"She must really love you."

"Yeah, we're a close family. When my dad had a heart attack last summer it was a wake-up call for all of us. Ever since then, I've been helping out a lot more than before. I was running one of the smaller resorts in California, but after that, I knew I needed to be back here. Home."

I reach over and squeeze his hand. He wraps his tighter around mine and then stares at our grasp as if it means something to him. I shiver, and maybe it's partially from the cold, but mostly it's because whatever this is between us is starting to feel very real.

"Come on." He rises, picking up the lantern on our table. "It's cold out here and I have one last surprise for you before our date ends."

"Now I'm intrigued."

He leads me away from the edge of the cliff, past our snowmobile toward the mountain's rock face. My boots crunch on the glittering snow illuminated by the lantern swaying at Noah's side. The first pinpricks of stars cut through the fading blue sky above.

"This place is magical," I whisper, soaking it all in as we step through a group of trees. "It's like the world is only for us."

A rustling in the bushes snags my attention and I freeze.

"Don't worry." Noah protectively wraps his arm around me. "It's just the camera crew."

"Right." I shake my head, realizing they've been here the

whole time. Of course, they have, I chide myself. "I almost forgot about them."

And this game we're playing. For a moment there, I forgot he wasn't only dating me and not ten other girls.

"Good, because I want this to be about us and not the show," he says as we stop before an ice-crusted rock wall shimmering like glass. "Ready for your surprise?"

"A snow monster isn't going to jump out and scare me, is it?"

He throws back his head in a laugh and tugs me forward into the entrance, holding up the lantern to light our way. A jagged crack in the rock, wide enough for me to walk through, cuts an entrance into the mountain. We slip into the narrow tunnel, rock and earth swallowing us. I clutch his hand tighter because it's so narrow that Noah has to turn slightly to fit his wide shoulders through it. I'm not claustrophobic, but it's still really tight. I'm tempted to turn around, but a camera person is following us from behind.

The tunnel spits us into a cave. Twinkle lights and garland are strung from the rock walls and tiny candles circle the perimeter, illuminating the place in a soft golden glow. A table and two chairs are set on top of an evergreen rug in the center of the place. Christmas carols echo across the intimate space and the air smells of earth, pine, and spices. A cluster of tiny, white-lit Christmas trees are in one corner where I spy a camerawoman hidden behind them, filming us.

Another reminder we're not alone.

"What do you think?" Noah asks as he escorts me to a chair draped with another thick fur blanket.

"I love it. It's incredible. I never thought a cave could look this beautiful."

He pulls the chair out for me, and as I settle into it, I pull off my hat and mittens and try to untangle my long blonde hair so I don't look like I've been caught in a windstorm. Then I unzip my jacket and wrap the cozy fur blanket around my body. A small heater has been set up by our chairs, and I rub my hands in front of it. Thankfully, it's warmer here than outside.

"Also," I add, smiling at the camera crew. "Whoever thought to bring this electric heater is my new favorite person."

The crew smiles at me but makes a point to not interact. Candles, garland, and berries are scattered across the table.

"Please tell me this is food because I'm famished," I say and lift the silver dome covering my plate.

I'm not disappointed. Stuffed chicken, sliced to show off the cranberry, spinach, and goat cheese stuffing, is arranged beside sliced sweet potatoes and asparagus with berries and rosemary garnish.

"This looks amazing," I say, practically drooling. "Like Christmas on a plate."

"That's Chef Stefan's doing," Noah explains as he opens the bottle of wine and pours us each a glass. "I think he's one of the best chefs in the world, and we like to hire the best."

"I don't think I've ever eaten anything this fancy." I hold up my wine glass. "My biggest excitement on the meal front is when our cafeteria has pizza Fridays. Should we make a toast?"

"To finding love," he says, gaze locked with mine.

My heart does this little flip as we clink glasses. But a bunch of questions crowd my mind. Will he find love in this process? Do I dare to even think it could be me?

Don't go there, I remind myself. This whole experience is about finding myself and having fun. Noah is dangerous because in the few hours we've been together today, I could totally see myself falling for him. I can get over a douchebag like

Ted, but Noah? I don't think my heart would ever recover from him.

I take a sip of the wine. It's smooth and rich. Another reminder I'm out of my league here. Noah Frost might wear flannel shirts and zip around on a snowmobile, but he's also a millionaire used to a life that belongs in movies and books.

"So you eat pizza on Fridays," he says, cutting his meat. "What is it you do?"

"I'm a third-grade teacher. So my days are full of teaching kids how you can get sucked away into another world in books while trying to remind them that yes, they will use fractions in real life."

"A teacher? Wow. That's a noble occupation. I respect that."

"I suppose. It seems like a great life, having summers and holidays off and making a difference in kids' lives, but between standardized testing, report cards, and managing parents, it's a lot. Still, my students are my life and I really love teaching."

We spend the rest of the meal with me sharing stories about how a kid got locked in the snake room at the zoo during a field trip and I had to rescue him. And then about a time I volunteered for the play and had to learn how to sew on the fly when our lead pirate's pants ripped in the butt.

"I had to sew him up in less than one minute before he had to go back out on set." I shake my head at the memory. "The worst part is he didn't believe in underwear. I had to sew him up with eyes half-open, half-closed."

Noah chuckles. "I'm surprised you didn't stab him with the needle."

"Well, I might have accidentally pricked him." I give him a knowing look. "Suffice it to say, I think he has found a new love for undergarments."

He shakes his head, eyes staring at me brightly. "I'm not going to lie, I'm surprised a girl like you hasn't already been snatched up."

My heart sinks and my laughter dies. This is it. This is the moment I need to tell him about The Cheater and Liar who broke me and made me never want to date again. I swallow the lump in my throat but my eyes dart over to the cameras, staring at me like a big eye.

I can't say the words. Can't admit how much he hurt me. If I say it to Noah on television, the whole world will hear. And so will Ted.

I clear my throat and shove away my pain and hurt into a secret compartment inside me and clamp that door shut.

"I guess I just haven't found the right guy yet." I attempt a smile.

Noah's eyes dim just a little as if he knows I'm keeping something from him, but then he nods as if he understands.

"I have something I'd like to give you." He takes my hand and escorts me to the cluster of trees. A candy cane with a big red bow hangs from one of the branches. He plucks it off and holds it between us. "I'm taking this whole process very seriously. I want to find the woman I'm going to spend the rest of my life with and every time I give one of these out it means I see a possible future with that woman. So this candy cane means I can see a possibility with you. Will you accept it?"

The room spins a little and my pulse ticks up a notch. I want to believe there could be a chance for us even if it's only for tonight.

"Absolutely," I say, taking the candy cane.

I lift up my eyes to see his face inches from mine. His lips taunt me and every fiber in my body yearns for him. With my free hand, I splay my fingers across his hard chest and then lift up on my toes.

Our lips meet, soft as snowflakes. A need for him urges me closer and I press my body against his, deepening our kiss. He sighs against my mouth and the sound sparks every cell within me. Our tongues meet and fire surges through me. I wrap both of my hands around his neck, loving the way his mouth fits mine. The scent of him calls to me, and it's hard to think about anything other than him.

His hands run up and down my back and then slip beneath my sweater just at the edge of my jeans, his skin touching mine. Heat pools into me and I gasp from the touch.

He breaks contact like he's been snapped back to this world. He's breathing heavily and his eyes are hooded, unreadable. But then he leans in close once again.

"Evie," he breathes into my ear, words meant only for me. "You've totally captivated me. I wish our time together could last longer."

My heart soars. I cling to him and this moment. It feels too good to be true and maybe it is. But for tonight, I'm going to keep this kiss, these words, this date as my own.

Because tomorrow nothing is guaranteed.

CHAPTER 8

Worst Case Scenario

ALEX

"Today is a new day. Time to put on your big girl panties and get back out there," I tell my reflection in the mirror as I put the finishing touches on my makeup. I've got on more than my usual, but much less than most of the other girls. I've just never gotten the hang of false eyelashes. No matter how hard I try, they end up askew and make me look more hot mess than sophisticated fashionista, so I've settled for ultra lash-building mascara and a smoky eye instead, hoping like crazy it'll be enough to make me look good on camera.

And yeah, maybe that makes me vain—caring how I come off to the television viewers. But it's inevitable my readers and my publishing team will tune into the show and it's important to me that I give the right impression. So I'm shooting for a very wholesomely sexy Andy from *The Devil Wears Prada* after her makeover vibe today. God, I love that movie. Just thinking about it puts me in a better mood.

Today is the first group date with Noah and I'm on it. Not exactly as exciting as our gazebo-under-the-stars moment the other night or Evie's snowmobile and ice cave by candlelight adventure, but it'll have to do because despite my intention to be pragmatic about this whole experience, I want to see Noah again even if it means doing it in the company of more than half the other girls. Every time I think about the way his eyes held mine when we talked, I get this flutter of nerves in my stomach. He read my books.

And liked them.

"You better hurry up! You can't be late," Sophie calls from the other side of the door. Yesterday she and I cheered on Evie before her date. Now it's *their* turn to cheer *me* on.

I step out of the bathroom and do a little spin. I'm wearing a faux fur vest over a creamy white turtleneck and dark-washed jeans that hug me in all the right places because of the Spanx I've got on underneath them. Thank the little baby Jesus this is a winter dating show, not some tropical-island-summer thing. Being a full-time writer is not exactly conducive to having a tight ass even if I do work out regularly.

"Très chic." Sophie nods approvingly. "Just the right amount of sexy."

"Enough to steal his attention away from Bianca?" I ask, biting my lip, heat flooding my face. Every self-help book I've ever read warns about the dangers of competing with anyone but yourself, but apparently, I haven't elevated to that level of maturity yet.

"Absolutely," Evie says, making a face. "That girl thinks high fashion is wearing heels with her string bikinis instead of flip flops."

A snort of laughter erupts from the doorway on the other side of the room.

Whoops. We're on camera.

Evie winces, her cheeks flushing bright pink as she puts her back to the cameraman.

Sophie clears her throat. "What time do you need to be downstairs?"

I glance at my watch, belatedly remembering that it doesn't work. I am the worst at maintaining my time pieces. To me they're mostly just for looks, so none of them actually tell time. I usually check my phone, but I had to turn it into the production crew when I got to the lodge so...

"Shoot!" I mutter. "I'm late."

I hurry from the room, the cameraman-spy hot on my heels.

"Have fun!" Sophie and Evie yell in unison from my bedroom doorway.

I can't help noticing the envy laced in their voices—well, Evie's anyway. Sophie's barely mentioned her impressions of Noah so far. Is she playing it close to the vest because she's working some kind of strategy? Or does she just not have feelings for him? Given how nice and handsome he is, it's hard to believe she's not interested at all. As much as I like her and Evie, I make a mental note to stay wary around them. This is a competition of sorts for Noah's heart, after all. And Evie is definitely developing feelings for Noah.

By the time I find the lodge's theater space where the group date is supposed to take place, the other girls are already there. Carianne's got them seated on stools center stage. Of course, Bianca's smack in the middle of the group, her dark hair glossy under the lights. I take the only open stool—all the way at the end next to Bella Grace, the Christmas tree costume-wearing Southern belle. Today, she's got on a more subdued sweater dress with cowgirl boots, limiting her quirky themed fashion elements to a pair of Christmas wreath earrings and a jingle bell bracelet. Her auburn hair is piled atop her head in a messy bun that accentuates her swan-like neck. Without the costume, it's so much easier to see how beautiful she is.

"Apparently Noah's running late too," she tells me as I settle onto my stool. "So it's okay you just got here." Then she looks sidelong at me. "Hey! Y'all weren't somewhere together, were you?" The other girls turn in our direction, waiting to hear my response. "I mean it's a bit of a coincidence that you're both late. You got the first private conversation after all."

"No," I say loudly with what I hope is just the right amount of hesitation so they aren't sure whether or not I'm lying.

Bianca's eyes narrow as she flips her hair over one shoulder. She's wearing a white-fur-trimmed red sweater with a v-neck so deep I can practically see her belly button. She leans over and whispers something in Kristin's ear and both of them laugh as their gazes slide over me.

"Okay, ladies!" Carianne calls from the orchestra pit. "Get excited because your date is about to begin! Cameras, start rolling." The show's crew hurriedly gets into place.

Jake Logan, the show's host, strides on stage, a big TV-announcer smile spreading across his face. "Good afternoon, contestants!" he says, his voice as smooth and rich as eggnog. "Who's ready to see Noah again?"

The other girls start cheering and bouncing up and down on their stools. Bella Grace grabs my hand and squeezes it excitedly. Jesus, I'm *so* uncomfortable. I am definitely not the type of person who bounces. Or cheers for that matter. But I'll look ridiculous if I'm the only one who doesn't, right? I force a big smile and squeeze Bella Grace's hand back.

She frowns and leans closer. "Try not to look like you're constipated, honey," she whispers. "Relax."

I make my smile smaller, with fewer teeth showing. I force myself to think of something relaxing. My kayak, being out on my lake. It's been less than forty-eight hours and I miss my cabin already.

"Better," Bella Grace murmurs approvingly.

"Noah, why don't you come on out?" the TV host says.

On cue, the double doors at the back of the theater swing open and Noah walks in carrying a huge basket full of red velvet gift boxes. Involuntarily, I suck in a breath. He is the definition of cozy-ski-cabin-hot. Navy cable-knit sweater that intensifies the blue in his eyes. Dark hair curling perfectly at the ends. Jeans that hug his ass just right and a pair of well-worn leather boots that manage to look both comfortable and stylish.

The girls' squeals increase exponentially.

I try to tamp down the snowstorm of nervousness spreading through my stomach.

"Hey, everyone," Noah says, his smile almost boyishly shy. "Thanks for joining me today. Growing up, this theater was one of my favorite places to hang out. I loved to watch the performers rehearse. Still do. Once I got older and started a band with a few of my friends, I even played a gig or two here myself."

He joins us on stage and hands the basket to Jake. "Being with someone creative is important to me." His gaze travels over each of us, but it lingers on me when he says the word "creative" and my stomach snowstorm becomes a full-out blizzard. Bianca notices it too and makes a face, elbowing Kristin not-so-subtly in the ribs. Both of them glower at me.

"So. For this date, I'd like you to unleash your inner artist and perform for me and the Everpine locals. And to help inspire you, I've gotten each of you a gift."

Jake starts handing out the red velvet boxes.

When Carianne gives us the signal, I pry the lid open and peek inside. The notebook and pen comfort me, but the ukulele? Not so much. Oh *no*. This performance is musical?

"I want each of you to spend the next hour creating a song," Noah says. "But don't panic. It doesn't have to be original. If you want, you can adapt the lyrics to say, your favorite Christmas song or something. Just have fun with it. Once it's written you'll get another hour to rehearse. Then we'll open the theater doors to all my friends and neighbors so you can perform it for them—and me."

Oh my god, this is my worst nightmare. He wants us to sing? In front of his whole town? I cannot think of anything more terrifying to have to do in this moment.

Kristin does a little happy dance with her feet. "How fun!" she exclaims, hugging the ukulele to her chest. Of course she's excited; I watched her bio reel. Out of high school she was a busker in New York City, serenading people in the subway for money. Her voice is amazing.

Noah grins at her, obviously pleased. "Feel free to spread out across the theater. Find a quiet spot to work. Then I'll be around to check on each of you to see if I can help you with your songs."

The other girls break out in applause at this, but I'm still gripping the sides of my gift box, staring at the ukulele like it might turn into a snake and bite me. I can't sing. Like, at all. Not even the shower has acoustics good enough to smooth out my pitchiness.

Jake clears his throat as he returns to Noah's side. "And there's one more thing you should know. At the end of your performances the town will vote on which one they liked the best." He pauses for dramatic effect. "And the winner will get some very special alone time with Noah."

Noah's grin turns mysterious as he and Jake exchange a glance.

What kind of special alone time?

The girls go wild, everyone talking all at once. I try to look as excited as they are, but there is no way I'm winning this competition. No. Way. That blizzard brewing in my stomach? It's quickly morphing into a Nor'easter the size of Vermont. I'm literally trembling.

"Your time starts now, ladies," Jake says as he guides Noah to the side of the stage.

Everyone jumps off their stools at once and eagerly starts hurrying off the stage to different parts of the theater, anxious to stake their claims closest to the cameramen. While they fan out across the seats, I slip behind the curtains backstage and climb a section of scaffolding so I'm literally above all the action, tucked away where the cameramen will be hard-pressed to follow. I need to be as alone as possible if I'm going to have any chance at this.

I set the ukulele out of sight behind me and flip open the notebook. Singing and performing are not my strengths, but writing is. If I write something original, not based on an existing Christmas song, maybe I can still stand out even if my singing stinks. I tap my pen against my thigh.

And tap.

And tap.

Twenty minutes pass and I've got nothing on the page.

I glance at the other girls below. Everyone is concentrating hard. It's so quiet I can hear the distant voices of people in the lodge's lobby outside the theater. All the other girls seem to be writing feverishly. A few are already silently mouthing lyrics.

Damn.

I rest my head on the scaffolding and close my eyes. *Come on, Alex. You write for a living. You face deadlines all the time. Writing romance is your superpower. You've got this.*

Except I don't. Because this time I'm not trying to channel a character's romantic thoughts. I'm trying to describe mine. And I've barely talked to this man and yeah, we shared a moment, and *yeah*, I get butterflies around him, but who is he really? I have no idea. All I have is his slick show bio and the few minutes' worth of conversation we had to go on. Nothing personal or intimate. I am dead.

A noise from somewhere beside me startles my eyes open.

"It's just me," Noah says, holding up his hands in surrender. He settles into a seated position beside me. "You get points for the most creative writing spot," he says softly, gripping the scaffolding beside him as he glances below. "You couldn't have chosen something closer to the ground?"

Just then a drone camera appears in the air in front of us. Jesus, I really can't escape the cameras, can I?

"Isolation helps me write better," I say, suppressing the urge to give the drone the finger. When I turn my attention back to Noah, I can't help but notice the tension in his face and how he's avoiding looking down. "Heights not your thing?" I ask.

He shakes his head. "Not since I was eight. I was climbing a tree and fell. Got a concussion and everything. I mean, I'm fine on a ski slope or somewhere enclosed like the gondola, but up here with the catwalk so narrow?" He shivers.

Seeing him nervous is apparently just the magic I need. Noah freaking out makes my freaking out lessen.

"I climbed trees too as a kid. It was a good place to hide from my family and read," I say.

Noah swallows and lets out a slow, shaky breath. "Any way I can convince you to continue this conversation on the ground?"

I can't hold back a laugh. "I would, but what's down there is definitely a lot scarier for me than what's up here." I gesture to the other girls just as Bianca starts twerking while humming *The Jingle Bell Hop*.

Noah lets out a burst of laughter. "Point taken."

"Besides, it's safer up here than you think. I won't let you fall." As soon as the words come out of my mouth, I realize how potentially laced with double meaning they are and my cheeks heat up.

Noah's gaze goes serious, as if he's sizing me up to see if I'm being sincere. Suddenly it's hard to meet his gaze. Something changes in the air between us.

"You're easy to be around, Alex," Noah says softly.

"Thank you?" I say, the question obvious in my tone.

"It's definitely a compliment," he says before clearing his throat. "So how can I help?"

"By buying yourself and your friends and family ear plugs," I say. "Because my singing sucks."

He laughs louder and harder this time before accidentally looking down again and shivering.

"It's not funny," I say, but I'm laughing now too. "I'm a writer for a reason. Performing is not my thing. I'm too shy." I feel ridiculous admitting it.

Noah considers this. "Being shy isn't a weakness. At least not to me. The competition is strictly for fun, I promise. You don't have to excel at singing to be entertaining. In fact, you don't have to sing at all." He swallows hard, his grip on the rail tightening even more. "Recite the song like poetry."

I meet his eyes with mine. "Actually, that's not a bad idea."

He grins. "Your words are musical all on their own. So let them shine."

Carianne calls to him from the stage. He's supposed to move on to the next girl now.

He sucks in a breath. "Welp, time for me to climb down. If I can." Without letting go of the rail, he gets to his feet and starts inching over to the ladder a few feet away. I fight the urge to laugh again. He's a big guy. Muscular. Rugged. And he's crossing the scaffolding like a ninety-year-old grandma. The drone flies beside him the whole way.

"Well, this is humiliating," he mutters.

And I can't help it, I do laugh.

He glances up at me, his face ashen. "I'm glad you're enjoying this so much."

"Don't worry. It's my turn next," I say.

And in what feels like mere seconds later, it is. The theater is crammed with people. The whole town's shown up to watch us perform.

Sweet Jesus.

My palms start to sweat. But before I have time to panic properly, Jake calls my name.

I'm up first?

"Go already!" Bianca shoves me out from behind the curtain and I stumble on stage.

The stage lights shine directly into my eyes. I can't see anything else. The audience is nothing more than a series of silhouettes.

I take a deep breath. I can do this. I'm just reciting poetry. Like in college. I strum the ukulele lightly.

We met as the snow came down
Strangers in a wintery town

Your smile caught me off guard
I don't know your story yet
But something about you feels so right
We don't need perfect dates or lines
Just snowfall and a little time
Maybe love begins like this
A moment wrapped in twilight's mist

I let my notebook fall to my side.

For a moment no one reacts and I nearly run off stage, but then there's a swell of applause and even a few whistles of approval.

From off stage, Bianca looks ready to strangle me. I must've done better than I thought.

I smile and take a bow. It's too dark for me to see Noah's reaction, but that's okay. I made it through and for now, that's all that matters.

I watch the other girls go. Kristin basically does Santa Baby without making any major changes and pulls Noah up on stage so she can dirty dance in his lap. It's wildly uncomfortable to watch and halfway through her performance, he manages to slip out of the chair and maneuver her into a slow dance instead. Sierra reworked "Jingle Bell Rock" so the lyrics relate to the show. Unfortunately, it's pretty clever and she sings it well enough to get a standing ovation.

Bella Grace does "Over the River and Through the Woods to our Bachelor's House We Go." Somehow she managed to find a stick horse and sings while riding it all over the stage. She purposefully hams it up and the crowd loves it. But the real showstopper is River, the most free-spirited of the group. Like me, she created an original song, but she sings it with a voice so clear, heartfelt, and charmingly folksy that she gets a standing ovation. Several people even cry.

She's the clear winner and no one's surprised when she gets the alone time with Noah.

And I'm not faking when I say I'm happy for her. She deserves the dinner and dancing moment they set up in the lodge's ballroom with a surprise serenade by Andrea Bocelli.

But I'd be lying if I said I wasn't jealous. I am. So much more than I thought I'd be. Tonight was a victory of sorts. I managed to face my fears and perform, but I'm starting to face an even bigger fear now: letting my heart fall when in the end there might be no one waiting to catch it.

CHAPTER 9
That's a Wrap!

SOPHIE

I perch on my bed next to Alex, who came back from today's date so completely despondent that I invited her into my room for a hangout party. Kristin is chilling with Bianca in the hot tub, so Evie and I have the room to ourselves. Evie is sitting on the floor, thumbing through a fashion magazine.

"It's not like a date really means that much," I tell Alex, even though I know better. Dates are the only real way to get to know each other, so those who don't get chosen for one will most likely be sent home earlier. "Especially early on. The first dates will probably just blur together in his mind, and he won't remember much from them."

Evie's head pops up, her expression hurt. Crap, I forgot she got picked for the first date. "Except that pivotal first date," I try to recover with. "You will always be the first person he chose."

Evie smiles, but Alex's frown deepens. I sigh inwardly. I was always good at managing people's emotions when I was an assistant producer, so why is it so hard now?

"Look, you both are the best here," I tell them. "And if he chooses Bianca or Kristin over you, well, then he isn't worth having."

"What about you?" Evie asks. "Don't you want to get one of those dates?"

For some reason, Jake's handsome face pops into my mind, and I push it away. But I smile and put an arm around Alex's shoulders. "Of course I do. And maybe I will. But I'm not going to sit here and worry about it when I can be enjoying myself with my new friends."

"Thank god for both of you," Evie says. "I don't know what I'd do if there were nothing but a bunch of Biancas and Kristins here."

The production assistant, Jane, pops her head into the room to advise us that we will be needed downstairs in thirty minutes and to dress in our "cute casual clothes."

Prior to flying the girls out here, the show provided a list of styles for everyone to wear with their corresponding "mood":

- Cute casual—wholesome
- Floor-length gown—elegance
- Cocktail attire—sexy
- Swimsuit—hot tub-ready
- Dressy casual—drinks with friends
- Sexy casual—looking for a hookup

That last one was Mack's idea and not my favorite, but I didn't say anything. It was only after she coerced me into being a contestant that I realized I'd also have to follow the dress code. I've never gone looking for a hookup, like ever. So it seemed like a joke trying to shop for something that I have zero clue about.

Now, cute casual, that's my jam. I grab a pair of jeans and my favorite soft gray knit pullover and take over the bathroom before Kristin can claim it.

At six-fifteen, all ten ladies are dressed in their cute casual outfits and are standing around the fireplace downstairs, waiting for our guy. I take a moment to examine River, fresh off her date with Noah. Her rounded cheeks are flushed and she looks incredibly happy as she talks with Zuri, so the date must've gone well. Both River's and Zuri's choice of attire is interesting. They're into fitness, so maybe it's not too odd that they are both wearing yoga-style pants and spandex tops under sweaters.

Kristin of course looks gorgeous in a green cashmere sweater that coordinates perfectly with her fiery red hair. Bianca also stands out, but her white silk blouse and form-fitting black leather skirt look more Gucci sexy than cute casual.

Mack is standing in a corner, texting on her phone, her eyebrows pinched together. I walk over to her and wait for her to acknowledge me.

"What?" she says without looking up from her phone.

"I've been getting to know some of the girls," I tell her. "They are an interesting group of contestants, to say the least."

"So?" she mutters, still fully engrossed in her phone.

"Kristin and Bianca are the front-runners for Queen Bitch, so I'd think you'd want to keep one around for most of the show. Probably not both, though, because they're too—"

"Look, you're here as a contestant," Mack says abruptly, slipping her phone into her pocket. "So unless you have actual real scoop, just be a contestant and let us handle our own jobs."

She walks away before I can respond and shouts at one of the cameramen to adjust the angle.

"Burn," a low voice says behind me.

I turn to see our esteemed host, Jake, grinning. "What do you want?"

He shrugs. "You know better than to bother Mack before she's finished her second glass of scotch."

I glance over to see Mack pouring herself a glass of Glenfiddich even as she's barking orders to the crew.

"How's it going up there with those girls, anyway?" Jake asks. "Any of the venom sneaking into your blood?"

"The girls are nice for the most part," I tell him.

He smirks. "Sure they are. And they're here for the right reason too."

"You know, that's one thing I always hated about you. You think you know everything that's going on, when you really know nothing."

"Oh?"

"A rock knows more about love than you do."

"Who's talking about love?"

"Not you. Never you."

"Bitter party of one," he quips. The corner of his lip lifts in that way that always used to set my pulse racing. I hate that my betraying heart still pounds harder around Jake. He's just another perfect-looking guy from Hollywood with a killer smile and a heart of ash.

I glare at him. "Just go do your job. Smile and nod like a bobblehead, hand out the candy canes, and steer clear of me." I spin around and leave him behind. Hot or not, Jake is no good.

As we gather in front of the fireplace, cameras set and rolling, Jake announces our destination for the evening: a toy store. We head to the charming village in vans and stop at the little shop. It's too small for all the cameras, so there is another larger space next door that will be utilized for the activity. We're each then given a slip of paper with a child's first name, age, and interests. We have five minutes to pick out three items that they would like and take them next door to wrap. I glance at my paper: Benjamin, age twelve, loves camping and nature.

Two things I know absolutely nothing about, and I have to buy three toys? For a twelve-year old?

I glance over at Evie's paper. Hers is a little girl, age six, who likes building things. So much easier.

Half of us are then sent into the store. Since it's so small, we have to take shifts. With a basket on my arm and a cameraman trailing me, I walk the aisles and scan the shelves. Most of the toys are for little kids. Plenty of dolls, Legos, and games, but nothing that represents a twelve-year-old who likes camping. I do find what looks like a nice magnifying glass and put it in my basket. I have a feeling we're being tested to see how creative we can be.

I'm musing over the board games when Jake calls out, "Ladies, you have ninety seconds to bring your items to the counter!"

Great. I cruise down the aisles again, scanning the shelves as quickly as I can. Everyone else seems to be heading to or is at the counter already. I grab a pair of binoculars and keep searching for the final item. I find myself back in the games section. Monopoly isn't exactly camping-related but it's still fun for a preteen. But then my eyes land on a microscope tucked behind the games. I remember using a microscope in school to examine leaves, so hopefully the boy will figure out how to use it for nature stuff. I place it in my basket and rush to the counter with ten seconds to spare.

We head to the space next door and wait for the other team to finish. Then, when we're all together, we stand at tables that have tape and scissors.

Jake steps in again, smiling that million-dollar smile. He's joined by Noah, looking very handsome in a red cable-knit sweater. They walk around to look at our gifts and take notes.

"Great job, ladies!" Jake announces as he steps back to the center of the room. "You all did very well, and I know there are a lot of children who are going to have a great Christmas. Now, you have five minutes—yes, five—to wrap the gifts you just purchased."

He directs a look at Bianca, who is frowning at the enormous stuffed bear she procured. "Some might be harder than others to wrap, but I know you'll be creative. The wrapping paper is along the wall behind me, so please be careful when picking out your rolls so as not to run over each other." He chuckles. "Ready...and go!"

We all take off running around the tables and head toward the wrapping paper. I grab a roll of blue paper with sparkling snowflakes and start to take it back to the table, when Bianca grabs it out of my hands.

"Finders keepers," she says, laughing.

What a bitch. I don't have time to fight over it, so I turn back to rifle through the remaining rolls. Most of the paper has been pulled except for a few bright pinks, a yellow floral, and one that looks like it's meant for a toddler with dump truck patterns. Ugh.

Looking over to the cameras, I notice Jake's curious eyes on me. I ignore him.

"Sophie, you can have some of mine," Alexandra calls out from her station as she holds up a roll of green camo. I smile at her gratefully as she cuts off a few pieces and hands me the rest.

The toys are pretty straightforward to wrap, and thankfully I'm pretty good at it. Years of practice at my first job at Kohl's helped prepare me for this moment. From the assortment of ribbon, I grab a natural-colored raffia and fashion it into a fancy bow.

"Look at her," Evie says in disgust as she wraps a Lego Star Wars set. She nods toward Bianca, who has given up on wrapping the bear and is instead wrapping Noah. Noah chuckles as she starts rolling the paper around him, standing in front so just her arms move the paper around his chest.

"He doesn't look thrilled about it," I tell her. Noah's expression has gone from slightly amused to decidedly uncomfortable as Bianca kneels in front of him to wrap his legs. Kristin joins her on the other side of Noah.

I quickly walk over to the scene and grab the roll from Bianca's hands. "Hey, can I borrow some of that paper since you aren't using it? Thanks so much." I tug on the roll, allowing Noah to spin out of his trap. He gives me a grateful look.

Bianca and Kristin glare at me as they scramble to their feet, but I'm already heading back to my station. Jake seems entertained by my intervention, grinning as I set aside the unneeded paper—my wrapping is already complete.

"Time's up, ladies!" Jake says. "Noah, please walk around and decide whose gifts are wrapped the best and which toys suit the child. The winner will join Noah tonight at the fire pit, complete with s'mores and hot cocoa."

Noah dutifully studies each person's wrapping, smiling and complimenting something about each. I get the feeling he already made up his mind. He ends at my station and compliments my professional wrapping and elegant raffia bows. Out of the corner of my eye I notice Jake watching us.

"Thanks, Noah." I lean over the table and run my hand along his arm, pouting my lips slightly, Bianca-style. "You had a piece of tape stuck to you," I whisper.

"Oh, um, thanks," Noah says, his eyebrows pinching together slightly, clearly confused by my attempt at being sultry. Now I feel a little stupid. That is, until I look over to see Jake glaring at me. Good.

Noah rejoins Jake in the center of the room, and they whisper in consultation for a few minutes. Noah raises his eyebrows at something Jake says, but then shrugs and nods. Alison takes the time to reset the cameras and adjust some positions before calling action again.

When the cameras start rolling, Noah smiles at us. "Thank you all for such a wonderful evening selecting toys for our community's children in need. This will be a very special Christmas indeed. It was hard to decide, so I'm going to select two of you to join me tonight."

Two? The buzzing around me confirms that this is an unwelcome surprise. It's harder to get to know each other when you're having to compete with another person on a date.

"So, Noah, which of these lucky ladies are s'mores-worthy?" Jake asks. I have to fight not to roll my eyes. He looks over at me then with a tiny smirk on his lips, and a suspicion starts to dawn on me.

Noah nods. "Noelle, I love that you paid attention to who the child is and chose a Barbie that will have special meaning for her. And Sophie, the raffia was a really nice touch, and I love the choice of camo for a boy who likes to go camping. Not only that, I know how hard it was to pick out items in a toy store for a preteen boy, and you did a great job. I have a lot of great memories of using a microscope to examine bugs I found from walks in the woods. It's perfect."

I can feel my face burning as I choke out a "thank you." Jake is grinning widely at me now. *Congrats,* he mouths.

Bullshit. He didn't want me to have time alone with Noah.

Why? Revenge? Or something else? I tell myself I don't care, then turn around, put my hand behind my back where the cameras won't see, and flip him off. I walk over to give Noah a big snuggly hug and a kiss on the cheek. Take that, Jake!

My smugness fades though as I catch Evie's sad gaze, though she tries to cover it up with a smile and congratulations. I quickly remove myself from Noah's embrace.

Bianca and Kristin huff and shoot daggers my way. I grin at them and give a little sarcastic wave. Hopefully the camera didn't catch that, or I may end up being positioned as the new Queen Bitch.

CHAPTER 10

Snowman Shenanigans

EVIE

The stockings are lined up in a neat row over the flickering fire. Our names glisten on each like they've been dusted in sugar with a little magic. The producer reminds us to wait until the cameras are rolling before we open them, which feels more like they're trying to make our nerves stretch even thinner.

And it's working.

My heart drums against my rib cage, creating its own chaotic carol. Sweat coats my skin beneath my flannel reindeer pajamas. I can't believe this, but I'm starting to like Noah. A lot. Which is scary and weird and definitely terrifying because if I don't open that stocking and get a candy cane, I'll be devastated.

"You don't look so good, Evie," Kristin says to me in that syrupy-sweet voice that grates on my nerves. "Worried you're going home today?"

I drag my eyes from my stocking to focus on her. Seriously, no one should look that good before nine in the morning, but this woman always manages to appear like she stepped out of a

Victoria's Secret ad. Her breasts spill out of her red satin lingerie that's so short, if she bends over, we're all going to see more than we'd like.

"Just excited to see Noah again," I say and flash her a smile. She's trying to wear down my confidence, and I refuse to let her.

"Right." Her eyes sweep over me, lips curling as if it's too hard to hold back a smirk. "And you look so...cuddly. Like a puppy."

"A puppy?" It's really too early to deal with Kristin.

"She doesn't look like a puppy," Sophie snaps, coming to my side. Her face is flushed and her brow is pinched in annoyance. "We need to get you a set of glasses, Kristin."

I wish I could hug Sophie right now.

"And we're rolling!" the producer calls out, which I've now learned means nothing. They've been filming us the entire time.

Jake steps in front of the fireplace, wearing a festive green sweater and jeans.

"Good morning, ladies," he begins, smiling warmly at us. "It's time for each of you to see if you've made a connection with Noah. And now here is the man you've all been waiting to see to share with you some final words before you open your stockings."

Noah strides out from behind one of the screens by the cameras. It makes me wonder how much he overheard. Bella Grace squeals and Zuri claps her hands, bouncing on her toes. He takes Jake's place in front of the fire. My heart swoops, drinking in the sight of him, remembering those strong arms wrapped around me and his firm body pressed against mine as we zipped through the forest on his snowmobile.

"These last few days have been incredible getting to know

each of you," Noah says in that deep, calm voice of his. "This decision was a tough one, but this Christmas I'm following my heart."

If my chest wasn't thumping before, now it's clanging like a bell. With a final smile, Noah exits into the lobby. The moment he's vanished, screams of excitement fill the living room. Everyone dives for the stockings, predators striking their prey. The room spins a little as I peek inside my stocking.

A candy cane waits for me. I pull it out and hug it.

Noelle bursts into tears and drops her coal like it's literally fiery hot. I feel bad for her. She'd been so enthusiastic and fun. Meanwhile, River starts shrieking, running around the room in joy while Bianca promptly unwraps her candy cane and starts to lick it slowly, clearly posing for the cameras to get a shot of her.

Quickly, I find Alex. She, too, is holding a candy cane and my heart leaps knowing one of my best friends here won't be leaving.

"Congratulations," I tell her, and we give each other a hug. "I'm so glad you're staying. That was pretty terrifying, wasn't it?"

"This whole experience is more stressful than I anticipated it would be," she agrees. "Did you see if Sophie got a candy cane?"

"You haven't gotten rid of me just yet." Sophie sashays over to us, waving her candy cane.

Alex and I cheer.

"If you found a lump of coal," Jake calls out over the mixture of cheers and crying, "please say your goodbyes to Noah. For the rest of you, there's a gift under the tree, waiting for you to open it."

I look down to find the present is right by my foot under

the boughs. It's wrapped in snowman paper and tied with a carrot ribbon. I pick it up and a gasp erupts from the group. I set it on the coffee table, and together, Alex and I rip open the present. Inside are scarves with our names on them. Sophie helps Alex distribute the scarves while I read the note out loud.

"Bundle up, ladies!" My pulse ticks up a notch. "It's time to show me who can handle the cold and bring on the heat. Join me in shaping up something unforgettable, and let's see what kind of magic we can create together. Noah."

Everyone starts talking at once about what we might be doing. Sophie drapes a blue scarf around my neck while a server comes in with a tray of hot chocolates and distributes them to each of us.

"Are these scarves made of sheep's wool?" Amber asks, scorn pulling at her lips. "Because I'm allergic to wool."

"No," Carianne assures her. "You should be fine."

"Right." Amber tosses Carianne her scarf. "Well, I only wear cashmere scarves. My skin is *very* sensitive."

Carianne takes a deep breath and then claps her hands. "Okay, ladies!" she calls out. "I want to get a shot of you all, toasting with your hot chocolates. Don't forget to smile."

She looks pointedly at Amber, slouched in the chair and curled up in what looks like a wool blanket to me. She's clearly upset she didn't get an individual date. But nothing can stop the smile on my face because I just got a few more days with Noah.

THE AFTERNOON SUN is hiding behind thick clouds as our group clamors out of the van and into Everpine's town square.

Cold bites my cheeks and excitement dances down my spine. We trail after Carianne, my boots crunching on the snow. One glance at this place and I'm already in love. Multi-colored brick shops line the streets. Wreaths hang from brightly colored doors and twinkle lights drape from windows as if to chase away the chill. Cobblestone sidewalks twist through the town with lanterns wrapped in garland, brightening any thoughts of winter gloom.

Carianne leads us off the sidewalk and across the snow, covering the town square like a blanket. A gazebo sits in the center where the camera crew is huddled, drinking from Styrofoam coffee cups and laughing.

"I wonder what we're going to do," Alex says, joining me.

"As long as we get to hang out with Noah," I say, "I'm good with whatever."

"Be careful what you wish for," Amber grumbles behind me, her breath puffing into a cloud before her. "It's damn freezing out here. We better be going somewhere warm."

Carianne stops beside the gazebo, grinning at us. "I'm afraid that's not the case. I need you all to make a nice line here and wait for Jake to give you instructions on what to do next. When Noah arrives, I'll hold up the sign so you know when you're supposed to cheer. Have fun!"

"Why does everything that woman says make me nervous?" Alex asks, buttoning up her black coat. She looks like a model with her sleek hair pulled back in a ponytail and fitted jeans tucked into heeled boots.

"You would think I'd be used to them being so cryptic," I agree. "Whatever we're doing, looks like we'll have a live audience too."

My nerves zing around me as the camera crew grab their equipment and position themselves around our group. Three of the townsfolk gather before us, setting crates on the snow, while others sit on the benches or stand by to watch.

Sophie slips into line beside me, pushing her red hat further over her ears. She looks so pretty with her brown hair flaring out and hazel eyes dancing as if she can't wait for what's next.

"I'm excited about this date," she says, rubbing her gloves together.

"You act like you know what we're going to do," Alex points out, chuckling.

"Oh, I just love snow." She waves a hand. "My day job normally doesn't allow me to do the fun things so I'm going to take advantage of this."

"What is your job again?" I ask.

We're interrupted as a van pulls up and Jake and Noah exit it, striding across the snow to join us.

"He's coming!" Zuri exclaims, practically bouncing up and down.

Noah's wearing a black coat and leather gloves, strolling through the snow like he was born to live in it.

"You know who's really hot?" Sierra says. "Our host. I mean, damn. That ass. If things don't work out with Noah, I'll climb Jake's tree."

I gasp. Sophie's eyes narrow and Alex rolls her eyes, clearly dismayed by what she's just heard.

"She really said that out loud," I whisper to my friends. I glance behind me, wondering if anyone else heard her.

"Maybe you should tell Noah you have the hots for another guy," Sophie says, loud enough for the townsfolk.

Sierra huffs, flicking her shiny brown curls. "None of you are any fun."

"Oh. My. God," Amber wails. "I already feel my skin

cracking and wrinkling in this cold. How much longer are we going to be out here?"

"Maybe if you had a scarf," Sophie says with a smirk, "you wouldn't be so cold."

Carianne waves her cue card frantically, and we all cheer as the two men step before us. Noah presses his lips together in a tight smile, but his body stiffens as he catches sight of Carianne's card that reads CHEER LOUDLY. He pales, obviously uncomfortable with how everything is so staged.

"Ladies, winter's chill is in the air," Jake begins, "and so is love! Today, you'll be putting your creativity to the test in a frosty challenge. You'll be working in a team of two or three to build a snowman, but not just any snowman. This one should capture the charm and irresistible good looks of our very own bachelor, Noah!"

Zuri squeals and jumps up and down while Bianca claps like a princess.

"We're playing in the snow?" Amber grumbles. "You've got to be kidding me."

Noah's gaze flicks to Amber, which tells me he definitely heard her. But he just smiles in that easy way of his that pulls on the lines of his face and makes him so endearing. I clench my fists. I need to put my thoughts and emotions in check. If I'm not careful, this guy could really hurt me, and after Mr. Cheats-A-Lot, I promised myself to never let that happen again.

"I know this isn't an easy challenge for you all," Noah adds. "But I have a special surprise for the winning group that I think you'll like."

Carianne's holding up her APPLAUSE sign but Noah's eyes have caught mine, intense and warm. A gasp escapes me and a thrill shivers down my spine. This man is dangerous to my soul.

"Our kind folks from Everpine have brought to you some accessories you can use for your snowman," Jake says, and the people in front of us open their crates. "Team up and then grab some scarves, carrots, and whatever else you wish because you have one hour to sculpt this guy out of snow. The townsfolk will be our judges. Let's see who can bring the *coolest* version of Noah to life!"

Instantly, I turn to Alex and Sophie. "Since there's an odd number of us, do you ladies want to team up?"

"Absolutely," Alex says.

"Let's kick some ass." Sophie holds up her palms and we give each other high fives.

"We should get our accessories now so we can get the first pick," I suggest.

Sierra and Zuri form a group and start planning out a design in the snow. Bella Grace and Bianca hurry off to make their snowman first while Kristin and Amber race us to the crates. I reach the first crate and go to grab a baseball hat, but Kristin snatches it out of my hand.

"Thank you very much," she says, lifting those perfect eyebrows.

"You literally stole that from me," I exclaim.

"All's fair in love and war, Evie," she says haughtily, and then scoops up the rest of the clothing, taking off with it all. I glower as she marches past Noah, winking at him. "I'd do anything for you, baby."

"Did the bitch just take off with all the clothing?" Sophie asks, horrified.

"Unfortunately, yes," I say, trying to tamper down my fury.

I remind myself that I'm here to have fun and spend time with Noah. "But we can improvise."

"I got us a carrot, a handful of rocks, and some cabbage leaves," Alex says, obviously able to keep a clear head in this madness.

Noah strolls over to us, hands in his pockets, eyes twinkling. "Cabbage leaves? I'm a little scared about what that's going to represent."

"Oh, you should be worried," I tease. "It's payback time for this little snow carving."

"I'm thinking it could represent his hair. What do you ladies think?" Alex holds it up beside Noah and the three of us laugh in agreement while he reddens.

Bianca magically returns, stepping up to Noah. "Hey, you," she says, batting her lashes at him while looping her arm through his. "I need to borrow those muscles of yours for a moment."

"Right. Of course." He flashes us an apologetic look before allowing Bianca to drag him off to the other side of the gazebo.

"Bianca strikes again," I say, unable to hide my annoyance when her giggles drift our way.

"Forget about her," Sophie says. "Let's focus on making a snowman that will make Noah laugh. The poor guy looks a little stressed."

The three of us find an area to set our things down and each of us start rolling balls of snow. The snow is hard and perfect for packing. It crunches, crisp and deep, as I push the ball across the lawn, gathering layer after layer and patting it down to keep it smooth and round. I'm about to roll it over to my group when a snowball smashes against my arm.

I look up to find Noah scooping up another handful of

snow, packing it into a solid ball. A wicked grin pulls on his lips.

"Oh!" My eyes widen. Quickly, I form a snowball of my own. "So that's how it's going to be."

His arm pulls back for another hit but I duck out of the way just in time. Then I retaliate, hitting his leg as he tries to run away. Laughing, I create another snowball, keeping my eyes trained on Noah as he pretends to slowly make a new one. This time I dare to run closer to him so I have a better chance at a shot. My snowball lands smack on his chest.

"You'll pay for that one," he warns.

Before I know it, he's racing at me with a massive ball of snow he must have hidden off to the side. I scream and run away toward the far end of the park only for him to catch me, wrapping his arms around my waist and picking me off the ground.

"Caught you," he says into my ear. "If I let you go, will you promise to not snowball me?"

My heart swoops. My body is pressed against his. I'm airborne in more ways than one. I don't want him to let me go, but I say, "Only if you behave too."

He sets me back on the ground and I turn to face him, breathless and flushed. A couple of the women are eyeing us warily, but I don't care. He sought me out, and I'm going to savor every moment.

"I've been thinking a lot about our date," he says and reaches over to push a hair away from my eye.

"It feels like it's been forever."

"And sometimes like only moments ago that we kissed."

I blink up at him, my heart thudding. "It was a good kiss."

"Very good." He glances over his shoulder and then steps

closer to me so we're a whisper apart. "Maybe we could do a repeat."

He goes to lean down when a dog rushes up to us, barking. We jerk apart in surprise. It's a golden retriever with big puppy-dog eyes and a tail wagging like it drank a bottle of energy drink.

"Browser!" Noah chuckles as the dog starts licking his hand. "What are you doing here, boy?"

"Is this your dog?" I bend down to pet his soft fur. Instantly, he starts licking my hand.

"My mom's dog really, but it appears as if he likes you too. He must have broken free from her grasp. He's bad like that."

"Well, I love him." I rub both hands on the side of his head. Maybe it's the rollercoaster of emotions or just touching the dog's fur but my eyes tear up.

"You okay?" Noah asks.

"I'm fine." Quickly, I wipe away a tear before one of the TV cameras catches me crying. So embarrassing. "He just brought back memories of my own dog. She was a doodle. Naughty thing but she also liked to chew on my ex's shoes so maybe she was the smart one, after all."

"Was?" he asks.

"She's in dog heaven now. She was a rescue and didn't have many years left. But the ones I had with her were the best and I like to think they were her best too."

"Wow. I'm so sorry." Noah draws me to him, and I lay my cheek on his hard chest. "That must have been hard but also that was a really cool thing for you to do."

Standing here, being in his arms feels too good to be true. A guy can't be this nice, right? River and Zuri are edging closer to us, exclaiming how cute the dog is, but I'm guessing they're just here to get some Noah time. The two of us pull apart.

"Thanks for that," I say. "It meant a lot to me and seeing your dog totally made my day. But I really need to get back to my group. They're probably hating me right now, making them do all the work while I'm having fun with you."

"I'll walk over with you," Noah offers. "Sounds like I need to apologize to them."

We head over to where Sophie and Alex are sticking in the carrot for the nose and adding stones for the eyes.

"There you are." Sophie waves a celery stick at us, teasing. "I can't believe you ditched us for this guy!"

Alex, though, is quiet as she tries to arrange the rocks. My chest tightens. She's upset.

"I'm sorry you had to do all the work," I say.

"Let me make it up to you," Noah offers. He pulls off his hat and props it on top of the cabbage leaves. Next, he withdraws a pair of sunglasses from his pocket and slips it into the snowy face. "There. Now he looks a lot like me. You're going to win for sure."

Sophie rubs her chin and assesses him and the snowman. "It does look a lot more like you, especially the round belly."

"Ahhh!" Noah presses his palms to his stomach. "I need to fire the cooks here. They're food is too delicious."

The three of us laugh but Alex stays quiet as she continues pressing the buttons into the body.

"Hey, Alex," Noah says. "Want to take a walk with me?"

She looks up, brightening a bit. "I'd love to," she says, rising to her feet.

As the two take off, a string of conflicting emotions tumbles through me. I'm glad Noah's trying to make this fair and right and that Alex isn't upset anymore, but deep down I don't want to share him with anyone else. Is that bad? Probably. Alex is one of the coolest people I've ever met.

"Dating a guy who's dating your friends at the same time sucks, doesn't it?" Sophie asks.

"Sure does." I adjust the sunglasses. "You seem pretty cool about the whole thing. What's your secret?"

"My secret?" She snorts out a laugh. "If you only knew. I mean, I'm just waiting to see where the chips fall," she adds at my confused expression.

"Ah, okay. Guess I'm not that patient."

Soon, everyone has finished their snowman and Jake is ringing the bell, calling for us all to gather around him. Alex returns to our group, a smile on her face. We're in the middle of showing her the sticks we added for arms when Browser comes trotting up and clamps his teeth around one and runs off with it.

We shake our heads, chuckling as we join the others around Jake.

"It's time for the judging," Jake says and looks at the village volunteers beside him. "Are you all ready to choose the *coolest* version of Noah?"

"We sure are," the oldest lady in the group says as she looks over at Noah, who palms his face, shaking his head.

The three judges set off. First, they come to River and Zuri's snowman.

"Tell us a little about your creation," one of the judges says.

"Ours is called Noah, the Romantic Snowman," Zuri says. "We sculpted a snow tuxedo and used our scarves to make a cravat. Sometimes he forgets to shave so the pine needles are the stubble."

The two bow and everyone claps.

"Nicely done," Noah says. "I never thought anyone would notice when I didn't shave."

This gets everyone talking as we move to Bella Grace's and

Bianca's. Theirs is slightly tilted and as Bella Grace tries to explain how this is Noah, the Skier Snowman, the head falls off.

"Yikes." Noah grimaces. "Please tell me that's not an indicator of what will happen the next time I ski."

Bella Grace pales. "No! It was purely an accident!"

"It's fine." Noah pats her on the shoulder. "I was just kidding."

"Oh, right." She tries to laugh but it comes out like a choke.

Bianca rolls her eyes, muttering, "We're definitely going to lose."

Next up is Kristin's and Amber's. There's a moment of startled shock as we circle theirs.

"We're calling ours, Sexy Noah Snowman," Amber says mischievously. "As you can see by his ample size and demeanor."

She points to the very large carrot pressed firmly in the bottom section of the snowman.

"Oh!" the elderly lady judge gasps, eyes widening.

"I see you've got big expectations to fill," Sophie tells Noah with a wry grin, nudging him.

He swallows and pulls at his collar.

"As you can see," Kristin continues, "he's only wearing a scarf, which can easily be taken off for good times."

She demonstrates this by slipping the scarf from the snowman's neck and tying it around his stone eyes like a mask. She winks at Noah.

"Wow." He clears his throat uncomfortably. "That's exciting."

None of the judges are smiling while my head goes to

places where it shouldn't, wondering what sort of things they do with Noah when they're alone with him.

Next, we head over to our creation.

"Ours is named the Real Noah Snowman," Sophie begins and points to the sunglasses. "Once you take off those glasses, you see who he truly is and discover he's the real deal."

"He's the guy you can be yourself with," Alex adds, pointing to his hat. "You don't need to wear different hats with him."

"But he's also the one whose dog might steal your stuff." I point to the missing stick hand. "That's okay though because you love everything about him, which makes it all worthwhile."

The judges beam and start clapping. But my eyes are on Noah, staring at me like my words touched him.

"That was just lovely," the lady judge says, shaking her head.

"Great use of props," the man points out.

"I'll give you judges a few minutes to deliberate who the winner is," Jake says.

"Oh, we don't need any time," the lady announces. "The winner is clearly these ladies who created the Real Noah Snowman."

The women clap half-heartedly but Alex, Sophie, and I jump up and down in victory, screaming. I feel like I'm one of my third graders, but I'm so happy to win that I don't care.

"I can't believe they won," Amber huffs. "They just stole Noah's stuff. No creativity whatsoever."

"Totally rigged," Bianca grumbles under her breath.

"Alex, Sophie, and Evie, you stay and find out what you have won," Jake says. "The rest of you, say goodbye to Noah."

A groan rumbles through the group but even Kristen's glare can't bring my spirits down.

CHAPTER 11
Cookies & Cuddles

ALEX

The *Santa's Most Eligible* crew leads us to the bakery situated in the heart of Everpine. It's a quaint little store all dressed up for the Christmas season with twinkling white lights outlining the entire building. Wreaths laced with mistletoe hang on the double doors and the display window has a mini kitchen in it with adorable little mice dressed as elves, animated to appear as if they're baking Christmas cookies and cakes.

There's a small crowd gathered across the street, sequestered behind barriers the show's crew put out. Sophie grins at them. "I'll never get over how wholesome this town is. Look at those adorable people in their Burberry scarves and woolen hats. Hallmark should consider filming all their Christmas movies here. They'd save a bundle on casting and wardrobe."

I swear, half the time Sophie is more intrigued by what's happening off-camera than on it.

"I'm so glad the three of us are on this date together," Evie says, smiling.

"Without bitches one and two constantly stealing time with Noah? Yeah, it's a dream outing." Sophie grins, jerking her head in Kristin and Bianca's direction. They're standing off to the side with the other girls, waiting for the show's van to pick them up. Sophie waggles her fingers at them, in a very "eff you" sort of wave.

I duck my head into my scarf and stifle a laugh. I haven't gotten to spend much one-on-one time with Noah lately, but having Evie and Sophie around has taken out some of the sting. I'm really starting to like them both. I hope they feel the same about me. If we can manage to make it through this ordeal without turning on each other, I think I might have found some friends ,which for me would be a real first.

The crowd cheers as we head into the bakery. I can't help noticing that Evie gets more cheers than Sophie and me. Is she the early favorite to win Noah's heart?

Ouch.

I steal a sidelong glance at her and suck in a breath. She doesn't seem to notice. Sophie on the other hand does, but instead of looking hurt, she almost seems proud of Evie. I wish I could be as unenvious as her.

Across the street, Jake is high-fiving a pair of teenage boys and posing for selfies. Bianca inserts herself into the picture next to him, leaning her head close to his, her red-lipped pout inches from his cheek. Jake not-so-subtly puts distance between them.

Sophie rolls her eyes. "For some people any attention— even if it's bad—is better than no attention at all. Come on, let's go inside. I'm freezing."

The inside of the bakery smells like cinnamon and vanilla, and the air is cozy and warm thanks to the gleaming stainless steel floor-to-ceiling ovens lining the back wall of the kitchen area. A blizzard of elaborate snowflakes made out of paper festoon the ceiling and a jazzy version of *Walking in a Winter Wonderland* plays softly in the background.

"Ladies, welcome to The Blushing Bun!" Noah is standing behind the counter beside a stunning older woman with a salt and pepper messy updo wearing an apron with the logo for the bakery and an image of a cartoon cinnamon bun with pink cheeks. He puts his arm around her. "I'd like you to meet my Aunt Julia."

Despite her cutesy apron, Aunt Julia is a little intimidating. There's something steely in her eyes. The way she holds herself is almost regal. "It's a pleasure to meet you," she says. "I'm looking forward to getting to know each of you a bit better. In particular, discovering whether or not you know your way around a kitchen."

Sophie and I exchange a glance. Is she the traditional type, the kind that thinks careers are for men only? If so, she and I are definitely not going to be on the same page.

Julia runs her hand along the marble counter. "I've always loved to bake. To me, crafting pastries, pies, and cakes is a form of artistry and one of the sweetest acts of love." She emphasizes the word "sweetest" and flashes a smile laced with good humor. "And it's also a wonderful pathway to becoming an entrepreneur for women. At present, they make up the majority of bakery owners in this country. And I am so proud to count myself among them."

Okay, liking Aunt Julia more now.

"I built this business from the ground up with my own two hands...and lots of support from the people of this town. But the person who inspired me most to keep on going was the love of my life—my husband." She gestures to a framed photo on the wall. "We were together for forty years when he passed."

Noah puts his arm around his aunt's shoulders.

Julia reaches up and squeezes his hand. "Baking together in this kitchen with him was one of my favorite things to do. So many good memories." She clears her throat, and her eyes, which had gotten sort of dreamy and far away, snap back into focus. "You learn a lot about a person when you prepare food together. Whether they are messy or neat. Methodical or spontaneous. Patient or not. So for today's group date, you will be preparing Christmas cookies with Noah. His favorites, actually: gingerbread Christmas trees with cinnamon pecan frosting."

"Oh, those sound delicious!" Evie exclaims, clapping her hands together excitedly. She must like to bake.

Beside me Sophie winces. "I suck at baking."

Julia clears her throat and continues. "Noah will be around to help you make your cookies. I've assigned you each your own workstation with recipe cards, but I'd like to see you veer from them just a little. In other words, put your own spin on your cookie—add something unique that speaks to who you are. You've got two hours to complete this challenge. Then, after they're done, Noah and I will pick the batch we like the best. And as you've probably already guessed, the winner will get something special—a candy cane, which means they will be guaranteed to stay in the competition for at least the next few days."

Every time anyone mentions the word "guaranteed" a current of electric excitement jolts through me. I hate those stupid Candy Cane Reveals and how much they tie me into knots. I keep thinking I don't want to compete, that he either sees me as "the one" or he doesn't, that I'm not going to fall all over myself trying to convince him and then I go and knock myself out to get him to notice me and give me a candy cane anyway. It's weird and disappointing and it makes me feel desperate. And maybe I am. Maybe being lonely as long as I have has made me that way.

The three of us spread out across the kitchen to our workstations as the cameras follow our every move. Noah and his aunt move to a quiet corner of the bakery to film a few more clips about the date, Julia's first impressions of the contestants, and what Noah's hoping he'll learn about us tonight. I try not to eavesdrop, but it's so tempting.

"Focus on your baking," I tell myself. I'm going to need to if I plan on doing well tonight. I'm not a terrible baker or anything; it's just that I don't do it very often. Baking for one is sort of depressing. But around the holidays I make cookies for my neighbors and friends, so I know my way around dough.

The recipe is pretty straightforward. Molasses, flour, eggs, etcetera. How am I going to make mine unique? I go to the kitchen's pantry and peruse the shelves, looking for something out of the box that I can use. There are so many options! Sprinkles and nonpareils in every shape, color, and size. Baskets of citrus. Spices I've never even heard of before. It's overwhelming.

Which of them speaks to who I am?

I have zero idea.

Evie appears beside me and grabs something totally weird.

"Black pepper?" I ask, wrinkling my nose.

She nods, laughing. "I'm going to add a teeny tiny amount. Enough to add a little heat. Trust me, it'll be good. I promise." She gives the pepper container a little shake as one of the cameramen films her. "A little unexpectedly spicy. Like me," she says into the camera with a wink. She's adorable. I can see why Noah seems so drawn to her. Is it more than he is to me? Looking at her now, I'm pretty sure the answer is yes. My stomach twists a little.

The cameraman pans to me.

I shrug. "I've got nothing yet."

He laughs. "Better hurry. Ten minutes have already passed."

Except even with all the many ingredients in front of me, nothing seems right.

Sophie slips past me and grabs some maple syrup. "It's sweet, and if it's good enough for Buddy the Elf, it's good enough for me," she tells the camera guy just as the show's host joins us in the pantry. Before he can get her to elaborate or maybe explain her *Elf* reference to the audience, she hurries back to her station.

Jake pretends to scan the shelves as he looks into the camera, addressing the viewers. "Each girl must find something that relates to who she is. Her uniqueness. So far Evie's picked something spicy and Sophie something sweet—which is surprising since I thought for sure she would pick something with a bit more bite. Now what will our Alex go for?"

He taps his chin thoughtfully then grabs a lemon from one of the baskets. "Maybe you're more of a lemon girl?

I shake my head. "No. Not today," I say.

This surprises a laugh out of Jake. "Not today," he repeats, shaking his head, a wry smile on his face. "Clever."

I head over to Sophie's workstation to tell her what Jake said. It's odd how often he finds ways to bring her up. I'm starting to wonder if he has a thing for her. I tell Sophie exactly this as I watch her crack a few eggs.

"What? No," she says, making a face. "There's no way." Color creeps into her cheeks. Wait. Is she sort of into him too? The more I think about it, the more sense it makes. That could be why Sophie's been so ambivalent about Noah—she's crushing on Jake instead. I make a mental note to ask her about it later when we're not around the cameras.

"You better get started, Alex," Sophie says as she eyes the wall clock across the room. "You don't want to risk not finishing in time."

I sigh. "I can't. I still don't know what my secret ingredient is."

Sophie glances around then leans closer. "At the back of the store is a second pantry. Maybe you can find something in there. But you need to hurry so the crew doesn't see you. Quick." She shoves me in that direction before I can object.

The bakery is a lot larger than it looks from the front. There's a pair of walk-in refrigerators in the hallway leading to the back, a beautiful office space beyond with a Christmas tree twinkling merrily in the corner beside a beautifully carved mahogany desk and a series of doors neatly labeled: Dry Goods, Spirits, and Equipment.

Spirits. As in alcohol.

I can't help grinning. Sophie is a genius. I know what my secret ingredient is going to be.

I glance around to see if one of the cameramen followed me. Nope, I'm on my own. Yes!

I slip through the door, shutting it quickly behind me...and run smack into Noah.

I let out a small shriek of surprise. A tumbler filled with amber liquid slips from his hand and crashes to the floor.

"Oh my god, I'm so sorry!" I exclaim, crouching beside the mess. "I didn't know you were back here."

Noah bends down beside me and stops me from picking up the pieces. "Don't. You could cut yourself," he says gently. "And it's okay. Just please don't tell anyone you saw me back here." He stands up and grabs a broom from the corner. "I needed a little break. All the cameras and the girls all day every day. It can be…"

"A lot," I finish for him.

He smiles and nods. "Yes." Then he sweeps the broken glass into a dustpan. "So why are *you* back here?" He looks up at me and raises an eyebrow. "Hiding out like in the theater?"

The way his dark hair curls over his forehead is adorable. It looks so soft. I want to reach out and run my hands through it. Pull him close…

I shake my head to clear it. "I was getting my secret ingredient. For the cookies."

He glances around at the shelves flanking the walls of the room. Bottles of various kinds of liquor are lined up neatly on each of them. "Hmm, interesting. Which one were you going to use?"

"Bourbon," I say. "It's what I drink whenever I finish a book, so it reveals something about me. One glass of Woodford Reserve—two if the book was particularly hard to write." I shrug, smiling self-consciously. "I was hoping your aunt might have a bottle in here. It has a sort of citrusy-caramel-chocolate vibe that should work well with the gingerbread."

His eyebrow arches. "Bourbon. You drink bourbon?"

I fold my arms across my chest. "Why's it so hard to believe? Because I'm a woman?" As soon as the words are out of my mouth I wince. I had meant them to sound playful, flirty even, but instead I sounded almost defensive. Not sure where that came from. Noah hasn't displayed any chauvinistic tendencies so far. And here I am sounding all accusatory. *Yeesh. Take it down a notch, sis.*

He holds his hands up. "Whoa. No. Because that's what I was drinking when you came in. It's sort of my end-of-a-long-day drink. The fact that you like it too is good. Sexy." He raises an eyebrow at me.

"So bourbon. Something else we have in common," I say, repressing a nervous shiver. The way he's looking at me...I'm not a woo-woo girlie, but it's interesting that we're both back here for the same thing. Feels a little like fate is conspiring to create something between us. But then, that's probably just the writer in me.

Noah's voice softens. "Yeah, I guess it is."

Click.

The sound has us both turning toward the door that leads back into the bakery.

I left it open when I stepped inside, but now it's shut. I hurry back to it and try the knob. It turns easily enough—but the door won't budge.

"The lock's not engaged or anything," I say. "I think something must be blocking it from the outside."

Noah tries it too, frowning. "Or someone," he says, raking a hand through his hair as he looks at me.

"Do you think someone shut it to keep me out of the competition?" I start knocking on the door. Then when I don't hear anyone coming, I start pounding. I'm going to run out of time to make my cookies.

"Or it was someone on the crew. Carianne, maybe. Creating a little drama." He laughs under his breath. "An opportunity."

"For what?" I say between knocks. Then it hits me. "Oh." My heart literally skips a beat. I turn around to face Noah, but he's moving across the room, inspecting the corners for hidden cameras.

"I'm sorry about this," he mutters. "You know I would never try to trap you into spending time with me."

The fact that he's bothered and embarrassed has me feeling strangely bold. "Don't be," I say softly. "I'm not."

Noah stops his search and turns to me.

"I mean, I'm not a big fan of small spaces, but somehow it's not so bad with you here," I say, avoiding his gaze because suddenly I'm too self-conscious to meet his eyes.

When I do finally look up, he's closed the distance between us. "Alex?" He says my name somehow as both a question and a plea. He reaches up and touches my face, his palm cupping my cheek, his thumb tracing my jawline.

I lean into his touch, turning so my lips graze his palm. My insides are a jumble of anxiety and anticipation. I haven't kissed someone in so long. What if I've forgotten how?

He brings his other hand to my face, then leans down and presses his mouth gently to mine. Every nerve ending in my body goes electric. I am buzzing from the feeling of his body against mine as he pulls me closer. I wrap my arms around his neck, winding my fingers through his hair.

Our kisses get more intense. His hands drop from my face to the small of my back and I can't help the soft sound that leaves my mouth. The heat of his hands radiating through the fabric of my sweater feels so good. Hot. I want this. I want him. I press myself closer, and his tongue slips inside my mouth.

"Noah?"

A voice cuts through the moment. Someone is on the other side of the door. Carianne. "Hello? Noah? Alex? Are you back here?"

A door opens nearby.

I untangle myself from Noah. *What am I doing?* I barely know this guy and I'm practically throwing myself at him, letting down all my defenses too early. There are so many other girls here who are also kissing him and I have no idea where I stand compared to them. I'm playing fast and loose with my own heart and that is a recipe for disaster.

"I guess we should let her know we're in here," I say. I start calling for help because I can't stay this close to him much longer.

"Alexandra?" Carianne's voice is right outside the door now. "Some boxes fell in front of the door. Hold on, I'll have you out in a second." There's a beat of silence and then she clears her throat. "Is Noah in there with you?"

I can tell by her voice that if he is, she's not happy about it. Probably because of the lack of cameras. That and technically, it's against the rules for me to be alone with Noah outside of filming. Crap! I could get disqualified.

I glance back at Noah. He seems to realize the gravity of the situation at the same time I do. But unfortunately, it's too late to do anything about it. Carianne's opening the door. There are two cameramen behind her, already filming.

"I didn't know he was in here," I explain, my cheeks heating up. "I came looking for some bourbon to put in my cookies and he was already here, and I was getting ready to leave and the door shut and then we couldn't open it." I am babbling like a total idiot.

"This is all my fault," Noah says. "I was taking a break from the cameras. Trying to steal a few minutes alone."

Carianne holds up a hand. "Relax. It's okay. No one's getting disqualified. At least not right now." She glances at the boxes stacked beside the door. "There's no way you could've trapped yourselves in here. If I had to guess, someone was trying to sabotage Alexandra so she couldn't participate in the baking. Whoever it was didn't realize you were back here too, Noah." She scrutinizes us both and laughs. "I'm betting they'll be pretty pissed if they ever do."

If?

"Wait. So you're not going to say anything? About us being trapped, I mean?" I ask.

She glances at the cameramen then motions for them to stop recording. "No." She studies her Apple watch. "You weren't in there that long. There's still time for you to bake if you hurry."

I turn and grab a bottle of bourbon. It's not the one I wanted, but it'll have to do. "Thank you, Carianne," I say. I turn to Noah, but I have no idea what to say. "See you back out there," I finally manage before turning around and hurrying off.

I'm so tweaked, the baking time goes by in a total blur. My head's completely mixed up after kissing Noah *and* discovering someone's out to sabotage me. I end up forgetting to add the baking soda to my dough, so the cookies turn out all wrong. What a mess!

In the end, Sophie wins an early candy cane and some private time with Noah tomorrow. But I'm almost relieved. I need to spend some time investigating the other girls and figure out who put those boxes in front of the door.

Because the one thing I'm certain of after tonight is that if I'm not careful, I'm going to get eliminated before I even have a chance to win Noah's heart.

CHAPTER 12

Not That Kind of Diamond

SOPHIE

I'm actually stoked that I got a date with Noah. What's even better is that Jake doesn't look too happy about it. He appeared stunned when Noah said my name as the winner of the cookie baking contest, though he quickly recovered and offered his million-dollar smile to the cameras.

I wait for Noah downstairs in the lobby, dressed in an oversized red knit sweater, white belt, and white leggings. Carianne had told me to wear "cute casual" again, which suits me fine.

Jake is in the lobby, talking with Mack. He glances over at me very briefly then back to Mack with what I swear is a guilty expression. I have to admit, he looks pretty hot in his dark jeans and black button-down shirt.

Look away, Soph. That's how he trapped you the first time.

"Hey, Sophie," Noah says as he comes down the stairs. He's dressed in a very appealing white turtleneck sweater and black pants that hug his legs perfectly. He looks very handsome, so why are my eyes trying to sneak another look at Jake?

I smile at Noah. "Hi! What are we going to do today?"

He shrugs. "Your guess is as good as mine. I was told we would find out when we get there."

Mack walks over to us. "Hi, Sophie, Noah. Come stand by the Christmas tree; the light is better."

We allow Mack and the other producers to position us just-so. The makeup artist touches up my face powder and adds a few sparkles to my cheekbones. My reflection in the small mirror is cuter than I would've ever thought. Feeling confident, I thread my arm through Noah's and receive an approving nod from Mack. She calls for cameras rolling.

Jake grins at me, his eyes dancing with a mischievous twinkle. "Congratulations again, Sophie, on achieving a coveted individual date with Noah. Would you like to know where you are headed today?"

"Yes," we both say, even though I already know they won't tell us here.

"Well, you're going to have to wait a little longer until we get there. We have warm coats and blindfolds for you both."

We put on the coats, then Jake hands us each a blindfold and instructs us to wear them. Feeling a little mystified at the secrecy, I place mine over my eyes and hold Noah's hand as someone leads us outside. I know we didn't have a secret blind-fold date when this was planned, so they must've just come up with it. Hopefully it's somewhere fun...and warm.

We feel the van making one turn after another, until finally it stops. Another hand takes mine to guide me out of the vehi-cle, one I know very well and makes my heart skip a beat. As sweet and handsome as Noah is, holding his hand doesn't give me the fireworks that I wish it would. The only person who gave me that feeling, ever, was Jake. But that was forever ago.

The wind is blowing, making me shiver even through my coat. It feels empty around us, like we're not near any structure.

"Okay, Sophie, Noah, please remove your blindfolds," Jake says.

I tug mine down and gasp. No!

No!

No!

We're at the bottom of a ski lift. I stare up at the impossibly high mountain. No, this can't be happening. Blood pounding in my ears, I throw a panicked look at Mack as she stands behind the camera. She pulls her forefingers across her mouth in an exaggerated grin. *Smile for the cameras*, she's saying. I try my best as my eyes catch Jake's. His grin falters slightly as he sees my obvious discomfort. Now he looks guilty.

Asshole! He *knows* I hate skiing. As clear as if written on his face, he's the one behind this "special" date. I guarantee he suggested this to Mack.

If he was standing next to me on a cliff, I'd give Jake a good hard shove down this mountain with my boot.

But for the cameras, I can only smile and try to look thrilled about flying down this mountain to my death.

"I'm so excited to take you up," Noah says, oblivious to my angst. "This is one of my favorite hills near the lodge."

Hill? I blink at the slope in front of me, wondering if Everest is even this high. Still, I smile and nod. What else can I do?

"Once you're down the hill, you'll be treated to hot cocoa in front of a cozy fire before enjoying a special dinner prepared by the lodge's world-renowned Chef Stefan." Jake's voice is enthusiastic. "Have fun up there!"

With the camera lens still tight on us, we put our gear on, then head over to the ski lift. I try to look as excited as Noah, and I think I've fooled him well because once we're on the lift, he puts an arm around me and is super chatty about how happy he is that I'm sharing this experience with him. I snuggle into his arm, more for warmth and comfort than anything else. Hopefully he can't feel me shaking.

"So how is it with the girls?" Noah asks casually when we're not even halfway up.

"Huh?" My eyes haven't left the mountain in front of us, my mind on whether I've chosen a beneficiary for my accidental death and dismemberment policy.

"The girls. Any drama going on in the house? I'll admit, I realized a little late that I haven't tapped into one of my best opportunities for really learning about these girls: you."

"Huh?" I ask again. I'm brilliant that way.

He laughs. "You're spacing out, aren't you? Look, I know you are doing this as a favor to the show, and I know your mind is somewhere else right now. Maybe with a...certain host?"

I stare at him, and he flushes. "I mean, right? You and Jake?" he asks.

"There is no 'me and Jake.' What gave you that idea?" *Oh, god, was I staring at Jake too much?*

He wipes his forehead with one gloved hand. "It's kind of obvious. At least, I thought so. Maybe I misread it."

"You *definitely* misread it, Noah. There was once...I mean, we used to date. But that was a very long time ago. We're not into each other now—at all. He's kind of a jerk, to be honest." A jerk who is setting me up on a date that he knew I'd hate.

He shrugs, obviously not convinced. "Okay, so back to the girls in the house. Any thoughts?"

Glad for the distraction, I share a few thoughts on each girl, being as careful as I can not to sabotage the show's efforts. I don't talk about how Kristin lied about having a dog on her application, or how she takes up all the space in our room. Or how Bianca is a complete bitch to all the other girls. Instead, I talk up Evie and

Alex and how incredibly kind, sweet, and smart they are. He nods and smiles, like I'm confirming some of his own initial thoughts.

"But Bianca," he says, frowning. "I don't know. I would've sent her home by the second round if it wasn't for Mack telling me by contract she gets the final say of who stays through the fifth round. I just hope she's in it for good reason."

Knowing Mack would kill me if I sabotage this, I just say, "Well, maybe you just have to get to know her a little better." I want to kick myself for saying that, but I don't want to kill my career.

Too soon, the lift slows and we're off and sliding down a ramp. I follow Noah through the snow to the top of what the trail sign says is a black diamond. Black diamond? I swallow hard, still trying to smile for Bob, the cameraman who's got the lens on me but is frowning from behind it. Clearly he can see I'm upset. Why can't anyone else?

"You okay?" Noah asks. "You've skied before, right?"

"Yes," I say, choking out the word. I know my teeth are chattering, but I can't tell if it's more nerves or cold. It doesn't help that the wind is picking up and it's starting to snow. "I'm okay. Just a little chilly."

He puts an arm around me. "Okay, well, as soon as we get down this hill, we'll enjoy the fire and hot chocolate at this really amazing little cafe. This slope is honestly more of a blue than a black diamond, so it's not too intense."

"Great," I squeak out.

Noah pulls the visor down over his eyes. "Ready?"

I nod. "You first. I'll be right behind you."

He looks like he's going to argue, but I give him a gentle push. "Go on, silly. I'll meet you at the bottom. I'm right behind you," I say again.

He laughs, kisses me on the cheek, then turns to ski down the first slope. I watch him, my knees knocking so bad they're probably going to break.

"Stop rolling for a minute, Bob," Jake says behind me. When did he get up here? "Hey, Soph, you okay?"

I glare at him. "You knew I don't ski, so you arranged this? How despicable can a person get?"

He winces. "I'm sorry. I didn't think you'd freak out this bad."

"Freak out? I nearly killed myself last time I went skiing, something I know I told you about. But fine, whatever. Guess this mountain will finish the job."

"Wait, maybe I can get them to let you go back down the lift," he says.

I scowl at him, picturing Mack's anger if that happened. She would never let me forget it if I ruined the shot of this "perfect" date. I'm supposed to be having the time of my life on my individual date and make the viewers think I'm a real contender for Noah's love. That's how it's supposed to play out. If I ruin this, I can kiss my career goodbye. With a final glare at Jake, I yank the visor down over my eyes and turn to face the mountain. I close my eyes for just a moment in a silent prayer, inhale deeply, then take off down Noah's "not-too-intense" hill.

The first part of the slope isn't horrible. Even though it's been years, I'm able to find my groove and start maneuvering my skis back and forth down the mountain. They slide over the freshly powdered snow with ease. Maybe I'll make it down after all. A movement to my right catches my eye, and I glance over briefly to see Bob skiing right along with me, cameras strapped to his chest and forehead. Impressive. For some reason, Bianca's face pops into my mind, and I wonder how she would handle this date.

I crest the hill and gasp as I take in the sharp slope in front of me, one second before my skis hit it. My face is hammered by snowy wind as I cruise forward at breakneck speed. Fast—too fast. As if on cue, my skis hit something and I flip upward, my legs and skis a complete tangle as I roll down the mountain. I slide to a stop on my butt, teetering just barely on a narrow ledge. Just beyond is yet another steep slope...and another. My eyes burn as tears well up in them. Yep, skiing still sucks. And I am going to die.

Bob stops below, shouting something up to me but I can't hear him. My gloved hands dig into the snow like I'm trying to hold onto a lifeline. I'm frozen, more from fear than the cold.

I hear a motor in the distance, getting closer and closer. A snowmobile is gliding toward me slowly, its rider stopping a few feet away.

"Soph! Soph, you okay?"

Why is he here? *I'm okay*, I want to say, but I'm frozen to the ground. Jake drops down next to me, his eyes full of genuine concern. "You're okay, right?"

I manage to mumble "Leave me alone" but he wraps his arms around me anyway.

"I'm not going to leave you. I'm so, so sorry about this," he adds in a low voice. "This is all my fault."

You're damn right it is, I want to shout. I shove him away as hard as I can, which in my condition isn't very hard at all. I punch him with a gloved hand, and it has exactly zero impact through all his layers of jacket and clothes. Unsatisfied, I yank off my glove and throw a fist at his face, a little harder than intended. He yelps and puts his hand to his nose. A few drops of blood trickle down and stain the snow red. Good lord, I didn't mean to almost kill the guy!

"Are you okay?" I ask quickly. I gather up some snow in my ungloved hand and press it to his nose.

"I'll live," he says. He sighs and takes my hand, holding it between his to warm it. "I'm really sorry, Soph. I was so annoyed that you seemed to be connecting with Noah, I guess I lost my mind."

"I'm only doing this because Mack asked me to," I remind him.

"I know. But you seem to be really into Noah now," he says in a sullen tone.

"Why do you care?" I ask.

He shakes his head but doesn't answer my question. "Come on, let's go. Can you stand?"

"I think so."

He removes my skis and gently helps me to my feet. A quick glance up the hill shows zig-zag tracks that end in my skiing demise. I can't believe I made it down at all. Trembling slightly, I allow him to lead me to the snowmobile. He gently helps me onto the vehicle, then gets on in front of me, taking my arms and wrapping them around his waist. We slide through the snow to a path on the other side that is a little flatter. The wind is not as strong as it was earlier, and the snow has stopped. I press my cheek against the back of his jacket. Now that I realize I might not die here after all, I can take in the snow-covered pines, smooth slopes, and the summits in the distance. It really is lovely up here, and incredibly peaceful. For a brief moment, I'm able to lose myself in the beauty of these mountains.

Then the cafe nestled at the bottom of the slopes appears in view, and everything comes rushing back: Noah waiting for me down below, the cameras likely fixed on him drinking his hot cocoa alone, and confusion about where I am, though I'm sure word has gotten to Mack about my skiing incident. I can picture her fuming and swearing up and down that my career is over if I screw this up.

I tap Jake's shoulder when we get to the last hill. "Stop for a minute."

He glances over his shoulder and nods, then slows the snowmobile until it comes to a stop. "You're worried about Mack, aren't you?" he asks as I sit there, staring at the cafe.

I climb off the snowmobile and walk over to the edge of the slope that cascades down to the cafe, a much gentler hill than the ones at the top of the mountain. "Well, Mack's part of it. I feel bad for leaving Noah stranded too."

"Don't worry, I already called down that you are okay and had a run-in with an ice patch."

"Good." I tilt my head. "Why did you join us up on the mountain? Just to watch me fall down?"

"No, not at all." He frowns. "After I saw the panic in your eyes, I felt horrible about picking this as your date. So I wanted to make sure you were okay."

I cross my arms and scowl at him. "I knew you were behind this choice. But why?"

"I was irritated with you, and I guess I wanted some retaliation for you being all cozy with Noah when you'd told me you weren't ready for a relationship. I remembered you didn't like to ski, but I swear, I never wanted you to get hurt. I figured you'd be angry with me but make it down with no problem."

"You could've killed me!"

He frowns. "I know. It was childish and stupid, and I'm really sorry. And don't worry about Mack. I'll sort it out with her."

"Wait a second." I narrow my eyes. "Me not ready for a relationship? As I recall, *you* didn't want to be with *me*."

"Not true. You were so focused on your career that you didn't have time for us, remember? Your words. 'I need the time to figure my career out without being tied down.'"

"I never said the tied down part. Just that I needed to focus on my career. And what about you? You were set on being a big star. There was always an interview or an audition or some networking thing to go to. Many date nights I was left sitting at a table for two by myself."

His eyebrows pinch slightly as he considers that. "I guess you're right. We were both chasing our dreams, and neither of us wanted anything to come in the way of that. I'm sorry, for my part."

His eyes cast to the ground. He looks honestly so sad about it that my heart gives in. And for the first time, I realize what he's saying is true. I didn't make time for us at all back then. I often worked twelve- to fourteen-hour days, seven days a week, trying to make an impression on a business that's never given two shits about me. He did the same to me too, but that's all I focused on. Neither one of us were ready to get serious, and neither one of us is more guilty than the other.

I give a heavy sigh. No use blaming him for something I'm partly responsible for. "I'm sorry too," I tell him. "I should've been more present in our relationship."

The moment his head raises and our eyes connect, it hits me. I no longer hate Jake. I really have forgiven him, and maybe I can forgive myself too. If only we had met years later...

I clear my throat. "We should go. Mack will have both our heads."

He nods. "And Noah will be waiting for you."

His voice has a slightly bitter tone, but he tries to smile as he helps me onto the snowmobile. I press myself against him, determined to leave my irritation on that hill behind us. The heat from his body warms me as we move slowly down the rest of the mountain. The ride will be over in a couple minutes, but I find myself wanting to stay. I slide my hands under his jacket, feeling his abs tighten as my arms wrap around them. My body is tingling all over, inside and out. It's been a long time since I felt that way. It's weird that only a half hour ago I thought I hated Jake, and now I can't get enough of him.

Too soon, the snowmobile comes to a stop. I take Jake's hand to climb off the equipment.

"Thank you," I tell him. "For being a knight in shining armor and rescuing me."

He chuckles. "I'm tempted to whisk you off to my castle."

"I'm tempted to let you." I grin and start to turn toward the cafe.

"Sophie, wait," he says softly, still holding my hand. But he drops it as a furiously ranting Mack comes running over, yelling that the production is behind, thanks to me. Carianne is there too, ushering me away from Jake and into the cafe. Noah comes up to me and gives me a warm hug.

"Are you okay?" he asks in my ear.

I nod. "Never been better."

As Noah guides me to a cozy couple of chairs near the fireplace where mugs of hot cocoa wait, I glance over my shoulder at Jake. His warm eyes are still on me, melting the final shards of ice on my heart.

Never been better.

CHAPTER 13

Sleigh Bells and Secrets

The idea that I'm falling for a guy I've only known for a short amount of time is unthinkable, ridiculous, and definitely dangerous. My heart has been tossed on a rollercoaster. It was a blast for a few days, but today, I want off.

The girls all hurried down to the hot tub the moment Cari-anne popped by suggesting it, but knowing cameras will be there, my feet are dragging down the steps. Not going to lie—it's a little terrifying seeing some of those women in their bikinis with perfect bodies. I'm the teacher who grabs a choco-late donut in the teachers' lounge on Fabulous Fridays and doesn't shy away from that second slice of pizza. I've never thought much about how small my breasts are or how large my thighs might look.

Until today.

It doesn't help knowing Noah is starting to make connec-tions with other girls here too. And can you blame him? Bianca is Miss Texas, Kristin's some sort of model, while Zuri is an Olympian. Then there are my two best friends, Sophie and

Alex, who are the nicest girls I've ever met and both have incredibly successful careers.

With a lineup like that, I don't know why Noah would pick me.

With my robe firmly tucked around my waist, I push open the large glass door and step outside into the pool area. Cold air swooshes around my body and a few snow flurries dance across my face. The main pool is closed up for the winter, but the large hot tub where the girls are gathered inside glows a cerulean blue. Twinkle lights blink from the bushes and garlands drape from the trellises.

I wonder how many cameras are hidden in those bushes.

"Hello, Evie," a server says, stepping up to me with a tray of sparkling red plastic cups. "Would you care for some Jingle Juice?"

"That would be nice," I say, taking a glass. I could really use something to relax me. "Thanks."

Fortified with my drink, I slip out of my robe, tossing it on one of the lounge chairs. The cold pavers bite at my toes and I quickly edge up to the hot tub, shivering in my bikini. The girls are laughing over something Sophie said. Steam curls up from the bubbling water into the cold night. A quick scan tells me everyone is here except for Zuri and Bella Grace.

"Evie made it!" Alex exclaims, looking genuinely happy to see me. Instantly, I relax.

"There you are." Sophie beams and waves me in. "Come on out of the cold and into the warmth."

I ease my way into the hot water, smiling as I sink onto one of the benches.

"This feels nice," I admit.

"Of course it does." Sophie clinks her glass against mine. "Cheers."

"This is the life, isn't it?" Alex leans her head back against the edge of the hot tub. "Way better than rewatching *Bridgerton* and drinking alone."

"Who does that?" Amber snorts.

"Sounds like something a loser would do," Kristin says, and the two giggle.

Beside me, Alex stiffens. This is why I had been resistant to come down here. These girls are wolves, hungry to devour.

"It's also way better than eating an entire box of pizza alone on a Friday night," I quickly add.

"I'll toast to that." Sophie lifts her glass. "How about eating a whole tub of ice cream alone?"

"Or a chocolate cake alone?" River pipes up. "Done that."

The four of us clink our glasses together while Amber just rolls her eyes and Kristin looks slightly disgusted.

"Ugh. I just couldn't," Bianca says, eyeing the bubbles warily like they might ruin her perfect curls. "I'd be so bloated afterward."

"Since we're all being honest here," Amber says, sipping from her drink. "You'll have to tell us, Evie, what you were chatting with Noah about at the snowman competition."

"Not much." The last thing I want to talk to Amber about is my dog. "Just stuff about life."

"You were talking to him for a *long* time," Bianca points out. "You were waiting forever to talk to Noah, weren't you, River?"

"I wouldn't say *forever*." River stares at her drink. "But you were kind of hogging him all to yourself."

"I honestly didn't mean to take time away from you all." I shift uncomfortably on the stone bench. This water is starting to feel a little too hot. "He was chasing me with a huge snowball and..."

Their faces warn me I'm making them angrier.

"Look, I don't need to know what you two were doing," Bianca says loftily. "It just felt targeted, you know?"

"Targeted?" Alex snaps. "Like someone locking me in the bakery pantry sort of targeted?"

Bianca rolls her eyes. "You should leave your active imagination to your books." But I don't miss how she throws Kristin a victorious look.

"How was she targeting you?" I press, needing to throw the bitch off her game. "Sounds like Noah was just trying to have some fun."

"She purposely drew Noah away from me after I kissed him," Bianca says pointedly, a slow smile curling across her lips. "God, that man can kiss."

Dread pools into my stomach, cold as ice. I mean, I know he's kissing other girls. He has to so he can find the right connection, but does she have to tell us all about how amazing it was?

"You kissed him?" Amber asks. "At the snowman competition?"

"He kissed me, actually." Bianca presses a hand to her chest, breathing in deeply. "I was so scared but he broke through my fears and kissed me first. It was beyond magical. I think we really had a connection."

Alex sucks in a breath. I glance her way. She looks oddly pale and her lips are pressed together. Something Bianca said definitely hit a nerve with Alex. Leave it to Bianca to spoil everything.

"I bet you did," Sophie mutters, clearly not buying Bianca's story.

"It's true," Kristin confirms. "I saw them, but it's not like a big deal. I kissed him at the last group date. I mean, who hasn't he kissed?"

I feel sick. Here I thought I had a connection, but that was all in my head. The memory of My Biggest Oops kissing my coworker on her desk slams back to me like a nightmare.

"I'm going to bed early," I say, standing. "Tomorrow's a big day."

"Just don't ruin it for the rest of us," Bianca reminds me. "This isn't an Evie Winters show. There are others, too, who are here for the right reasons."

I stop halfway up the stairs. I know the cameras are likely catching all of this, but her words unleash so much fury inside of me that I don't care. "Are you insinuating I'm here for the wrong reasons?"

"I think Noah's money is too good for a teacher like you to pass up."

I'm frozen in shock. My mouth won't close.

"That was low, Bianca." Alex wraps her arm around me. "Even for you."

"Things sure are getting heated around here," Sophie says. "Think it's time to cool off. Come on, ladies."

"I went to college and got a degree to get a teaching job so I can do exactly what I love," I say. "I don't need Noah's money to find happiness."

And with that, I storm out of the hot tub, Alex and Sophie following in my wake. The air feels even colder than it did when we got in, but I'm so mad, I don't even care. Shivering, we quickly slip into our robes and shoes and hurry inside, back up to our room, complaining the whole time about Kristin and Bianca.

"If those two weren't here," Alex says, pulling her towel closer, "this whole experience would be so much better."

"But they're perfect for the TV ratings," I grumble as I slip into a pair of jeans and my thickest sweater. "They basically accused me of being a gold digger."

"If anyone is a gold digger," Sophie mutters, "it's Bianca. But don't let any of them determine your feelings."

"You know, you're right." I pace the room. "Noah came to talk to me. I didn't seek him out. But then again, who knows what kind of lies Bianca is feeding him if she's telling them to my face."

"She's just doing it for the cameras," Alex says. "She feeds off of drama."

Finally, Alex goes back to her room to take a shower while Sophie pulls out a magazine and curls up beneath her thick blankets. I move to stare out the window. The ski slopes are all lit up, shining across the glistening snow. "I wish I could talk to him without the cameras and when I'm not worried about taking another person's time."

"You know," Sophie says, not looking up from the page, "the cameras aren't on all the time."

I consider her words and then grab my coat. "I'm just going to walk around and get some fresh air."

"Have fun!" Sophie says.

The hallway is quiet but when I peek over the balcony, I spy a few of the crew members sitting in the lobby. Technically, I'm not allowed to roam the resort without letting someone know where I'm at. But right now, I don't want to be found so I opt for the back stairwell. I wonder where Noah sleeps. He must have a room somewhere around here, maybe even in this lodge. If I could figure out where he is, I could talk to him without the cameras or annoying other women lurking about.

Once I'm on the first floor, I dart into the back hallway, only to run into Noah's dad, Victor, who must have come from outside. He's wearing a thick jacket and pulling off a hat dusted in snow. We all got to meet him and his wife earlier and he seemed like he was really hoping that Noah could find his true love through this experience.

"Victor!" I exclaim. "It's good to see you."

"And you as well. But what are you doing? You should be out having fun at that party they set up for you girls by the pool."

"Actually, I just came from there. I realized I needed a break from all the show drama."

"Sure, sure. If anyone likes to avoid drama, it's me." He chuckles, and I wonder how much he's overheard.

"You wouldn't happen to have seen Noah around, would you? I really need to talk to him."

"Oh, yes." He nods, eyeing me carefully. "In fact, I've just left him. He's working in the barn, taking care of the horses. If you go out this door and follow the path to the right, it'll take you right to him."

"Really?" I clasp my hands together. "Thank you so much. You don't know how much it means to me."

He chuckles warmly as I hurry out through the back door and clip down the path until I spy the barn just up ahead. Golden beams of light spill out of the windows and music escapes into the night air. Now that I'm here, my heart starts thumping again. I don't think he'll be upset with me for showing up uninvited. Or I could be wrong, and he's not really into me and has only been putting up a front for the cameras.

Pushing aside my fear, I pull back on the door and step inside. Christmas country music floats around me from a speaker sitting on a bench. Horses lift up their heads, assessing who has invaded their territory. Hay litters the floor and the air smells of animals and barn. A sleigh is tucked in the corner of the room and the walls are cluttered with tools and harnesses. I find him in the last stall, placing a blanket on a horse.

"Hey, you," I say, inching closer, crossing my fingers he won't be upset.

He jerks at the sound of my voice but when he sees me, his whole face lights up. "What are you doing here? This is unexpected."

"I'm kind of breaking rules coming to see you." I shrug, crossing my arms. "But I couldn't stand another night without talking to you. Like really talking to you without all the fanfare of the show."

He pats the horse down and then shuts the door to the stall. He tosses off his gloves and then comes up to me.

"You have no idea how happy I am that you broke the rules." He takes my hands in his. "I haven't been able to stop thinking about you."

My heart misses a beat. He can't stop thinking about me? Really? That feels too good to be true.

"I love hearing you say that." *More than you know.* "But I also know you've got lots of other women here. Even though I signed up for that, it's still a lot."

"I get it completely." He brings my hands up to his mouth and kisses my knuckles. Warmth floods through my body. "Your hands are cold."

"I forgot to grab my gloves when I left," I say breathlessly. "I didn't know you'd be outside but your dad tipped me off."

"Come on." He pulls me toward where bales of hay are stacked up. "I've got something that will warm you up."

"I don't know if I'm ready for that..." I hedge.

"Ah, not like that." He chuckles and grabs a thermos and two mugs. "I was thinking more along the lines of the coffee version of warmth."

My face flushes at my mistake. "That sounds wonderful."

He grabs a few blankets off the shelf and spreads them over the hay bales. Before long, he's made up a makeshift area for us to sit. We settle onto the blankets, each with a cup of hot coffee. He pulls me close to him, draping another blanket over us. He smells like a mix of horse and spice, and I'm not sure I'm going to ever want to leave his arms.

I've fantasized about having a moment like this with him without the cameras so often that this feels like a dream.

"There's another reason I wanted to come see you tonight," I begin. I suck in a deep breath, half-terrified to admit the truth. "I needed to find out who we really are together. Like how we interact and talk to each other without the cameras, cue cards, and fancy drinks."

"I think that's the best idea I've heard since we started this whole show." He takes a sip and then clears his throat. "So, if we're being honest, I was touched by what you said about me at the snowman competition. You mentioned that I made this experience worthwhile. Was that for the cameras or was that real?"

"That was one hundred percent real. And I guess that's what makes all of this so scary."

"You don't have to be scared with me, Evie. I like you. A lot. And I'm not saying that to every girl here."

My hand finds his, warm and calloused. My heart takes off in terror, a freight train at full speed because I need to tell him things about me that aren't cool or fun.

"At our date in the ice cave when you told me about your ex," I continue, "I really identified with you at that moment. I wanted to tell you about my own dating experience then but I wasn't quite ready. My ex-boyfriend, I have a lot of nicknames for him, but we can call him Mr. Cheats A Lot."

"Wow. That's a name you don't forget."

"The truth is he was not a nice guy and finding out he cheated on me—with one of my coworkers, no less—was painful. I don't ever want to feel that kind of pain again."

"I'm so sorry." He trails a finger along the center of my palm.

"When I caught them, we got into a huge fight. He said it was my fault. That I gave too much attention to my students and not enough to him. He said I pushed him away, and that's why he had to find love elsewhere."

"What an asshole."

"A part of me wonders if he's right." I lean my head back against the bale of hay. "Like I wasn't watering the plant and putting enough effort into growing it."

"The plant?"

"It's an analogy. The plant is the—"

"Relationship. Got it. Also, I bet you're a great teacher. The fact he used that against you is a real jerk move."

"But there's probably some truth to what he said. When I do something, I give it one hundred percent. And when it comes to teaching, I'm passionate about it."

He shifts so we're facing each other. "First of all, I love that you're passionate and committed to your work. You should never have to apologize for that or question yourself. Second, a relationship takes two people. If he was committed to you, he should've talked things out with you, rather than taking his passions elsewhere."

"I'm scared, Noah." My voice is a terrified whisper.

"What scares you?"

"I guess I'm just scared of not being enough all over again."

"I don't know what our future holds. But as long as the

two of us are together, I'm going to do everything I can to show you how great you are. And you're a hell of a kisser."

"Yeah?" A smile escapes my lips and I set both our mugs aside. "Maybe we should try that again."

"I'd like that." His voice is a whisper.

He drags a finger along my lips, eyes drinking me in like I'm the most special person in the world.

Our lips meet. A brush, teasing of possibilities that I can only dream of. My eyes flutter closed, drinking in the scent of him, memorizing the feel of our kiss.

"There's something special about you, Evie," he whispers into my ear.

His arms tighten around me and our kiss deepens. His tongue sweeps into my mouth and I let out a low groan. Hot hands press on my cheeks and then he's cupping the back of my head and dragging his mouth along my neck. His five o'clock shadow scrapes across my skin, sending shivers dancing up my spine. When his lips find mine again, hungry and passionate, all reason flies out the door.

I forget he's dating other women.

Forget we're on a TV show.

Forget that I'm not the smartest or most beautiful girl here.

All I can think about is that before Noah, my world was broken and stagnant. But now he's set me into motion. Everything is bright and wondrous again.

"I thought I knew what kissing was like," I say. "I was so wrong."

"Oh, Evie, that's just the tip of the iceberg."

The sound of ringing breaks through the silence, ripping me back to reality. In a daze, I haul myself off Noah. I'm flushed and sweaty. He's chased away the chill of the night, but I'm aching for more.

"Sorry. Phone," he says with a groan, holding it up. He checks his texts. "I'm supposed to be doing a one-on-one interview with the film crew right now. As much as I hate it, I should head back."

We climb to our feet, and after Noah turns off the lights, we head out of the barn, back to reality.

"No one has ever kissed me like that," I admit. "It was really great."

"It was amazing for me too."

He tucks my hand in his and we stroll back to the lodge, snow drifting around us like we're walking through a Christmas card. In this moment, I can almost believe we're meant to be together and nothing can come between us.

CHAPTER 14

From Pumpkin to Princess

ALEX

I've been holed up on the lodge's back deck in a chair in the corner under a mound of blankets all morning when the show's alert goes off—a series of chimes that sound like wedding bells over the lodge's intercom system. I've managed to steal several pads of paper from all the contestants' rooms and have spent the past few hours brainstorming an idea for a new novel—a thriller where lots of people get murdered. I needed some sort of outlet for all the frustration I'm feeling watching Noah get closer to some of the other girls—especially Evie—while I haven't managed to spend a single solitary second with him alone since we kissed in the bakery. And I still don't know who locked us in at the bakery, though I have a growing list of suspects.

Groaning, I untangle myself from my comfy flannel nest, hide my notepad in the back of my jeans under my sweater, and trudge to my usual spot by the fireplace between Sophie and Evie. The crowd of contestants is quickly dwindling. Now that River has been eliminated, there are only nine of us left.

"You okay?" Sophie asks. "What's going on?"

"I didn't sleep well is all," I say. I can feel Evie watching me too, her forehead puckering with concern. She was so happy last night after she spent time with Noah; she was practically glowing. I don't want to admit how upset it made me feel—hearing how their relationship got stronger—because I know it'll steal some of her happiness away. And while I want Noah as badly as she does, I also like her and don't want to make her feel bad for doing exactly what she's supposed to. Vying for Noah's heart is what we're all supposed to do. But then a small part of me, a selfish part, resents that she seems to be so much better at it than me. Why didn't I think of going to see him on my own?

Because after the pantry incident, I've been scared of being disqualified for pushing my luck.

And besides, Noah hasn't exactly sought me out on *his* own. And this is what has me the most upset. After that kiss I hoped he would.

Carianne clears her throat. "We start filming in five, ladies." She scans the room. "Anyone seen Jake?"

"Not today, unfortunately," Sophie says under her breath.

"Unfortunately, huh?" I ask, nudging her hip with mine. "What does that mean?"

Sophie snaps out of whatever she's thinking, her body visibly flinching. "It doesn't mean anything," she says a bit too quickly. "I just know he's supposed to be here so we can start filming and I don't want to be stuck waiting around for him." She eyes me once more. "You sure nothing's wrong?"

There's no time to answer. Jake rushes into the room with the show's makeup artist hot on his heels, still trying to dab powder on his nose. He waves her away and gets into position.

"And rolling!" Alison says.

Jake launches into his usual introduction. "Good afternoon, ladies! How's everyone doing today?"

"Good afternoon, Jake," Kristin and Bianca say in unison, their voices all sing-songy while the rest of us nod our heads that yes, we're doing okay even though there's tension in everyone's faces. We are over halfway through our time here and all of us are worried about the next elimination. I know because it's all anyone can talk about when they're not busy gossiping about each other, me included. This environment is designed to make us feel insecure and vulnerable and it's working.

Jake clasps his hands in front of him. "I've gathered you all together because—"

Before he can get whatever announcement he's trying to make out, he's interrupted by two very buff, very hot shirtless men clad in elf costumes complete with jingly shoes carrying a glossy red trunk with a large gold lock on the front.

"We have a special delivery from Noah for one very lucky lady," Jake finishes.

"Please say it's the elves," Bella Grace murmurs and several of the girls start giggling.

The elf guys set the box down on a table next to Jake. He takes a moment to inspect it. "But there's no tag. Who could it be for?"

He's just drawing out the moment, building the suspense so the viewers—and us—are practically salivating to find out. He looks at the elves. The one with full lips and blond hair that's tousled to perfection clears his throat and begins to recite a poem.

Oh brother. The drama is at its peak right now. But if I'm honest, I'm only rolling my eyes because I'm trying to temper my expectations. Of course, I want whatever it is Noah sent. I want some sign that the connection I felt with him still exists.

The poem is undeniably cute.

Inside your stockings snug and small,
Lies a golden key—one each for all.
It's a holiday touch of fate,
But only one unlocks the date.
If your key fits just right,
You'll join Noah for an epic night.
So come take your chance,
And see if it leads you to romance.

The blond elf gives a little bow once he's done reciting, then he and his buddy head for the lodge's front doors, the bells on their elf shoes and hats jingling merrily.

Kristin grabs Bianca's hand and bounces excitedly in place. "Oh my gosh, how cool! It's just like *Cinderella*!"

It *is* just like *Cinderella*. Damn it. I don't want to love this, but I do. That Disney movie was always my favorite. Most writers choose Belle over Cinderella, but I was always more drawn to the riches to rags to riches aspect of the latter. And maybe I relate to the loneliness she faced, ostracized by her stepmother and stepsisters. Also, the whole makeover thing just like in *The Devil Wears Prada*. I am nothing if not consistent.

"Well, ladies, it sounds as if you might want to check your stockings." Jake points to the fireplace.

There is practically a stampede to get to them. Evie, Sophie, and I hang back.

"Extra points to us for being classy," Evie whispers, and both Sophie and I laugh.

Most of the other girls have their keys, so Jake starts lining them up in front of the gift box.

I head for my stocking and pull out my key. It's surprisingly heavy, made of brass and ornate enough to look antique. The producers definitely went all out for this one. It doesn't take a genius to guess that whatever's in the box has to do with Noah's next one-on-one date, but what the date is? *That's* still a mystery. However, the keys and the elves are not so subtle hints that this date will be the biggest one yet. My stomach fills with nervous energy as I line up behind Evie. It's no secret that Noah seems to like her a lot. Will she get it? Not likely since she had the last one. She seems to realize this too, because she's not as excited as everyone else.

Sophie lines up behind me, last in line. She turns the key over and over in her hands. She keeps whatever she's feeling so close to the vest it's hard to tell if she wants to be the one or not.

Bianca is first to attempt to open the box. Her key doesn't work. Yes! I was hoping really hard it wasn't her. God please, *anyone* but her. And maybe that makes me a terrible person, but there's no way that girl is here for the right reasons. If pressed I'd pick her as the one who locked me in the spirits pantry at the bakery.

Girl after girl tries. None of their keys open the box. Before we know it, it's Evie's turn.

She sucks in a breath and tries her luck. The lock doesn't budge. She plasters on a smile as she turns to Sophie and me. "I'm so happy it's going to be one of you!" she says, squeezing both our arms excitedly. One of the best things about her is how supportive she is, even when it must hurt to be.

I step up to the box. My hand is trembling a little as I slip my key into the lock. *Please, please, please work*, I plead silently. I imagine Noah's face. His lips. How they felt on mine in the bakery. My nerves ratchet up a thousand notches. I turn the key. It resists the movement, and my heart starts sinking to my shoes. The disappointment is so acute I feel tears prick my eyes. But wait. It's not pushed into the lock all the way! I adjust it and try again.

Click!

I can't suppress a gasp. It worked! My key worked! I can feel everyone's eyes on me, waves of jealousy radiating off each of them. Stomach jittery enough to make my whole body tremble, I lift the box's lid.

Inside is a beautiful sapphire-blue velvet evening gown. Floor length, off the shoulder, and gathered at the waist. Lying beside it are a pair of long white dress gloves. And beside them is a shoe box. I open it and discover a pair of jewel-encrusted Louboutin heels the exact same shade as the gown, so high and pointed they could be considered a deadly weapon.

I'm so overcome I can't find words. It's all so wonderful—and familiar. Wait. This really is just like *Cinderella*. The gown is reminiscent of the one she wore to the ball, just a more modern silhouette. How did they know it was my favorite?

I hold up the dress and say all of this out loud to the camera because I know I'm supposed to. What takes me off guard is how emotional I'm feeling. I've written moments like this into my novels, but I never once thought I'd actually experience one.

The other girls' faces are crestfallen. I get it. This is a lot. Overwhelmingly romantic. Of course they all want it for themselves. Knowing this makes me feel a little bad for being so elated for myself. I can't quite look them in the eyes.

Jake clears his throat. "Congratulations, Alexandra! If Noah's gift is any indication, tonight's going to be a fairytale. We can't wait to see it unfold."

And with that, the crew stops filming, and surprise! I am ushered out of the room and led to the hair and makeup trailer where a very well-known makeup artist and a hair stylist on loan from the Kardashians turn me into a version of myself that I hardly recognize. I have never looked so glamorous in my entire life.

It's all such a dream that at first, I can't quite comprehend the nightmare waiting for me back in my bedroom. The dress is hanging from my closet door, but it's completely ruined. Jagged tears run the length of the bodice. The Louboutins sit just beneath it, sapphire velvet fabric stuck to the heels.

"Oh my god," I breathe. Someone used the shoes to eviscerate my dress!

Carianne walks in a moment later with a pair of cameramen. "Hurry, Alexandra, it's nearly time to go," she says, her eyes on the clipboard she's carrying. "And we'd like to get a few shots of you putting the final touches on your outfit. Slipping into your shoes. Pulling up your gloves, that sort of thing."

"Um, I can't. M-m-my dress," I stammer.

Without a word, the cameramen hoist their cameras onto their shoulders and start filming. I look away, too hurt to face the lens right now.

Carianne glances up and lets out a slew of curse words each more graphic than the last. Her outburst is loud enough to draw attention and soon several of the other contestants appear in my doorway.

"Good gracious me!" Bella Grace drawls. "Your dress! Someone's sabotaged you, Alex."

"You think?" Sophie pushes into the room and pulls me into a hug. "Whoever did this needs to be thrown off the show. Immediately," she snaps. "And really? You're filming this? Jesus."

Carianne gives her a warning look then turns to me, her

face softening. "Alex, I am so sorry this happened. I promise we will find out who's responsible and they will pay." She directs this to the girls standing in the doorway.

Bianca is among them, as are Kristin, Sierra, and Evie. Kristin's the only one who looks upset by what's happened. Her eyes actually look glassy with tears.

"Who would do such a thing?" Kristin says, tears falling down her cheeks as she looks from the dress to me.

Beside her Bianca is suspiciously quiet. I glower at her. If she did this, I will get her back if it's the last thing I do.

Evie looks from me to Bianca and nods subtly as if to say she knows it's Bianca too and she's got my back.

Carianne claps her hands. "Okay, everyone out. Except Alexandra. Honey, here's what's going to happen now." She strides into my closet and pulls out the terry cloth robe with the show's logo on it, the one we all got the night we arrived. "Put this on and then in ten minutes, go down to the lobby. Noah's going to meet you there."

"You want me to go on this date in a robe?" I ask, frowning.

"Just trust me," she says, a smile spreading across her face. "I've got a plan."

And then she's gone.

Ten minutes later I'm standing in the lobby just like she asked, clad in nothing but my delicates, the robe, and a pair of slippers.

Noah is there, beaming the moment I step out of the elevator. "Alex," he says. "You look beautiful."

I glance down at the robe and give him a dubious look.

He shakes his head, his gaze running over me in a way that makes my stomach twist. "You could've just rolled out of bed wearing a literal garbage bag and you'd still be gorgeous," he says.

I can't stop the smile spreading over my face. "Flattery will get you everywhere," I say, laughing.

"Shall we?" He offers me his arm. I take it, and together we walk outside to the stretch limo waiting in the lodge's porte-cochère.

Ten minutes later we are in the heart of downtown at a high-end boutique a few doors down from the bakery. There are five evening gowns hanging on a rack, each more elaborate than the last from designers I've dreamed my whole life of wearing, but could never afford.

"Take your pick," Noah says. "Whichever one you like best."

I take a peek at one of the price tags and nearly faint.

"You're still getting your Cinderella moment," Noah says softly. "I've wanted to give it to you since the moment we met. I know it's something you've always wanted."

"But how did you know that?" I ask.

He takes my hand and kisses it. "I've read your books, remember? That fantasy is written into most of them in some form."

It takes me less than a minute to pick the dress I want—it's dark blue, like the one he gave me originally, but made of silk instead of velvet and it's simpler with spaghetti straps and a deep V in the back. It fits me perfectly and compliments my pale skin. I love it more than I thought was possible to love a dress.

Noah's expression when he sees it on me sends a thrill through me. He looks awed and it makes me feel good. Powerful somehow.

The store's owner, a petite French woman with icy blonde

hair, brings me a faux-fur wrap to go over the dress. I slip it over my shoulders.

"You look amazing, but you're missing something," Noah says. He holds up a black velvet box and flips open the lid with a flourish.

Inside are a pair of diamond earrings and a necklace made of sapphire and diamond hearts.

"It's perfect," I whisper.

"It's yours," Noah says softly. "Well, for tonight anyway."

I lean over and very lightly run my fingers across the necklace. "Thank you," I breathe.

Noah puts it on me. "Stunning," he says, his eyes twinkling.

It's heavier than I expected. I still can't believe I'm wearing something so fancy. It must cost more than my cabin back home.

Together, Noah and I leave the boutique...and find a helicopter parked at the center of the street.

"Your chariot awaits," Noah says.

I stop short of the helicopter door and turn to him. "If I get too caught up in the moment and forget to tell you later, I had a really nice time." I'm referencing another one of my favorite movies here. I can't help it. The moment is so *Pretty Woman*.

Noah leans down and kisses me softly. "Me too."

The helicopter flies us straight to New York. When I see the Flatiron Building, I can't help myself and let out a little squeal of delight. "That's my publisher down there," I say, pointing to the approximate spot where Owen's office is.

Noah smiles and nods, but I can tell he isn't as excited. But then again he's a reader, not a writer. The inner-workings of publishing probably aren't something he's all that interested in.

Still, I can't help feeling a twinge of disappointment. But that's silly. He's a great guy and he's told me how much he loves my books. Is it really a big deal?

We land on a helipad nearby and are taken by car to a showing of the Nutcracker at Lincoln Center. The whole place is buzzing, all the audience members watching us more than the show since episodes of Santa's Most Eligible have already started airing. At first, I'm too caught up in the romance of the night to notice, but as the show goes on, I can't help being distracted.

"Everything okay?" Noah whispers in my ear.

"I feel like we're in a fish bowl," I whisper back, nodding at the crowd.

"Ah," he says, smiling. But the attention doesn't seem to bother him at all. If anything, he seems to like it—at least more than the ballet.

"This is not really my thing," he confesses during the inter-mission. "I'm more of a football game or rock concert kind of guy."

My heart sinks a little. It looks like I have found something about him that isn't perfect—at least not for me. I love the ballet. And I absolutely hate sports. Sitting through a football game is my idea of torture.

I shake my head. I'm being silly. He doesn't like ballet and yet he came to one tonight to please me. Is there anything more romantic than that? No. We don't have to have all the same interests, do we? If he's the one for me, maybe sitting through Sunday football won't be so bad.

After the show, we have dinner in a private penthouse at the top of the Central Park Tower with the whole city spread out beneath us, a collection of glittering lights that mirror the stars. As I nibble my way through the first course, I start peppering him with questions.

"So I know you like skiing and football, but not ballet. What else should I know about you?"

Noah takes a sip of his beer. "Well, um, let's see. I love to travel."

I brighten. "Me too!"

He grins and leans closer. "I particularly love adventure travel. Spelunking in Mexico. Rock climbing. That sort of thing. Roughing it under the stars." I must make a face because he laughs. "Not your thing?"

I shake my head. "I'm more of a museum and shopping sort of girl," I say. "Spelunking in a cave is the stuff of nightmares for me. Being under so much earth?" I shiver. "No thank you."

Is it my imagination or does he look a little disappointed?

I clear my throat. "But camping isn't out of the question. I've always wanted to fall asleep under a blanket of stars."

He perks up at this.

We spend the rest of the meal talking about our families and jobs. The conversation flows easily and before I know it, we're back at the lodge, saying goodbye.

Instead of taking me inside, Noah steers me toward the lodge's terrace. The stone walls are festooned with Christmas lights and garland. I pull my wrap a little closer as Noah disappears around the corner of the building. A few seconds later, all the lodge's outside lights snap off.

I gasp in surprise.

"Look up," Noah whispers as he comes to put his arms around me.

The sky is crystal clear and encrusted with what must be a

million stars. Nature's own Christmas lights. "A blanket of stars," I murmur, remembering our conversation earlier.

Noah kisses the top of my head. "And you didn't even have to go camping."

Standing here on this cold December night under all this twinkling beauty, I really do feel like Cinderella wrapped in the arms of her Prince Charming, hoping despite all the odds—and differences in favorite pastimes—that I'm headed for my own version of happily ever after.

CHAPTER 15

Secrets, Secrets

SOPHIE

My mind is full of Jake since that strange but wonderful night on the mountain. Whether I'm talking with Evie and Alex about what could happen at the next reveal, lining up for omelets at breakfast, or climbing into my bed at night, my thoughts drift to him. Even this morning at the Candy Cane Reveal, when poor Bella Grace received the coal and we were all feeling a little sad about losing the quirky but sweet girl, I couldn't keep those familiar butterflies from fluttering up in my stomach as Jake's eyes touched on me. Every moment I'm around him is electric. A brush of his finger against mine as I pass by him, a smoldering side glance as the cameras shift from him to Noah.

There's still a part of me that is afraid of opening myself to Jake again, to allow him access to my vulnerable heart. But the other part of me, the one that dreams of being in his arms, in his bed, tempts me into wanting to strip down the defenses I've built.

"Sophie, did you hear me?" Evie asks, sitting next to me on my bed and nudging me with an elbow.

"What?"

Alex laughs softly. Already showered and dressed in her PJs, she returned an hour ago from her date with her face glowing. Because she's kind and could see how left out Evie felt, she didn't go on about Noah. Still, I can tell she's really into him.

"I think she's daydreaming about a certain guy," she says.

Evie groans and flops back on the bed. "Join the club." She props herself up on her elbows. "Seriously, what do you think, Sophie? Don't you agree with Alex? Bianca must've destroyed her dress."

I shake thoughts of Jake away. "I do, but there's no proof. I wish there were cameras in the rooms."

Evie gives me a raised eyebrow. "Really? Because that would totally creep me out. I don't need anyone seeing me in my pajamas."

"You're in your pajamas every morning at the Candy Cane Reveal," Alex reminds her.

"Not my fake pajamas. My real ones that have Winnie the Pooh on them."

Alex and I laugh, and for the tenth time I think to myself how lucky we are that the production team allowed us to room together, since Alex's roommates have been sent packing and Kristin decided to move in with Bianca. "I'm going to go for a walk," I tell them, standing up. "I'll be back in a bit."

I head to the dining room to see if they have any chamomile tea, but stop at the bottom of the stairs when I hear a low and familiar voice.

"I told you," Bianca says quietly.

I quickly slip behind a door and peer around to see Bianca leaning against the wall, a phone to her ear. Considering we locked phones away when contestants arrived, I'm guessing she had a burner stashed in her luggage. The production team does its best to ensure that doesn't happen but it's not too hard to smuggle one in.

"I know, babe, I know. I don't care about him. Just you."

She pauses, then says, "No. I told you, I need to see this through. As soon as it's over, I'll get plenty of bookings, and then we'll be set. I just need to make it to the final two."

Another pause, then Bianca sighs loudly. "Fine, but quick. There's a shed out back with some farm equipment. I'll be there in two minutes. This is the last time 'cause I've got to focus on the show."

She makes kissing noises, then there's the sound of a door opening and closing on the other side of the room.

So, Bianca has a lover on the side. I chuckle as I forego the cup of tea and go looking for Mack. I turn the corner and collide right into Jake.

"Whoa!" he says, his arm wrapping around my waist to steady me. For a heartbeat, we're pressed together in an empty hallway. This is the only time since that moment on the mountain that we've been alone. He's wearing a white T-shirt and jeans, his "off-camera" look. The light but heady masculine scent of his cologne makes me want to melt into him, and my pulse is beating so fast he's got to hear it.

"Sorry," I mumble, backing away and bumping into the wall behind me.

The corner of his mouth lifts. By the look in his eyes, he knows exactly what I'm thinking. "You okay?"

"Yeah." I clear my voice. "Did you see Bianca?"

He tilts his head. "Yes, just a second ago. She said she's going for a walk. Why?"

I roll my eyes. "A walk. Apparently, she's got a guy on the side. I heard her talking to him on the phone."

His eyebrows lift. "Phone?"

"She must have a burner. She made plans to meet him in the equipment shed out back."

Jake stares in the direction Bianca went. "Well, well, well. Interesting. Mack will want to know about that." He sighs. "So much for signing affidavits swearing they weren't in a relationship. I'm guessing Mack will have her cameras out there within the minute, though." He gives me a lopsided smile. "Makes for good television."

I bite at my lip, guilt chewing at me. The cameras will catch her hooking up with some other guy, and Mack will have no qualms about airing it if she thinks it will boost ratings. I can't stand Bianca, and what she did to Alex was awful, but embarrassing her like that on national TV was not my intention.

"Wait," I tell him as he pulls out his phone. "Don't tell her. Not right now."

Jake raises an eyebrow. "Protecting Bianca?"

"No. Well, sort of. I don't know. I just don't think it's cool to have camera crews listening in on...that."

"Isn't this what you signed up for?"

"Yes. Well, no." I stare at the ground. I *did* sign up for this, and if I was on the other side of the camera, I'd probably have sent those cameras out to catch her in a compromising position as quickly as I could. So why my hesitation? Have I gone soft, being a contestant? Do I care more now than I did before because I'm one of them? I don't know, but one thing's for sure: I can't do that to her, even if she is the Queen Bitch.

"I don't care," I say quietly. "It feels icky to do that to another woman. If you feel the need to tell Mack right now, that's on you. I'd rather tell her later than have her run out there to film the whole thing."

He stares at me for a moment like it's the first time he's seeing me. "You've changed."

"Meaning?"

"The Sophie I used to know who was on the fast track to a film career would've run to Mack immediately with all the juicy details."

I narrow my eyes at him. "Maybe you don't know me as well as you think you do. I'm still going to tell her about it. Just on my own terms, when I don't have to sacrifice integrity for a scoop."

"I get it." His eyes soften. "You're full of surprises, you know."

"I guess," I say. "I better go back upstairs. I'll see you tomorrow."

"Soph." He reaches out to take my hand, glancing around quickly to make sure we're alone. "About, um, us."

He stops abruptly, his eyes searching mine for an answer to a question he hasn't even asked. Here in the dimly lit hallway, my other senses take hold. Jake smells so good, his familiar cologne faint but intoxicating enough to make my heartbeat pound in my ears. His hand is wrapped around mine, warm and strong, but gentle at the same time. He pulls me to him, his other hand slipping around my waist.

He's nervous, I can tell. Probably wondering if I'm going to pull away or punch him again. I wrap my free hand around his neck and press my lips to his, welcoming the heat building quickly between us. His mouth is hot on mine as he drops my hand and pulls me closer to him. I know he wants me as much as I want him.

A noise somewhere jolts us apart. I fall back against the wall, then turn toward the stairs and move as fast as I can away from him. I try my best to remind myself that Jake is the host here, and according to our contract, completely off limits. Not to mention arrogant, overly confident...the one guy I should avoid.

The one guy I really want.

But at the staircase is an unfortunate surprise. Alex and Evie are staring at me, their eyes wide, expressions shocked.

Shit.

CHAPTER 16

Tangled in Tinsel

EVIE

"Explain yourself," I snap at Sophie as soon as we step into our room and Alex closes the door. "You're supposed to be here for Noah, so why were you making out with the host of the show?"

"Yes, spill," Alex says. "What's going on with you and Jake Logan?"

Sophie sighs. "Everything."

She sinks down onto the bed and presses her face into her hands. I almost feel sorry for her when she lifts her face, practically glowing. Her cheeks are flushed and her eyes are sparkling.

"What if Noah finds out about this?" I swallow the bitterness in my mouth. I'm not going to lie, but cheating is definitely a trigger for me. "He's the one who could be getting hurt in this situation."

"Noah's not going to get hurt. He already tried to get us togeth—" Sophie stops mid-sentence.

"You're not serious!" Alex blurts out. "He knows about you two? And you're still here?"

"There's no way Noah knows about this," I say.

Sophie bites at her lip, looking from me to Alex as if she's carrying a secret she's not sure she should share. Anger simmers beneath my skin. I can't believe she would so blatantly cheat on Noah and break the rules we were told about in the beginning. They literally said no flirting with the host, and here she was, making out with him. This isn't the Sophie I thought I knew.

"How would the producers feel if they knew about you and the show's host?" I ask, not bothering to keep the irritation out of my voice.

"Please don't say anything," Sophie pleads. "I'll tell you what's going on, but you have to *promise* me you won't say anything."

"I can't keep your secret from Noah." I shake my head, my heart aching as I remember his story about how his ex cheated on him. "He deserves to know."

"He already does," Sophie says.

"So you weren't lying? He really does know?" Alex's sceptical tone matches my own.

"He's known from the very beginning," Sophie says, and then she tells us how she was a producer and had been volun-told to take the part.

"Oh my god," I say, sinking onto the bed beside her, trying to process what she just said.

"Wow," Alex agrees. "I mean that's a plot twist even *I* didn't see coming."

"Whew." Sophie grins. "It feels good telling you all this. It's been hard keeping the truth from you both."

"So you and the host, huh?" Alex sits on Sophie's other side and nudges her playfully with her shoulder. "Nice."

"Jake and I have a history. We've known each other forever. It's a bit of a love/hate relationship."

She tells us how they met and the rollercoaster of their relationship. Listening to her talk, I can see she's really fallen for this guy.

"I shouldn't have jumped to conclusions and let you explain yourself," I say. "It's just cheating is a big trigger for me. My ex cheated on me."

"I'm going to order room service," Sophie says. "And then you're going to tell us all about this ex that sounds like a douchebag."

We stay up until two in the morning, eating warm brownie sundaes and thick-crust pizza. I tell them about the snake-in-the-grass and Alex shares a horror date that has us laughing so hard my stomach hurts. And just like that, our friendship is back in place and maybe even stronger than before.

THE NEXT MORNING brings a whirl of excitement when we all find a gift below the tree after breakfast. It's a shoe-sized box with a red bow on top. It's a nice pick-me-up after Zuri's emotional elimination this morning. We all really liked her, and I know most of us wish Bianca had been sent home instead.

Kristen swoops the gift up in her arms but frowns when she reads the card.

"It's addressed to Evie," she says with a glare. "That's not fair. She already got a special date with Noah."

Everyone is talking but all I can focus on is opening the card. Breathlessly, I read it out loud.

"It's the most magical time of the year, and I can't think of a better way to spend it than by your side. Let's spread a little holiday cheer and make memories that will last all year. Noah."

I rip open the present to find a Styrofoam cup and a hot chocolate packet.

"Looks like I'll be making some hot cocoa today," I say, holding up the gifts.

"I'm kind of glad I didn't get that date," Amber says. "It sounds boring."

I don't care what I'll be doing as long as I get to be with Noah. The note tells me to dress in comfortable clothing so I change into a flannel shirt and jeans. An assistant escorts me through the lobby to a car waiting outside. My pulse is racing by the time we pull up in the town center of Everpine. The whole place has transformed from the last time I saw it when we were doing the snowman competition.

Wooden booths decorated with thick garland strung with white lights form a circle around the perimeter of the square. A stage is set up on one end and people are gathering on it, testing the mics. Noah is waiting for me on the sidewalk along with a number of spectators. I slip out of the car and run into his arms.

He twirls me around and then kisses me right in front of what feels like half the town. When we pull back, I'm breathless, soaking in the sight of him in his brown jacket and jeans that show off his lean form.

"Are you ready to be put to work?" he asks me.

"As long as I'm with you, I'm up for anything."

"Excellent." He slips his hand into mine and leads me across the square. "Then you're hired."

"This sounds like serious business."

"It is." He nods solemnly. "Together we're going to be working the cocoa and cookies booth for the Christmas market that Everpine Lodge runs every year. It's a small gesture we do to give back to the community."

"I love that."

People are making final preparations to their booths, and as we stroll along, Noah introduces me to the locals. Booths are full of handmade crafts, homemade knitted scarves and mittens, artwork, and delicious foods like mulled cider, hot gingerbread, and roasted chestnuts that fill the air with their festive scents. There's even a craft booth where kids can write and decorate letters to Santa.

"This place is so perfect," I tell Noah as we arrive at Everpine's booth, the sides decorated with pine boughs and red ribbon. "I get why you love this town so much."

We slip into the booth. Noah lines up the cups and then we pour the chocolate powder into each one.

"I'm glad you like it," he says as he passes me an apron. "It's really important to me that my future wife wants to be a part of all this. I know it's a lot to ask someone to just drop their life and come live here with me, but I hope you see the reason why I can't leave Everpine."

We've barely finished getting everything set up when carolers break into song, singing "Jingle Bells" on the stage and guests start wandering their way through the market. I'm amazed at how well Noah and I work together. It doesn't take us long to become a well-oiled machine. I greet each guest who stops by, encouraging them to grab a cookie while Noah pours hot water into a cup. After a quick stir, I pass the steaming cocoa to the guests and Noah thanks them on behalf of Everpine Lodge.

In the back of my mind, I consider Noah's words. Would I want to leave my life back home? I have my students and my book club friends. It would be really hard to just get up and leave all that behind. But seeing how Noah's face lights up as he jokes and laughs with the townsfolk, I know that this is his home and where he belongs. If he were to leave this place, it would be like he'd be leaving behind a part of him. And to ask that of him wouldn't be right.

Time flies by so it's a surprise to me when Noah's parents arrive to take the next shift.

"I've got to confess," Tessa says, a twinkle in her eye. "We were secretly watching you two work for a bit."

"Still regretting not applying for a secret agent role?" Noah teases his mom and hugs her.

"She'd have been a great agent," Victor agrees. "Thankfully, she likes skiing more."

I laugh as I take off my apron. Noah's family always knows how to make me feel relaxed and comfortable like I fit right in.

"I saw right away what a great team you two make," she continues. "Thank you, Evie, for coming out today and working the booth. It meant a lot to us, but also to all of the guests."

After we say goodbye to Noah's parents, wishing them good luck, Noah takes my hand once again and we head back toward the car.

"You did awesome," Noah tells me. "You can come back every Christmas and help out."

My thoughts spin as we slide into the car and I think about our future. Who will he be engaged to next Christmas? What does that mean? Does he see me more like a friend than someone he's going to marry? I'm so confused right now. I wish I knew what he really was thinking.

"That was a fun date, but man, I really don't want it to end," I say as the car pulls us away from the village and back up the mountain to Everpine Lodge. "I mean, we got to spend time together but we didn't really get time to talk."

He smiles and kisses my forehead. "My thoughts exactly,

which is why I'm glad I insisted we have a second part to this date."

"A second part?" My hopes lift.

"I wanted to show you a little side endeavor we are doing at Everpine Lodge," he says. "And get your help for one more thing."

The car turns left just before we're supposed to go further up the hill to the lodge.

"I'd love that," I say, taking his hand and squeezing it. "I'm not ready to leave you yet."

"Good, because I think you're going to like this."

The car pulls into a rocky parking lot. Stretched before us are lines upon lines of evergreen trees, tucked in neat rows like toy soldiers. We step out of the car, and instantly, I'm enveloped with the scent of pine mixed with fresh snow. The wind whispers through the boughs, and if a second car hadn't pulled up with the film crew, it all would've been perfect.

"The air smells like a slice of Heaven," I say, trying to pretend away the cameras that are suddenly capturing our every move.

"This is our tree farm that we've been developing," Noah continues. The cameras don't seem to bother him as his eyes sweep across the trees with pride. "We have so much land that is used for skiing but a lot of it just sits here so we figured we should put it to use. Next year, we're hoping to open it up for the public where people can come and chop down their own real tree."

"That's amazing. I've never had a real tree."

"What would you say about the two of us heading out and cutting down a tree for my cabin? Then we could decorate it together if you're up for that."

"That sounds like a blast. Sign me up."

The sounds of bells clang through the frosty air. A man sits in a sleigh drawn by two horses trotting our way. A squeal of excitement escapes me as the sleigh stops right before us.

"Care for a ride?" Noah asks.

"Absolutely," I say, and Noah helps me into the seat.

He settles in beside me, tucking a thick blanket over our laps. A cameraman leaps up last, sitting in the corner across from us. Annoyance itches at my skin, but I remind myself that this is what I agreed to when I signed the contract. I need to have fun and not let anything ruin that.

The sleigh takes off and we speed across the snow, whizzing through the lines of trees. The wind shivers over my cheeks, but I don't care. I squeeze in close to Noah and wrap my arm through his, soaking in the whole experience. As we ride, he shares with me how he came up with the idea of starting a tree farm while watching a Hallmark show with his mom a few Christmases back.

Soon we come to a clearing and the sleigh stops. Noah helps me out. Standing here in this forest of evergreens feels like we've entered a hidden world meant only for the two of us. And I'd have believed it if there wasn't a camera guy in front of us.

"This area has the oldest trees," Noah explains. "We should find something we like here."

"I never thought of you as a Christmas tree farmer," I say as we tromp through the snow. "Do you find it takes away from your time at the ski lodge?"

"It's been a great side hustle. I think it's because I get to watch the growth. With the lodge, we're on a continual loop. A customer walks through the door, we try to give them the best experience possible and then the moment they leave, another customer takes their place. But seeing these trees develop and mature over time allows me the satisfaction of a job well done."

"Teaching is a lot the same way," I agree, taking in the thick evergreens. "Every year, I get a new group of students. I give them my all, teach them everything they need to know to move to the next grade, and by the time we get to the end of the year, I can really see their growth."

A perfectly A-framed tree catches my eye up ahead. I point it out and we investigate it. The pine needles are soft as I rub my fingers along them. It's the same height as Noah and shaped in a perfect cone.

"I think this is the one," I declare.

"I think you're right." He leans in and his lips press soft as a snowflake against mine. My breath catches, and my heart tumbles about like it's dancing. "Let's take this one home."

Home. That word clatters around in my chest. It's a scary word, but it's also one that fills me with yearning. Noah takes off his jacket and grabs a saw. He drops to the ground, tackling the stump like he was born for this job, muscles straining from the effort that I can't help but admire. I hold the tree trunk to keep it from tipping over. My thoughts wander again, wondering what his house is like and if I would like it too. It's weird that we're dating and yet have never even seen each other's places.

Together, we lug the tree into the back of the sleigh. The camera guy films every moment of it, even the boring parts. And then our driver sets off again and we're flying over the snow. We leave behind the tree farm and take a snowy trail through the forest. With the boughs draped in thick, glistening snow and listening to the whoosh of the sled, it's like we're being whisked into a winter wonderland. The horses' hooves create a steady rhythm as they clomp along.

The trail takes a turn, and up ahead a cozy cabin sits at the end of the trail. Smoke curls from the stone chimney as if inviting us inside. It's made of wood and the pitched roof is topped in powdery snow. A small porch juts out from the front where a neat pile of wood is stacked by the front door. Parked off to the side is the familiar black van of the film crew.

"So this is where you hide out after you leave us each day," I say.

"Let's keep this a secret just between the two of us," Noah says with a wink. "There's a few ladies back at the lodge that don't quite understand the word privacy."

"Considering we have a camera crew, I wouldn't exactly use the word private."

He chuckles, but he does have a point. Some of the women would sneak here in a flash if they knew where he lived. And it would likely not be during daytime hours.

The driver and Noah lug the tree inside, and I trail after them, trying not to look at the camera guy. I can't quite get over how awkward everything has been with him videoing my every move. Will he be here with us the whole time or will we get to have some privacy?

When I step inside, it only gets worse. The cute little cabin is bursting with people. Two cameras are set up around the place where they're putting in the tree. The tiny kitchen is packed out with two people setting up more cameras while another three are placing pots on the stove, arranging knives and a cutting board on the counter, and stacking up vegetables like they're preparing for a kitchen show.

Carianne pops before me with a hurried smile. "Glad you made it back okay. How are you feeling? Do you need any water or anything?"

"I'm fin—"

"Gerry!" she calls over her shoulder. "Get Evie some water. Hurry."

"I'm sure I can get some water from the sink."

"Nonsense. I want to get a few shots of you two decorating the tree and then making some dinner together. You know, romantic stuff. The viewership of the cooking date for our last show, *Golden Hearts*, were off the charts, so this is going to be a big one for the ratings."

"Okay," I say, wringing my hands as I take in the chaos and the word *ratings* rattles around in my head. I know Sophie has been sent to do something else, but I really wish she were here instead of bossy Carianne.

The romantic day seeps away like spilled coffee as the reality of the show takes over. Suddenly, everything that we're doing feels fake and forced. I know I began this whole adventure to have fun and show the Cheating Scumbag how awesome I really am, but now that my feelings are involved, it's changed everything.

"If you'll just stand here," the director Alison instructs, pulling me by the tree. "Noah, you move beside her and pretend you're having a great time."

"Pretend?" I lift my eyebrows.

Noah laughs at my expression. "The only pretending I'm going to do is try not to show how crazy I am about you."

A box of ornaments, red plastic balls, and silver stars is pushed into my arms while another person dusts my nose with powder. Noah peeks inside the box.

"Those are definitely not my ornaments." He chuckles, rubbing the back of his neck. "Sorry about all of this. It's a little much."

"That's what this is all about, right?" I shrug, trying to be the better person here. "If nothing comes out of all this, at least I might make my ex jealous."

His brow puckers and his eyes grow worried. Something I said didn't sit well with him, but there's no time to discuss it because Alison yells out, "Rolling!"

"I guess this is when we decorate the tree," Noah says, grinning.

"Why don't you tell her about your favorite Christmas?" Alison throws out.

And that's when he shares with me about his first real skis, not the ones for beginners.

"They were immaculate." Noah hangs up a red ball. "They're fine-tuned to deal with a mountain in any condition and the whole experience changed for me. I think that's when I knew that I would be carrying on the family legacy of running the business and lodge. Skiing was a part of my blood."

"That was great!" Alison says, interrupting the moment.

I jerk at the sound of her voice after being so caught up visualizing Noah racing down the slopes. The box of ornaments is ripped from my hands by Carianne while Alison ushers us to the kitchen.

"Now you'll make pasta together," Alison says. "I mean what's more romantic than that, right?"

"I could think of a few things," Noah says, rubbing his chin and grinning mischievously at me.

A delicious shiver dances down my spine. Damn...he just went there.

And just like that, my smile slips back into place. She positions us at the island, handing me the knife and Noah the bowl and spoon.

"Woah!" Noah teases. "You're not going to stab with that, are you?"

"Try to think of more romantic things to say," Alison admonishes, clucking her tongue.

"Yeah, Noah." I hold up my knife with a wicked grin. "Otherwise, I'm coming for you."

He cocks his head to the side, assessing me. "I like the sound of that. Well, without the knife, of course."

My eyes slip to his chest, wondering what it would be like to run my hands across his bare skin. How it would feel to lean in and feel our bodies connect.

"Evie!" Alison exclaims. "Start on the carrots."

We do some shots of me chopping the veggies with Noah's arms wrapped around me, hands on mine. His scent drifts over me and feeling him so close reminds me of the passionate kiss we shared in the horse barn. If only all these people would just leave, maybe we could actually have time to bond.

At Alison's direction, Carianne hands us a plate of premade pasta.

"I want you to each feed each other a bite," Alison says.

"But this isn't pasta that we made," I point out.

She waves her hand dismissively. "The viewers don't need to know that."

My whole body is stiff as a board as Noah brings the fork of pasta to my mouth because there are ten people huddled around watching us. But even though it's incredibly awkward, there's something visceral about him feeding me. His gaze lingers on my lips, and as soon as I swallow the food, he kisses me.

At first, I become rigid from shock. But the passion in his kiss sends a shiver of delight running through my veins. This is the sort of man that has me wanting to leave behind my whole life and embrace everything he has in store for me. It's a terrifying realization.

His mouth moves to my ear and he whispers, "I'm about to kick everyone out just so I can give you a real kiss."

My heart leaps. My skin is hot and cold all at once. I press my hands to his firm chest, gazing up into his eyes. Wondering if this is all too good to be true. Hoping for impossible dreams.

"Perfect shot!" Alison interrupts. "That will be a great scene to air before the Candy Cane Reveal."

Those words rip me back to the fact that this is a reality show and there are too many other beautiful, amazing women vying for his heart and likely feeling exactly how I am.

"It will be weird watching this on TV later," I admit, taking my apron off.

"Right." Noah kneads his forehead, almost as if he's having those same thoughts.

I can't help but wonder if there's another woman who he has just as much or more of a connection with than me.

"You can ride with us back to the lodge," Carianne tells me as the crew finishes packing up.

Except I don't want to go back. I want to stay here and never leave Noah's side. I want us to leap in that sleigh and race away from all this madness.

"When does she need to be back by?" Noah asks. "Because I could drop her off. You all could head back and do whatever you need to do."

Carianne's eyes flicker between the two of us in indecision. "Well, I guess it couldn't hurt. We've got to get back to do some interviews with the other ladies. Just have her back before ten."

"I think I can do that," Noah says.

We watch the staff pack up the last of the items, leaving the kitchen island sparkling clean and two plates of food that were clearly created by Everpine's cooking staff on the back counter. A few of the camera crew linger, trying to get some more shots in but Noah shoos them away, saying, "Don't forget that based on our contract, my quarters are off-limits unless I agree."

This motivates them into their vans.

"Nicely played," I tell him, squeezing his hand.

As the roar of the engines fades away, Noah turns to me, laughing and shaking his head. "Now *that* was a wild experience," he says. "But you handled it way better than I could have ever asked of you. Thanks for going along with it all."

"When she said you had to pretend to like me I almost died." And then I start laughing too.

"I want to know where she got those ornaments. Like, were mine not good enough?"

"Apparently not." I wag my finger at him. "From now on, red balls and silver stars are all you get."

"I had a great time with you today even with the cameras and almost-cooking-a-dinner together."

"I might be wrong, but I think we passed as professional chefs," I joke, nodding to the plates of gorgeous pasta and shrimp with veggies. "I'm seriously impressed by what we whipped up without even using hot water or a stove."

His eyes twinkle. "You know, something tells me that you could do anything you set your mind to, Evie."

His face grows serious and he moves in closer, pushing back the loose strands of hair that have fallen out of my ponytail. Then he cups his hand behind my neck and leans down, kissing me. Not for the cameras or the show.

For me.

For us.

My body is electric under the spell he's cast on me. He picks me up like I'm lighter than air and sets me on the island, cocooning himself between my legs. I run my hands through his feathery soft hair. Hot lips trail along my neck, leaving behind sparks that set me on fire. A moan drags from my throat. He runs his hands along my side and, as I unbutton the front of my flannel shirt one by one, a low rumble comes from his chest.

Eyes, dark as midnight, drink in my breasts and his hands skim over my bra like if he touches me, I might burn him. Maybe this is a bad idea getting so intimate, but right now, this feels like the best idea of the century. I unclip my bra, tossing it aside, and drag off my shirt. His hands gently cup my breasts like they are sacred. Our mouths meet once again, and this time he pulls me off the edge of the counter and hauls me over to the couch.

Breathlessly, I climb onto his lap, straddling him like I've dreamt of every night since I arrived. His body instantly hardens between my legs. His hands grasp my waist, palms heated like he's on fire. The need to feel him against me sends me rocking back and forth on him, a rhythmic grind that has him groaning with pleasure.

I'm losing myself in the moment, and that is a very dangerous thing. With a groan, this time of frustration, I stop. What am I doing? This is all wrong, very wrong.

"We shouldn't be doing this," I say, climbing off him. "You're dating so many other women right now. And this... We can't be doing this and that at the same time."

He blinks up at me, half-dazed, half-shocked. "You're right. I'm sorry." His face morphs into a pained expression and he rakes a hand through his hair. "When it comes to you, I don't think of anything but us. It was wrong of me. I didn't mean to take advantage of you."

I quickly button my shirt back up, my head yelling at me for letting things get out of control while my heart is screaming to race back into his arms and feel his mouth on my skin.

"I think you should take me back to the lodge now," I say firmly.

Noah looks stricken, full of regret. "Of course. Whatever you want."

I toss on my coat like armor and make a beeline for the door, needing to get as far from Noah as I can. This man could destroy my heart and rip it to shreds.

I don't think I'd ever recover.

CHAPTER 17

A Literary Escape

ALEX

Envy is a horrible, nasty thing. I know this. I write about this. But still, I can't fight it, no matter how much self-help advice I mentally give myself. Evie is talking about her date with Noah last night at his house and with every new detail a fresh wave of jealousy crashes over me. Even if it ended badly, it's clear she has very strong chemistry with Noah and that he's really into her, even if Evie worries he's not.

The tree trimming and the intimate moment they shared after is way more intense than anything I've shared with Noah. All the little romantic moments—it's an onslaught I was ill-prepared for when I sat down for breakfast. I was freaking humming on my way to the dining room for Christ's sake reminiscing about my Cinderella date. Despite the few tiny misgivings I had about our lack of things in common, the night was perfect. And I survived the next round of eliminations. Even though it was a sad moment for Amber, it's always a thrill to get that moment of validation.

But now, I feel like slipping out of my seat at the table and creeping back to my room to hide under the covers.

Still, I force myself to smile, to comfort Evie with the same level of enthusiasm that Sophie is, but inside I am dying a little. All the good feelings I had from my last date with Noah erode one by one. He took Evie to his cabin. No other girl's been there. My gut is churning, and I regret the small amount of food I managed to eat before Evie showed up.

"I mean the way I feel when he kisses me," Evie whispers, eyeing the tables where the other girls appear to be caught up in their own conversations. "It's this connection deep in my soul. Like I have butterflies and all, but it's more than that. It's like I feel this certainty that he's my person, but how can I? We're not exclusive. We may never be. But somehow I *know* him—like on a spiritual level if that makes sense. Even though I haven't spent much time with him. It's as if he's always been meant to be in my life, but that's stupid, right? To feel this so soon?"

Evie is a mess, her face tear-streaked. She really likes Noah. Last night obviously terrified her because it made her realize just how much. It's unsettling to see. Do I feel this strongly? My stomach churns. I want to. He's a great guy. What's holding me back?

Sophie squeezes her arm and looks thoughtful before snapping her fingers. "I think it's the string theory thing."

Evie sniffles and wrinkles her nose. "The what now?"

Sophie laughs and leans in closer to us from across the table, so we're less at risk of being overheard by the others. Evie's tears have turned a few heads and more than one girl is eyeing us over their egg white omelets. "Basically, the theory states that we all have a soulmate, someone attached to us by this invisible thread and that thread connects us our whole lives, then slowly pulls us together at the exact right time. When you're with Noah, you're feeling that kind of connection. Which is probably terrifying, but I don't think it's unfounded. He invited you to his private house. That's something, isn't it?"

I force a grin, trying to match Sophie's enthusiasm. "She's right," I say, each word a struggle. I want Evie to be happy. To find her person. But I want that for myself too. Noah is the nicest guy I've ever met. He ticks so many of my boxes. I want this string connection too. But then I immediately feel selfish for wanting it at the expense of my new friend's happiness.

Evie brightens just a little.

Sophie keeps talking. "Watching from off-camera I can see how strong the connection is between you two. I have since the very first night."

Her words hit me like a punch to the gut. Evie is a sweet person. Adventurous, full of energy, so nice that it's impossible not to like her. And yet, in this moment I'm starting to hate her. I can feel it building. I don't like it, and I don't like myself for feeling it. But there's this monstrous bit of me, a piece I try to keep buried deep, that is ready to rage. I like Noah. *I* might be in love with Noah. Every date and moment we've had has made me like him more. And I've been alone for *so* long. Every time I like someone it seems as if they choose someone else. What is wrong with me? Am I doomed to just write about love, but never experience it?

What I'm feeling must be plain on my face—I've never been very good at keeping my feelings hidden—because Sophie and Evie frown in unison.

"I'm so sorry," Evie says. "I'm making this morning all about me. Talking incessantly about my date and I—"

"No, don't be sorry," I say, forcing a grin that I know doesn't look sincere. I feel bad because I don't want to make her feel any worse. She is really freaked out about whether

Noah's legitimately into her. But after everything Sophie said, her take on what's happening between the two of them, I can't keep the tears building behind my eyes at bay for much longer. I push my chair away from the table.

Sophie grabs my hand. "Wait. I know he has feelings for you too, Alex."

Evie swallows hard and nods. She doesn't like hearing this. Good. Now maybe I'm not the only one feeling jealous. But then, that's awful to wish what I feel onto her.

I nod because I don't trust myself not to let out a sob if I try to speak. I wriggle out of her grip. "Pull it together, Alex," I silently tell myself. Then I take a deep breath and swallow hard. "I want you to find the love of your life, Evie. Truly," I say. "I just wish it wasn't the same guy I'm hoping will be mine." Then I hurry out of the dining room and into the lobby—and straight into a ladder.

"Oh my god!" I can't help crying out as I grab the bottom of the ladder to steady it. I look up, tears streaming down my face, only to discover Noah's at the top of the ladder, dabbing paint on the wall. He gasps as the ladder teeters left then right, threatening to topple.

"I'm so sorry!" I wince as Noah wobbles, his arms flailing a bit as he struggles mightily to keep his balance. For one heart-stopping moment I'm sure he's going to fall, but then he manages to grab onto the top of the ladder and steady himself. But unfortunately, the brush in his hand and the pail of touch-up paint resting on the ladder's little shelf near the top get tossed in the process and tumble down, down, down, crashing across the lobby's travertine floors by my feet. Paint erupts from the pail, an ivory explosion that peppers my face and clothes.

Every person in the lobby is staring at me with startled expressions. Cameramen hustle over, capturing it all on tape.

"Are you okay?" Noah asks as he starts to climb down.

I can't talk to him right now. I just can't. Not after everything Evie and Sophie just said. I need to get out of here.

Fast.

I make a run for the lobby door, the same way I did that first night when Noah chose me for his first private conversation. It was a mistake, not leaving that night. If I had, I wouldn't have this ache in my chest and all this awful, bitter envy.

The lodge's transportation shuttle is getting ready to pull out. I just manage to slip on as the driver is shutting the doors. I settle into a seat in the back and wipe tears from my cheeks. I have no idea where the shuttle is going, but I start praying like mad that it's to the airport because all I want to do right now is leave and never look back.

But curse my rotten luck, the shuttle turns onto the road that leads into town and not the highway. It comes to a stop in front of The Blushing Bun, the bakery where I got trapped with Noah. It's even more adorable in daylight—and crowded. There must be a hundred people lined up outside the front doors.

"It's because of that show," the woman next to me says as she gently rocks the baby on her lap. "Ever since it started airing, people have been pouring into town. I'm so glad this is our last day on vacation because it's getting ridiculously crowded. Stupid reality TV." She shakes her head. "I don't get it, I mean why would any girl volunteer to compete against a bunch of other girls to win over some guy? I don't care how rich or handsome he is. It's just plain crazy and desperate if you ask me. Having to convince someone that you're the one they should marry. I mean, shouldn't they just know? You can't tell me he hasn't figured out who he wants from the first night. Because he has. And deep down all those girls know it."

She's being unnecessarily harsh, but her words strike to the heart of what I've been privately thinking. What am I doing here? Am I desperate? Maybe. Probably. I need to get off this bus. Now. But I'm all the way in the back. And no one is in a hurry to disembark.

The woman babbles on. "It's the same on every single dating show. He knows from that first meet and greet thing, but he pretends like he doesn't. Like he's all confused. And he kisses all these girls. So many! And every single girl is ready to let him off the hook for it if only he'll choose her. It's degrading if you ask me."

She's getting so fired up that several people in the shuttle aisle start glancing back at us.

"Hey, aren't you—" one of them starts to say, eyeing me.

And that's it. Before they finish, I open the shuttle's rear emergency exit and bolt. An alarm starts to blare. I turn around to find half the passengers peering through the open back door. More than one of them has a phone aimed at me. They're recording me. Crap.

I start to run and veer off down a side street, hit a patch of ice, and nearly crash into a trio of trash cans before I manage to right myself and keep going. I turn down another street and then another, my only goal to put as much distance between myself and the shuttle passengers as possible. It doesn't take long before I am well and truly lost.

I do a quick spin and nearly sob when I spot a charming little bookstore, Oleander & Ink, to my right. It is the perfect place to hide. Maybe whoever's working there will let me borrow their phone so I can call my editor, Owen, and demand he gets me the hell out of here.

The moment I walk inside, I feel better. The familiar smells of leather, paper, and fresh-brewed coffee waft over me and suddenly I'm home, even if I'm technically not.

"Welcome in," a man with salt-and-pepper hair and black-rimmed glasses calls out, giving me a warm smile as he looks up from a copy of *The New York Times*. He's sitting in a deep leather chair by the store's front display window with a steaming cup of coffee beside him and one leg crossed over the other. He looks a bit like a college professor from the neck up, but from the neck down he is all Christmas in his crimson sweater with the collar of a green and red plaid shirt peeking out at the top and a pair of expensive-looking leather boots with green laces. He's even got a pair of gold Christmas wreath cufflinks. He's somehow both elegant and silly-looking at the same time. I like him immediately, especially his smile...and choice of reading materials. I can't help noticing the paper is open to the arts section. My favorite.

"Thank you," I say, acutely aware that I am covered in paint speckles and probably have mascara smeared under my eyes from crying. If he notices, he doesn't let on, and I like him even more.

He folds up his paper neatly and sets it beside his coffee. "I just made a fresh pot. You want some?"

I realize I'm shivering. I left in such a hurry that I didn't have time to grab a coat.

"That would be amazing, thank you," I say.

"Cream? Sugar?" he asks as he pours me a cup.

"Both," I say.

He smiles approvingly. "So, what brings you in today? Looking for the latest Patterson novel perhaps? We have two copies left. Given that it's Christmas-themed, it's going fast. Already sold two this morning."

I shake my head as I take the cup of coffee. "Thank you, but no. I'm more of a Lucy Foley girl."

"Ah," he nods. "Not romance?"

And by the way he raises an eyebrow and nods at the romance section where my latest novel is prominently displayed, I know he recognizes me. Thank god it's for my books though and not this stupid Christmas dating show.

"To write? Yes. To escape into? No," I answer.

"What about to live?" he asks as he leans against the coffee station counter. Well damn. So he does recognize me from the show too. But then again he is a townie. He was probably in the lodge's theater the day we had to sing. Recalling it makes me wince. I still can't believe I did that.

I swallow down a bit more coffee. "I'm starting to think maybe it's a no to that too," I say softly. I'm totally caught off guard when tears well up in my eyes as I say it. What is going on with me? I'm living a literal rollercoaster of emotions every single day I'm here.

"Is there any way you might let me borrow your phone?" I ask. "I don't have mine and I really need to get in touch with someone. My editor, actually." I wipe a stray tear.

The man's forehead creases with concern. "Hey now, what's wrong?"

I shake my head, the lump in my throat so thick I can't form words around it. More tears fall down my cheeks.

The man ducks behind the counter and digs out a box of tissues. "You know, I've been told I'm a pretty good listener. If you want to talk about it." He leans against the counter and smiles gently at me. "Or not. We can also just sit here and enjoy our coffees. Up to you entirely."

His manner is so comforting that I can't help myself. I start spilling all that's happened in one long litany of words. How I thought doing the show might help me be less lonely, but how most of the time the opposite is true. How I like Noah, but I'm having trouble really letting my guard all the way down. How I'm scared I won't be able to, not when every time I'm not with him, I'm forced to hear about his dates with the other girls. How I want to fall in love, and I might be with Noah, but I have no idea because I've never actually been in love before. Do you have to have everything in common? Should I feel this certainty that Evie does? And I'm scared that I'll look ridiculous on the show and lose all my readers. How I don't like competing for someone's attention, even if it's someone as handsome and amazing as Noah, and I think maybe I should quit. I talk and talk and talk, but the man doesn't seem to mind at all. He listens better than anyone I've ever met.

When I'm all talked out, he takes my coffee and tops it off before leaning against the counter and studying me.

"Do you want a bit of advice or did you just need to vent?" he asks gently. "I've learned when it comes to women it's always good to ask." His smile is soft, endearing.

Huh.

What do I want? I'm not sure. But now I'm curious what kind of advice he's going to give. "Maybe a bit of both," I say, returning his smile. Getting it all out has already made me feel better.

He chuckles. "Well if I were you, I would ask myself what I'll regret more: leaving before you know for sure who Noah's going to choose when you have no real proof it won't be you or staying and risking that on proposal day it might be you?" He takes a sip of his coffee. "My two cents? In my experience taking a risk on love is always worth it. Because there is a chance for a happy ending and even if it doesn't go that way , always staying open to the possibility ultimately increases your odds of finding the love that is meant for you one day."

He's right. I'm letting my fear rule me again. And if I keep doing this, I'm never going to get the big things I really want, especially love.

I set my coffee down and lean over and give the man a hug. "Thank you," I say.

"Anytime," he says, hugging me back. "Now get back in the game, girl."

I decide to do just that.

CHAPTER 18

Sweeter Than a Candy Cane

SOPHIE

Candy Cane Reveals are the best and the worst. Worst for anyone who is sent home, and best because if you stay in, you're one step closer to being with Noah forever. At least it's best for these other girls.

Okay, so I'll admit, in the very beginning there was a small part of me that kind of hoped Noah would fall for me and vice versa. He's handsome, kind, and genuine—the perfect guy. Call it vanity or lack of confidence or whatever, but receiving a candy cane in the mornings was something I looked forward to and hoped for almost as much as these other girls.

But now, the vibe has changed. Evie and Alex are clearly in love with the guy and, in my opinion, are the most deserving of his heart. I want to stay in the competition just to help them get ahead. At the same time, being in this competition is a little ridiculous when I've fallen for the host of the show.

Jake.

I shiver thinking about him. If you told me a month ago that I'd be completely head over heels for the guy who broke my heart years ago, I'd have said you were crazy. But here we are. I've tried to talk to him a few times after we kissed, but he always seems to be busy or talking with someone. I've caught him staring at me, though, and he's occasionally brushed my hand with his fingertips as he's walked past me, giving me a crazy case of goosebumps. With fewer people here there are more eyes and cameras on the remaining girls, so I know I need to be careful. I think he knows it too.

As for the show, I've already stayed in long enough to fulfill any expectations of Mack's. She seems happy with my portrayal of Sophie Hicks, not to mention the intel I've given her on the other contestants. That is to say she isn't yelling at me or firing me. She was angry when I told her about Bianca's burner phone and liaison with her secret boyfriend, so I'll admit I'm surprised that I'm the one going home instead of Bianca. It tells me the viewers probably prefer her over me, which stings a little. At the same time, I know Bianca's days on the show are numbered. Mack isn't going to put up with her shit much longer.

"You've done pretty well, kiddo," Mack says as Carianne adjusts my mic on my blue silk nightdress before the reveal begins. Carianne's eyebrows pinch at that, but she wisely doesn't say anything.

"Anything to help the show," I tell Mack. "Besides, it's more fun than I thought it would be. Except for having to live in a house with a couple of these girls."

"A 'couple of these girls' have boosted the ratings," she says. "That's all that matters."

Which is why Bianca probably isn't going home this morning. I wonder how Noah is handling that. I think of some of these other sweet girls who were sent home. I know he would've rather kept any of them around over Bianca, but it's not my place to say. Considering Mack's sovereignty over the show, it's really not even his place either. The worst part is that Mack knows how Bianca is and clearly doesn't care. Poor Noah.

"By the way," Mack adds in a low voice as she fluffs out my hair on the sides. "You need to be the last to check your stocking today. Just wanted to give you a heads up."

My heart sinks. The last to check the stocking—she wouldn't tell me that if it wasn't my turn to be ousted from the show. I appreciate her giving me a heads up, since they easily edit the morning reveals to the order they want to show them. A rare moment of kindness on Mack's part.

Even though I can freely admit that my heart's not in this, to receive a lump of coal is to be rejected. Rejection hurts, no matter how much I try to pretend otherwise. I look over at Evie and Alex, my friends on the show. Even though it will be good to not have a camera staring me down all the time, I'll miss hanging out with them.

Mack pats my shoulder. "Make the scene real, Sophie. Make it count. And you'll be back in the producer chair almost as soon as you step out of the gondola. But only if you play by the rules."

Her eyes narrow at me slightly before she walks away to direct the cameras. I'm frozen in place, my heart in my throat. As clearly as if she'd shouted it at me, she knows. Did Jake say something to her? Did the cameras catch us kissing that time in the hallway? Or did I give it away staring so openly at him?

I remember Mack's warning: No boyfriends, no fraternizing with the crew, no flirting with the host. I glance at Jake, who is talking with Noah in the corner. Would I be willing to sacrifice everything for a second chance at love with Jake? Would he?

Evie and Alex come down the stairs, followed by Sierra and

then Kristin, who's dressed in emerald-green satin pajamas that coordinate beautifully with her bright red hair. Bianca is behind her, looking grumpy as hell until a camera focuses on her. Then that frown quickly flips to become a lovely smile. Faker. I just hope Alex and Evie get a fair shot to be the final girl. At least they're in it for the right reason.

The crystal clinking of a glass draws our attention to Jake and Noah standing in front of the Christmas tree. "Ladies, it's just about time to see who gets a candy cane, and who will get the lump of coal."

His eyes skip over me as he smiles at the other women. The cameras won't notice that, of course. I wonder if he is glad about me being done, or if he's angry. I won't have to pretend to date Noah anymore, so surely that makes him happy.

"Before we do that, Jake," Noah interrupts, as scripted, "I'd like to propose a toast."

"Absolutely, Noah," Jake responds, stepping back and gesturing grandly.

Noah's mother Tessa walks around with a tray, offering a champagne glass filled with sparkling apple juice to each woman.

"Seems like they could scrape together some mimosas instead of this crap," Bianca mutters to the rest of us.

I try to hide my smile. Clearly Bianca doesn't realize Tessa is Noah's mom. *Not going to look too good for you, Bianca.*

Tessa ignores her and moves to Kristin, Sierra, Evie, Alex, and me, and we take our glasses and thank Tessa. I grin at Bianca and raise my glass in a mock salute. Bianca narrows her eyes at me. As nice as Bianca may come off to Noah, his family will give him the real scoop.

Noah holds up his glass, and we all hold ours up as well. "Ladies, I know this has been quite the journey for you all. I have valued the time spent here with each of you, and I hope it's been fun for you too. Unfortunately, one person will be going home today. If you didn't receive a candy cane, our adventures have come to a close."

His eyes linger slightly on me. "But that doesn't mean your knight in shining armor isn't just around the corner, waiting to whisk you off in a limo to his castle."

Well, damn.

I stare at Jake, who still is avoiding eye contact with me. My reaction may be cool and calm on the outside, but inside I'm a melted jumble of emotions. Noah couldn't have just randomly pulled those words from the air.

One by one, each girl checks her stocking, squealing as she reveals a candy cane. Evie and Alex hug each other, and I'm happy for them both. Sierra is smiling, and Bianca and Kristin look more smug than anything.

Finally, I step forward. The realization that I'm the last to check and everyone else has gotten candy canes seems to have dawned on Evie and Alex, whose smiles droop as they watch me dip my hand into my stocking. I'm all too aware of the cameras focusing on me when I wrap my fingers around the hard jaggedy lump, grateful Mack gave me a heads up.

I allow my hopeful expression to falter, then turn to despair as I pull out the coal. I close my eyes and think about *Marley & Me*, the movie I watch when I need a good cry. I turn to the other girls and show my coal, my eyes full of tears. Evie, Sierra, and Alex gasp and rush over to hug me. Even Kristin comes over to give me a hug. Bianca hangs back, and though she does say "I'm so sorry, Sophie," her expression is gleeful.

"Sophie, we're sorry to see you go," says Jake, still not looking directly at me. Damn him.

Noah comes over to give me a big hug, and I hug him back.

"I'm sorry," he says aloud. Then he whispers in my ear, "Thanks for all your help."

"I wish you nothing but love, Noah." And I do.

As we walk toward the front door of the lodge and outside to the awaiting gondola that will take me down the mountain, I give him another hug and whisper in his ear, "Just remember that not everyone is here for the right reason. Please be careful."

He nods. His eyes tell me he's not surprised. But he's helpless to do anything about it if the show feels keeping a contestant like Bianca will boost viewership. I know I can't be any more direct or Mack will make sure I never get another job in this industry.

Before I climb into the gondola, I step to the side to do the interview with the production team. I haven't been looking forward to this. Carianne usually steps in to encourage sobbing from the one who was kicked out of the house. But funny enough, even though I felt rejected for getting the lump of coal earlier, I'm not even a little bit sad now. I'm determined to help Evie and Alex be the final two, and it will be easier to do behind the camera than in front. Plus, there's Jake...

Snowflakes drift around us as I wait for Alison to finish consulting with the crew. I shiver and pull my coat tightly around me, painfully aware that all I'm wearing underneath is a thin satin nightgown and wishing I'd chosen my flannel pajamas this morning instead.

"Ready?" Charlotte asks with a smile. She's the best interviewer we could've asked for and has a lot of experience with contestants in reality shows. Mack put her in this position for a reason, but I've got butterflies in my stomach knowing she's probably going to hit me with questions I may not want to answer.

"Ready," I say, trying to keep my teeth from chattering.

She nods and gestures at the camera to roll. "Well, Sophie, you've received the lump of coal and your journey has ended. What are your plans now?"

I shrug. "I guess I'll go home." Clever it's not, but what else am I supposed to say?

Charlotte's eyebrows pinch slightly. She isn't happy with that response.

"How did you feel about not getting a candy cane?"

I give a heavy sigh. "Pretty sad. I really wanted to continue this journey with Noah. But I hope he finds the love he deserves here."

Charlotte smiles at that. My apparent sadness makes her happy. "Who do you want to win Noah's heart?"

I pretend to think about that for a moment. "Well, I think it should be Evie or Alex. They are both here for love and are the sweetest girls ever."

"Who do you think should be the next to go?"

"Definitely Bianca. She's no good and is sabotaging whichever girl she feels is getting too close to Noah. Or Kristin. If Noah wants to spend the rest of his life catering to a high-maintenance gold digger, Kristin's his gal."

I'm not worried about saying all of this on camera. They'll cut or keep whatever they want in the editing room. I'm just giving them the fodder they want while letting Noah overhear the truth about these girls.

The snowflakes are falling faster now and the wind is picking up. Alison spends a few minutes watching the footage on the camera while I bounce up and down, trying to keep warm. She finally removes her headset and nods her approval, allowing Noah to escort me to the gondola. He gives me a kiss on the cheek. The door slides open and I slip inside. I try to look forlorn for the cameras, though I can't help but give a sigh of relief to be out of the wind. I turn to wave at Noah. The door closes and the gondola lurches forward, ready to take me down the mountain, where a van will drive me to a nearby bed and breakfast reserved for recent show outcasts.

But I'm not alone.

Jake is sitting across from me, holding a candy cane and looking incredibly sexy in his made-for-TV pinstripe suit. "Your knight in shining armor, here to rescue you."

"Jake." I gasp and quickly look out the window, almost expecting to find a camera drone ready to send Mack enough footage to destroy my career. But we are already starting the gentle glide down the mountain, and the snow is falling thicker.

"Don't worry," he says, grinning. "Mack knows that with your insight into the contestant side of the show, she'd be crazy not to keep you on as a producer."

"You talked her into it?"

"I might've nudged her a bit, but she knows you're too good to lose. You're safe."

The gondola rocks gently as we move down the mountain. For a long moment we stare at each other. I wrap a finger around the candy cane and tug myself over to Jake's lap, straddling him and pressing my lips to his. The chill I felt in the wind earlier is gone now, and my body is on fire. He teases me with his tongue, his arms wrapping around me, his hands traveling down my back and around my curves. He draws a moan from me as his lips trace a path down to my breasts.

My nightgown hitches up around my waist and I rock into his body, welcoming the heat between me and my knight in shining armor.

I'm home.

CHAPTER 19

Santa Claus Village

EVIE

A big announcement must be in the works because Carianne looks more frazzled than ever as Alex and I join the other two girls by the lodge's fireplace. My heart pounds against my rib cage, a trapped animal desperate to bolt, as I stand on my assigned marker. Is Noah going to choose someone early? Will he send me home? After our last date, things have been super awkward and weird between us.

If only I could sit down with him and talk all this through, but deep down, I know the only way for me to feel good about any of this is if he were to pick me, and this whole crew would disappear, and it would be just the two of us.

To my right, Alex looks as pale as a sheet of paper while Kristin sashays in, all glossy smiles. Then Bianca enters, clicking in on heels with her confident walk. Her brown hair shines under the camera lights, and her chiseled jaw, red lips, and sleek, tight dress remind me that she's in a completely different league from me.

My cute green fit-and-flare dress with cutouts in the shape of holly leaves suddenly feels cheap and wanting in comparison. The terrible sensation, like I'm about to throw up, flares in my stomach, but then I spy Sophie popping her head into the room, waving at Alex and me, and then miming exaggerated breaths.

"Leave it to Sophie to make this moment bearable," I tell Alex, already calming down as I follow her advice.

"What would also make it bearable," Alex whispers to me, "is running out that door."

"Nope." I grab her hand. "You're not leaving me. I can't do this without you."

Thankfully, she flashes me that stunning smile of hers and says, "You're right. We're in this together."

Jake strides into the room and stands in front of the fireplace. Warmth lights up his face as he takes us all in.

"Ladies, I've got some great news for you. It's time to pack your warmest coats because you're headed to a place where Christmas comes to life—Santa Claus Village in Finland!"

"Finland?" I gasp.

Kristin screams with excitement while color returns to Alex's face. Even Bianca's cool and composed façade breaks into a smile.

"See?" I squeeze Alex's hands, jumping up and down. "Aren't you glad you stayed? Maybe it'll inspire your next book!"

Alex's face lights up at that. "That's not a bad idea."

"You'll get to visit reindeer and take an icy adventure," Jake interrupts our cheering as he tries to finish his lines. "Plus, this place is your last chance to spend time with Noah, so don't hold back showing him your true feelings. You have ten minutes to pack those bags!"

❄

THE SUV RUMBLES down the snowy road to the Nova Skyland Hotel. Excitement races through my veins at the thought of seeing Noah soon, but at the same time, my nerves are frayed. I couldn't sleep during the entire flight as my head spun trying to figure out where Noah's thoughts were. The other four ladies are gorgeous, smart, and successful.

I mean, Sierra is a beauty pageant winner. Every inch of her body and every movement she makes is honed to perfection.

Of course, Kristin is cruel as winter, but Noah hasn't seen that side of her.

I can totally see him choosing Alex at the end of all this. She's the complete package. Beautiful and incredibly talented, plus she's got her head on her shoulders. She would make Noah happy, I'm sure of that.

And I couldn't be terribly upset because both she and Sophie have become my closest friends. Maybe even friends for life.

The real danger is Bianca. That girl is cutthroat. She always says the right thing and acts the part, but I don't trust her, and I wouldn't put it past Bianca to spin some wicked lies to win Noah's heart.

The vehicle stops. We wait in the SUV until the camera crew is ready to record us.

"I hope we get our own rooms," Kristin says. "It's getting old acting like we're still in college."

"We've got a suite ordered for you," Carianne tells us, looking up from her clipboard.

Sophie is sitting beside her, instead of in the back with the rest of us. It still feels weird seeing her being on the production crew side of things, but at the same time, she fits the part perfectly. I was surprised no one got too upset about her role. I suppose knowing it's one less person that they have to compete for Noah's heart, it makes sense.

"Thank god," Bianca mutters.

"But," Carianne grins deviously like she can't stand the idea of us being too happy, "you'll still be sharing rooms."

The SUV door whips open, sending in the crisp winter air. We're directed into the hotel, a wooden-framed building sheltered within tall pines crusted in ice and layered in snow. The entrance doors swoosh open, revealing a lobby with a crackling fireplace and natural beamed floors and walls. The air smells of cedar and smoked wood, which instantly relaxes me as I drag my suitcase down the hallway.

Carianne escorts us to our suite, which has us all gasping over how beautiful it is. The one wall is floor-to-ceiling glass, overlooking the snowy forest. A fire burns happily in a wooden stove, and the large, soft chair facing outside looks so tempting. I can totally see myself curled up with one of Alex's amazing rom-coms, sipping hot cocoa.

"There are two rooms on either side," Carianne says. "You can decide which room you'd like to be in."

Sophie jerks her head, indicating for Alex and me and we follow her into the room on the right. "This is the nicer of the two rooms because the bath is amazing."

"I wish you were still our roomie," I say. "We'll miss you."

"Don't worry about me." Sophie waves her hand dismissively. "I've got a pretty decent room to myself. It's not huge, but at least it's bigger than Carianne's. Still, I'll miss hanging out with you like we used to, but now I can look after you two on the other side of things."

"We really appreciate that," Alex says, and then she announces in a loud voice, "Evie and I are calling dibs on this room."

I slap her a high-five, quickly putting my luggage next to hers.

"That trip has me utterly exhausted." Bianca collapses onto the plush couch dramatically. "Please tell me we're going to get some time to sleep."

"Feel free to sleep the day away," Sophie says. "But for those of you who want to see Noah, meet me in the lobby for your group date in an hour. And wear something warm."

"One hour?" Kristin wails. "That's not enough time to get ready!"

"Or decide on the perfect outfit," Sierra adds.

All thoughts of relaxing fly out of my mind as my heart soars at the thought of seeing Noah.

FINNISH CAROLS WAFT through the air, which is crisp and laced with pine. Snow crunches cheerily beneath my boots as our group strolls through Santa Claus Village. Square lights glow from lanterns, and the wooden buildings are all trimmed with garland and white lights. Carianne stops us at the line marked Arctic Circle. We pose for a group photo, pointing at the line.

My breath puffs into the Arctic air, but today the cold doesn't bother me. I'm just soaking up being in this beautiful country, and I decide that I refuse to let Kristin and Bianca infringe on my joy. We're escorted up to a reindeer pen where the animals are munching happily on grass. They stare at us like they haven't a care in the world.

Noah is leaning on the wooden fence, looking so sexy with those broad shoulders slightly dusted with snow like powdered sugar. A soft scruff shades his jawline, making me wonder how it would feel against my skin. His lips tip up into a smile as we approach.

"Noah!" Kristin screams, running and tackling him in a hug.

"Woah." Noah chuckles. Once she extricates herself from him, he moves to give each of us a hug. I catch a whiff of his spicy scent as his arms wrap around me. My heart takes off racing like I'm back on the sleigh. "It's great seeing you ladies again. Welcome to Lapland, home of Santa Claus."

Carianne holds up the CHEER sign. I resist rolling my eyes. Then she interrupts Noah to have the five of us move into a straight line before him, once again reminding me that this is a competition and everything about this moment is orchestrated. My stomach twists up like a tangle of Christmas lights. Noah smiles easily at us to calm our nerves, but everything about today suddenly feels weird because he isn't looking at me. Panic pulls up a chair and settles in my chest.

Jake strolls up in a sleek winter coat to give the day's instructions.

"Hello, ladies," Jake says. "I hope you're ready for your next holiday adventure because today you're going to be Santa's helpers by feeding his reindeer. You'll fill up your bucket with reindeer food from the barn and race to the trough, where you'll pour your food into it. The first to transport all of their food will win a reindeer sleigh ride with Noah."

Carianne waves her CHEER sign again, but my smile drops. If I don't win, it means I'm going to have a very limited time with Noah, which sucks big time. The thought of him cuddling up with another girl like he did with me on that sleigh ride back at his farm makes me want to vomit. I really need to win this.

Noah wishes us good luck, and fear creeps up my spine like

frost because it all feels so cold and clinical. This is my fault because the last time we were together I was freaking out on our ride back to the lodge.

Noah and Jake head over to a platform where a garland-draped table is set up for them. Meanwhile, the five of us are each given a bucket and line up in the snow.

"This is totally going to ruin my hair and makeup," Bianca pouts.

"I don't know about you ladies," Alex says. "But these games are starting to get old."

"I feel the same way," I say. "I just want some time with Noah."

"You don't need any more time with him." Kristin gives me a pointed look. "You already had two dates. Two *long* dates."

"Sounds like someone might be going home." Sierra lifts her brows at Kristin.

Jake rings a bell, and we take off with our buckets. Cold air bites the back of my throat as I race into the barn and scoop the reindeer food into my bucket. The long braid I wove my hair into whips behind me in the wind. In real life, I avoid running at all costs, but this is a race for Noah's heart. I need to show him I want to win. I burst out of the barn first, only to spy Kristin sashaying over to Noah's table.

What is she doing?

I toss my food into the trough located by the reindeer fence. I'm running back when I realize Kristen has perched herself on the table's edge, feeding Noah something.

What the hell?

My feet slow. A cold dread sluices over me. Kristin throws back her head in a laugh, and then lightly touches Noah on the chest, her fingers lingering on his jacket zipper. My mouth drops open. It's hard to focus on anything but the two of them. I need to keep moving. I need to win. I need to—

Something knocks into me, and I go flying.

I cry out and smash into the side of the fence, hitting my head. Desperately, I try to get up, but dizziness washes over me. The world shifts and blurs.

"Oh my god, are you okay, Evie?" Alex runs up, concern filling her eyes.

"Hey, I'm going to call for a medic," Sophie says in a calm voice on my other side. "You just stay put."

"I'm fine." I stand, wincing. "It's just a little bump."

"That doesn't look so little." Sierra grimaces like I've got a massive wart on my nose.

Noah is suddenly at my side. His hands cup my face. "Evie, are you hurt?" Panic streaks across his face. "What happened?"

"What happened is Bianca pushed her into the fence," Alex snaps, fisting her hips. "I saw it."

"That's a lie," Bianca says with an eye roll. "I was running and just knocked into her. She wasn't watching where she was going."

Sierra snorts and rolls her eyes. "Girl, you're totally lying. You might as well fess up and face the truth of what you did."

"You could've really hurt her," Alex says.

Noah's eyes flicker between the three of us. His eyes darken as they land on Bianca.

"I need you to come with me, Evie," Sophie says. "The medic is here."

"I'm fine," I assure Noah, who looks absolutely wrecked. Warmth fills my body that he looks so concerned for me. "Just a bump on the head. You all continue without me."

"We're not continuing," Noah announces. "I need to talk to Bianca."

Sophie wraps an arm around my body and ushers me over to a bench. A medic from the village meets me and does a quick check for a concussion, but all I can focus on is Noah talking to Bianca off to the side. Both their expressions look intense. Alex settles beside me on the bench, offering her support. Thankfully, the medic clears me of any concussion and offers ibuprofen in case I get a headache.

"Keep a close eye on her," the medic says in flawless English. "She should be fine, but if you have any issues, call me."

"I can't believe Bianca did that to you." Alex huffs as the medic leaves us. "What is this? Third grade?"

"Apparently," Sophie says, eyeing the cameras filming Noah and Bianca's argument. Their raised voices indicate things aren't going Bianca's way. "This might be Bianca's last straw. Noah's been wanting to cut her for a while, but Mack wanted to keep her on for ratings. Villains always add drama to the show. I'm just sorry you got caught in the crossfire."

Finally, Bianca and Noah leave the reindeer area and head to the entrance of Santa's Village.

"What are they doing?" Kristin asks, slipping on bright red lipstick. "I wish they'd hurry. It's damn cold out here. Whose idea was it to come to the Arctic Circle in the winter?"

Sophie rolls her eyes while Alex and I share a grin as I whisper, "Grumblelina strikes again."

A car drives up. Noah opens the door for Bianca. She climbs in, her mouth pulled into a firm frown.

"Looks like Bianca's leaving," Alex says with a gasp.

"Thank god," Kristin says, while Sierra looks the happiest I've seen her since we landed in Finland.

"She won't even look at him as he's saying goodbye," I note, watching it all unfold.

Am I evil that I'm glad to see her leave? The car drives away, and just like that, there are only four of us.

EVEN THOUGH IT'S only one in the afternoon, the sun is starting to hang low in the sky as the four of us remaining women cram into the SUV with Sophie and Carianne. The van rumbles down a remote road, tall pines and endless snow surrounding us.

Yesterday was such a weird day. After Bianca left, Noah and the four of us remaining girls hung out at Santa's Village together. We fed the reindeer and then had drinks at the café, but there was definitely awkwardness to the date. With only four of us, I think we all were feeling how real this was becoming.

Noah didn't give any of us preferential treatment, which only made me even more confused by his feelings for me. Before we left, Noah secretly slipped a note into my pocket, whispering to me to read it privately. I've read it a million times. I pull it out once again, soaking in the words and trying to believe in them.

Evie,

I know things have been awkward between us after that night in my cabin, but I'm willing to take this at your pace. Every time something happens, I find myself wanting to tell you about it. I miss your laugh and just hanging out together. When I'm with you, the world

*makes a whole lot more sense. Can we call that
our first fight? I feel like surviving the first
fight in a relationship is a big milestone.*
Missing your smile,
~ Noah

I slip the note into my glove, needing it to be close to me as the SUV finally rumbles to a stop. We clamor out to stand at the shore of a large frozen lake. Endless white ice coats the surface, glittering in the fading sun. A tiny round hut with a peaked roof is plunked in its center with a single curl of smoke drifting out of a pipe into the pink-streaked sky. I tuck my hood over my head to ward off the chill. The wilderness feels wild and untamed around us.

"What is this place?" Kristin's lips curl in disgust as she zips up her thick fur coat. "It's like something out of a horror movie."

"I think it's amazing," Alex says. "Atmospheric, not creepy."

"You have a weird way of looking at things," Sierra says as she checks her pocket mirror for the fourth time.

"Don't worry," Sophie explains as the film crew gathers around us. "The hut you're going to will have heating."

Jake comes to stand before us, a big smile on his face. "We are now down to three. Today you're going fishing for love."

"I love fishing and I adore the wilderness," Kristen says brightly, beaming as one of the cameras zeros in on her.

It takes everything in me not to roll my eyes.

"A snowmobile will take you out to the fishing hut to meet Noah," Jake continues. "There you'll spend some quality time with him, but even though there will be four of you heading out there, only three will be leaving with Noah. So be sure to use your time wisely."

My stomach sinks at the thought of never seeing Noah again.

"And there is the man of the hour," Jake points to where Noah has stepped out of the hut, waving to us, "eagerly waiting to talk to you."

Two snowmobiles are pulled off the camera crew's truck and transport us out to the fishing hut. As I step onto the platform, my breath creates billowy clouds—it's that cold. Noah opens the door and hugs each of us as we dart inside.

"Welcome to my humble abode," he says cheerily. "Please go ahead and have a seat and make yourself comfortable."

Benches are set up around the perimeter of the round hut with a small ice hole in the center. One of the benches has been converted into a food spread with a holiday-themed charcuterie board, mini champagne bottles in the ice, and a carafe of hot chocolate, which Noah pours into mugs for us.

"Should we make a toast?" Noah asks. As his eyes scan each of us, for the first time, I sense his awkwardness too. The air is tense, a snowstorm brewing on the horizon.

"To finding love," I offer and take in our group.

Alex beams at Noah while Kristin's eyes narrow on Alex like she's plotting her murder. Sierra looks bored out of her mind.

I start piling my plate with cheese and grapes and spot Sierra slipping an individual-sized champagne into her coat pocket. Guess she's stocking up for her own after-party later.

After the toast, we each try our hand at fishing. We make a pact that the first to catch a fish gets to talk to Noah first. Moments later, Alex catches one. It whips back and forth at the end of her line. Kristen leaps onto her bench with a squeal.

"Don't let it bite me," she exclaims.

Sierra pulls out her nail file and starts filing like she's already checked out.

Noah unhooks the fish and tosses it back into the water. After he cleans off, he turns to Alex, holding out his hand.

"Looks like luck is on your side tonight," he says to Alex. "Shall we go outside and chat?"

"I'll be timing you two!" Kristin calls after them as they head out.

Now I'm stuck alone with Kristin, Sierra, and the cameraman. So fun. The moment Noah leaves, Kristin tosses her hot chocolate into the fishing hole and pours herself a large glass of champagne from a bottle chilling on ice. She takes a long swig, purposely staring anywhere but at me. The hut is so quiet I can hear Sierra's file swishing over her nail. If it wasn't awkward before, it definitely is now. I try to strike up a conversation.

"So what's been your favorite thing we've done so far?" I ask.

"You don't have to rub it in, Evie," she snaps.

I jerk back. "Rub what in?"

Sierra freezes and looks up, a smile curling on her lips. "Oh, this sounds like fun."

"The fact that you've had more time with Noah than the rest of us. Honestly, I'm pissed because I've never done anything to you, but you continually try to take away not just others' time, but also mine."

"I'm not trying to take away anyone's time with Noah." My blood is pumping now, I'm so angry. "But you've got to know, Kristin, that this goes both ways. Noah is just as much a part of deciding who gets to spend time with him as the rest of us are."

"I guess it makes sense why you got those dates. He told me he feels sorry for you."

"What?" It's taking every fiber in my body not to storm out of the hut.

"You're a sweet thing. It's adorable that you're a teacher. But the reality is you're a walking mess. If yesterday isn't proof, just look at you now."

Kristin titters and sips her champagne. I swallow my annoyance. Okay, so my hair is a bit of a mess from the wind while riding the snowmobile out here, but that's reality.

"But me?" She waves a hand down her body. "This is what Noah needs. To come home to someone who can calm him down and not stress him out. But he is so blinded by his starstruck obsession for the famous author, Alexandra Ryan, he doesn't care about us."

I know I shouldn't let her get to me, but my insecurities and self-doubt are at an all-time high already, and her words just aren't helping me out. Especially because she isn't wrong. With flawless glowing skin, a perfectly toned body, and glossy hair that shines in the camera light, she is a model on the loose. While I'm a teacher who has no problem wearing a paint-stained T-shirt for the rest of the school day and joins in a game of tag at recess, dodging puddles to win.

"You think he's going to pick her?" Sierra asks, leaning forward, a frown puckering her perfect forehead.

"Obviously." Kristin rolls her eyes. Then she focuses on me, saying, "But you should be more careful who you trust, Little Miss Sunshine."

"You've been drinking too much," I say, rolling my eyes.

"I might have been eavesdropping while they were standing together feeding the reindeer," she continues. "I heard her tell him that you were only here for a good time and weren't looking for anything serious."

My chest tightens. Would Alex really say that? I press my lips together, afraid I'll say something on camera that I'll regret later.

Noah and Alex slip back into the hut. Alex's cheeks are flushed, and I don't think it's from the cold. I clutch Noah's note tighter in my hand. Kristen starts to get up, but Noah says, "Evie, would you like to chat?"

Sierra huffs in annoyance.

"I'd love to," I say, eager to escape Kristin's presence. On the way out, I whisper to Alex, "Good luck with her."

She lifts her eyebrows, chuckling. "Thanks. I've got a feeling I'll need it."

Outside, the sun hugs the horizon even though it's only two in the afternoon. The wind has picked up, swooping around us and kicking up snow. I shiver, but Noah pulls me to a bench. The camera crew and Carianne are sitting outside their tent, far enough away that we might forget about them, but close enough to get that perfect shot of me messing up.

"Watch out," he warns as we edge along the platform. "This patch of ice has been broken up for an outdoor fishing experience, so be careful."

"Noted," I say. "I've already completed my falling duty, thank you very much."

We plop onto the bench. He tucks a thick fur blanket over us and wraps his arm around me.

"Wild, isn't this?" he says, gazing at the chunks of ice breaking apart in front of us. "What do you think of Finland so far?"

"Other than falling and hitting my head, it's been good. I love the countryside, and the village is adorable. Plus, I got this really nice note from this cute guy, which made everything even better."

"Really?" He lifts his eyebrows. "Sounds like a pretty decent guy."

We're talking a bit cryptically due to the cameras, but at the same time, I love that we have something that only belongs to the two of us. I take his gloved hand in mine.

"I missed you," I say, referring to his note. "I missed you at breakfast because I wanted to know if you would eat rye bread with cucumbers. I missed you when I was staring at the stars last night because there was a falling star, and I wanted to know if you saw it too, and if so, what you would have wished for. But mostly, I realized you've ruined my days because they are empty without you."

He sucks in a deep, ragged breath. He hooks his thumb on my chin, gazing into my eyes with a fierce intensity that swoops my heart into a loop. "Oh, Evie. You have no idea how much your words mean to me. I've been a wreck wondering where your head has been at."

Then his lips are on mine, hot and full of need. I grab hold of his jacket, clinging to him like at any minute I might lose him. Like the universe might find a way to rip us apart.

I'm terrified, and yet, fire rushes through my veins, igniting me. I'm more alive than I've ever been. Deep in my soul, I know I've fallen for this man. A man that's not mine. At least not yet.

My heart aches for the what-ifs, for the possibilities that are stretched before us, wider than this snowy lake.

"It's my turn!" Kristin announces, stumbling out of the hut. Noah and I jerk apart. It takes me a moment to reorient myself after that passionate kiss. Kristin's eyes narrow on us. "Why are you kissing my boyfriend, Evie?"

Before I can answer, she laughs as if this is the funniest thing she's ever said. *Oh god, she's so drunk.* She stumbles to Noah.

"Come, darling," she coos. "Let me show you what a real kiss is like."

"Be careful," Noah warns, trying to steady her on the platform.

Alison stands up from her chair by the camera crew. "Cut!" she calls out. "Noah, it's time for you to come over and have a little talk with the cameras."

Kristin huffs while Noah apologizes, telling us he'll be right back. As he jogs over to the production tent, Alex steps out from the hut.

"Is everything okay?" Alex asks. "Kristin, you shouldn't get so close to the edge."

"You can leave now, Evie," she says, swaying. "And Alex, it's my turn. Go away. You already had yours."

With a sharp glare at Alex, she steps too far left. "Noah! Help me!" Her arms flail as if she's falling backward, but it's obviously an act based on her expression.

"Stop pretending you're falling in," I say, crossing my arms. This woman is really getting on my nerves.

But while trying to flail her arms, her heel slips over the edge. With an ear-piercing scream, she falls backward.

Into the icy water.

CHAPTER 20

Icy Accusations

ALEX

Kristin's sinking!

My brain registers this fact, but my body is frozen with panic. I can't move. I'm literally just watching her thrash around, desperately trying to get to the surface, to grab hold of something, anything.

"Help!' Evie screams. "Alex, we have to do something." She ducks into the tiny hut. It's just her, Sierra, and me beside the fishing hole. Everyone else went with Noah to film his narrative asides in the production tent.

She's back an instant later. "There's nothing we can use to save her."

The sound of her voice startles me back to life. Before I know what I'm even doing, I get down on my stomach next to the fishing hole. "Evie and Sierra, grab my legs," I order. "Make sure I don't go under."

Quickly, the two girls do as I ask, and I shove my hands into the water.

Jesus.

It's like a thousand needles prick my skin at once. The

water is so cold there are no words to describe it. It's almost maddening. I can't imagine how bad it is for Kristin. I let out a yelp, but somehow manage to keep my hands submerged. Kristin claws at my jacket sleeves and hands frantically. I feel my body slide closer to the hole. She's going to pull me under too. Her face is upturned, so she's staring straight at me. What the hell? Is she smiling?

Then suddenly Noah is beside me and then he's in, submerged in the depthless water, lifting Kristin out. The crew is running from the production tent, not as fast as Noah but closer to us.

I help Noah by gripping Kristin's arms tighter while Evie and Sierra pull my legs hard. Inch by inch I start sliding backward with Kristin digging into my jacket sleeves, her hands like claws.

She flops onto the ice next to me, coughing so hard she's choking, her body curled into itself. "S-s-s-o c-c-cold," she chatters. Her gaze darts to me. I suck in a breath. I never noticed before, but her eyes are as icy as the water, completely devoid of any real emotion.

Noah pulls himself out next, muscles straining, his face a mask of pain. Immediately half a dozen of the crew surround him. They wrap Noah and Kristin in oversized towels. No one seems to notice my soaking-wet, rapidly freezing arms. And the cameramen are back, filming the chaos with fervor.

"We have to get them out of here ASAP," Carianne orders. "Or they'll go hypothermic." She pulls out her walkie and starts barking orders.

Kristin begins bawling loudly. The camera crew keep filming, zooming in for a closeup on her face. She throws herself at Noah. "You saved me," she wails, looking very shaken up. She squeezes her eyes shut as if the whole experience is just too much to take and nestles her head against his chest. Noah looks stunned, like he can't believe what's just happened. He pulls her closer and wraps his blanket around them both. His lips are blue and his teeth chatter so hard I can hear them clacking together.

I glance at Evie and Sierra. No "thank you" for us, I guess. I narrow my eyes at Kristin. This whole thing is so odd. I can't get the image of her smiling from underwater out of my head. Was she really scared or just acting? Could she have gotten out of the water on her own the whole time?

Sierra ignores me and moves closer to Noah and Kristin so she can hand Kristin a tissue.

"What happened?" Noah asks Kristin once she's quieted a little.

She sniffles and wipes at her eyes with the tissue. Her mascara is smeared all over her cheeks. "It was h-h-her. S-s-she t-t-tripped me." She can barely get the words out her teeth are chattering so hard as she stabs her finger in my direction.

"I did not!" I sputter. Is she *high*? I was nowhere near her when she went in and she knows it. But then I start putting the pieces together. How the cameras were all with Noah, how no one was there to witness her go in except Evie, Sierra, and me. Oh no way, she's framing me to get me eliminated!

"She's lying. Alex didn't do any such thing." Evie folds her arms across her chest, her face flushing.

Sierra is uncharacteristically quiet all of a sudden. Jesus, she's not going to stick up for me.

Kristin starts sobbing again. "Evie's only saying that because she and Alex have formed some kind of partnership. That's why they're always hanging out together. But Evie's being naïve if she thinks Alex isn't plotting. She wants to get me off the show, so they're the final two. I just never expected that she'd put me in danger to do it. Be careful, Sierra. Because you're going to be their next target."

Sierra's eyes go wide as if she's starting to believe everything Kristin is saying. But how can she? She was right here.

"I didn't see Alex trip her, but she was standing next to Kristin when she went in. It makes sense that she tripped her."

Evie and I gape at her. She has to be crazy. Because what the actual hell?

Noah frowns, his gaze traveling from Sierra to Kristin to me. Doubt has crept into his expression.

Evie shakes her head. "Noah, it's not true."

The cameras swivel to me, zooming in, recording every nuance of expression on my face, waiting for me to react too, to deny what Kristin's saying. I didn't do anything wrong and yet, even knowing this, somehow under their unrelenting focus I can't help feeling as if I have. I don't like Kristin, or Sierra now for that matter. And if I'm honest, part of me was almost happy to watch Kirstin fall into the water after what she said to Evie—until I realized how serious the situation might be. If Noah believes Kristin over me, I lose any chance I had with him.

Damn it. I'm already imagining the upcoming episode. The replay on this moment. All those viewers. It's her word over mine. If they think I actually tripped her, I could get cancelled.

I start to deny all of it even though it probably won't do any good when Jake appears and interrupts me. Typical. They have him swooping in on camera to make sure he's somehow involved in the drama.

"Helicopter's on the way," he says. "We need to get you both outside and on board." He turns to Evie, Sierra, and me. "*You* ladies stay here until we can sort all this out."

Oh my god. I'm right. Even if they clear me from any actual wrongdoing, it'll be too late. There's no footage of her fall.

Noah locks eyes with me for a second longer. I try to put everything I want to say into the glance I give him. I didn't do what she's accusing me of. My feelings are genuine. But the moment is gone so fast I can't read his expression to see if he believes me, and then he's being ushered outside with Kristin.

A moment later, the helicopter arrives and two medics hop out. Evie and I watch them briefly examine Noah as he's loaded onto the helicopter with Kristin. It's so cold and he's soaked to the bone. Does he already have frostbite? I tuck my wet hands into a blanket one of the crew members brings me to try to warm them back up. I'm starting to wonder if I do too.

The medics seem calm, so I tell myself he'll be okay. I hear Evie murmur something under her breath to that effect too. We're both worried, but at least he's got medical help.

Once the helicopter's in the air, Jake hurries over to his snowcat.

"Wait!" Sierra runs after him. "Please take me with you. It's freezing out here!"

Seriously?

Jake and Sierra drive off, and Evie and I are suddenly alone on the ice. The crew is already busy breaking down the production tent.

Evie lets out a bitter laugh. "I can't believe her."

"Me neither," I say, genuinely shocked. "All this time I had Bianca pegged as the only real villain on set, but was she? What if Kristin was the one who locked me in the liquor pantry at the bakery and ruined my dress?"

Evie's eyes widen. "At the very least she was probably in on it given how often she and Bianca hung out."

Sophie hurries over to us, breathless. "Sorry. I was in the editing truck. What the hell happened?"

I let out a breath. "Kristin's saying I tripped her on purpose and that's how she ended up in the water. But Sophie, she's lying."

"I was right here." Evie folds her arms. "Kristin was nowhere near Alex when she fell in."

I shoot Evie a grateful look. If she were more of a schemer like Sierra, Bianca, or Kristin, she could've lied just now and backed Kristin up if only to get me out of the final two. But Evie is honest to a fault. It's one of the things I like best about her.

Sophie pulls us farther away from the remaining crew. "I believe you. But with no footage to review, it's her word against yours."

I groan. She is literally confirming my worst fears.

Evie exhales heavily. "So what do we do? How do we prove Alex didn't do it and I didn't help her?"

"Come on, let's get you both out of here." Sophie dangles a set of keys in front of us. "I've got a snowcat with our names on it. We can talk about how to fix this mess on the way."

Evie lets out a relieved breath. "You have a snowcat? Oh, thank god. I wasn't sure how long they were gonna make us wait out here until we could leave."

"So where did they take Noah and Kristin?" I ask as we follow her out to the snowcat.

"The hotel." Sophie climbs into the driver's seat. "They have a doctor on standby to check them out. If they get the okay from her, Carianne is planning to give them some alone time at the Ice Bar. If I had to guess, it's to mollify Kristin in case she decides to sue the show for reckless endangerment or something."

Evie groans. "Where she'll lean into the damsel in distress thing *hard* and keep pushing the idea that you somehow conspired against her." She secures her seatbelt and shakes her head. "Noah won't believe her B.S. He just can't...will he?"

I hop into the second seat. "I say we crash their private time to make sure he doesn't. Somehow trick her into a confession."

Evie turns to face me. "But if we can't, won't that just reinforce you as the bad guy—and make me one too?"

I shake my head and smile. "Oh, we'll pull it off. Leave it to me. Plotting is one of my superpowers."

Sophie starts to laugh. "I'm liking wherever your head is going already."

"Good," I say. "Because we're going to need your help."

KRISTIN AND NOAH are wrapped in fur blankets and cozied up in a booth made of ice and festooned with white Christmas lights when we arrive. The place is mostly all cameras and crew, save for a few townspeople gathered on stools around the actual bar staring at the TV screens flanking both sides. *It's a Wonderful Life* is playing. Combined, these elements add a sense of realism to the scene, so it doesn't seem like Noah and Kristin are completely alone. But they look downright eerie to me, bathed in the blue glow of the lights inside the bar's icy counter staring vacantly at the movie, pretending to watch.

Evie and I slip around the side of the space and into the women's bathroom. It at least is not made of ice and is instead blessedly warm. I suppose if it wasn't, no one would be able to pee in here. They'd be too cold or god forbid, the pee might freeze. The thought makes me laugh, quelling my nerves a bit.

"You ready to do this?" I ask Evie.

She grins. "I am beyond ready. Let's do this."

I grin back and squeeze her hand. As jealous of her as I've been the past few days, I really do like her a lot. I turn my attention to the last stall. "How about you, Soph?"

Sophie's head appears over the top of the stall door. She lifts up her cell phone and shows us the screen where her camera is recording the room. "I've hooked my phone into the hotel's TV system. We are good to go."

I leave the bathroom and walk up to Noah and Kristin's table. The cameramen positioned around their table immediately start filming me. The more drama the better, right? The moment she notices me, Kristin burrows deeper into Noah's shoulder like she's scared.

"Please leave me alone," she says softly.

Oh brother.

"Sorry to interrupt," I say with as much warmth in my voice as I can muster without coming off as completely insincere. "I was just so worried about you. I wanted to make sure you were okay."

Kristin sniffs. "I am, thanks to Noah." Her eyes start to glisten. "Why did you do it? I mean all this time, I've been nothing but nice to you. And I've had the least alone time with Noah so far compared to each of you. It's just not fair." She presses her fingers under her eyes to keep the tears from falling. "I don't understand."

God, she is an actress. Even *I'm* half-buying this victim routine she's got going on. But I had a lot of time to think on the snowcat and looking back, I am sure it was her, not Bianca, who has been undermining me this whole time. Now we just need to prove it.

I put a hand over my heart. "I would never trip you on purpose." I'm not an actress like she is, and I don't try to be. I want this to seem potentially insincere. I avoid looking at Noah, but I can practically hear the gears in his brain working as he tries to figure out what's going on.

Right on cue, Evie appears. "Don't listen to her. She's lying," she says. "I saw her trip you, Kristin."

Kristin's eyes narrow almost imperceptibly.

I wheel on Evie. "No!"

"Just stop, already," Evie says. "I'm not letting you get me caught up in this." She slides into the booth next to Kristin. "I am not conspiring with her, I swear. Until I saw her trip you, I was convinced she was the only person on this show I could trust, but then when you walked past her I saw her put her foot out."

"Liar!" I practically bellow, pounding the icy table hard in just the right spot so that Noah's and Kristin's drinks spill in her direction—and into her lap.

Kristin jumps up and the glasses roll off her lap to the floor and shatter. The entire front of her turtleneck sweater dress is soaked in booze. "You ruined my dress!" she hollers.

"Seriously?" Evie glares at me. "Leave her alone."

I let out a mock growl of frustration and turn on my heel and stomp out of the bar, my heart pounding. My part is over. Now it's up to Evie and Sophie.

I head over to the television by the lodge's fireplace. *It's a Wonderful Life* is playing on it too...or was. Suddenly the screen flickers and then the black and white image of Jimmy Stewart standing next to a Christmas tree is replaced with the Ice Bar's bathroom as seen through a crack in the door of stall number five.

"Sophie, you rock," I murmur to myself.

Evie enters with Kristin.

"Let me help you dry off," Evie is saying. She grabs paper towels and starts pressing them to Kristin's dress.

Kristin narrows her eyes and bats her hand away. "Leave it. What game are you playing?'

"Game?" Evie throws out the paper towel and then turns to Kristin. "I'm not playing any game. I am merely trying to survive the one *you're* playing. Alex didn't trip you and we both know it. But she's drop dead gorgeous and a successful author. I can't compete with that. No offense, but I have a better chance at winning with you in the final two with me than if she is."

Kristin gives Evie an appraising look. "Gotta say I'm surprised. I didn't think you had it in you. If I did, I might've framed you instead."

Evie clears her throat. "Thank you. That's all I needed to know." Without a word, she strides out of the bathroom.

"What the hell?" Kristin says and then the TV goes dark. I turn around to find a small crowd has gathered around me. Among them is Jake and Mack. Jake breaks into a grin when he sees me. "Well played," he says.

I try to suppress my own smile as Kristin and Noah emerge from the Ice Bar. She is pleading with him not to believe what he's just seen and it's clear he's not buying it.

The next Candy Cane Reveal isn't until tomorrow morning, but I'm pretty sure we all know who's getting the lump of coal.

CHAPTER 21

The Snow Hits the Fan

SOPHIE

I'm almost embarrassed to admit it, but the Candy Cane Reveal is kind of fun now that I'm on the other side of the camera. It's exciting to know who Noah will be sending home before the other girls do. Though, in this case, I'm pretty sure after last night's antics everyone here knows it's Kristin. Our audience doesn't, though, and she has plenty of fans out there who have no idea what she's really like, who believe she's easily going to be the final girl. They won't be happy, and I look forward to seeing their reactions on social media. The angrier they are, the better for our ratings.

Otherwise, being behind the camera has been more challenging than I could've imagined. Mack is breathing down my neck constantly to make sure everything is perfect. With Bianca's abrupt exit—which, even she has to admit, gave us great positive response from viewers who hated her—and Kristin's shenanigans, Mack's stress has become my stress. There are definitely moments when I wish I was still a contestant, spending my days relaxing in the hot tub and hanging out with Evie and Alex.

Everyone gathers for the reveal. Evie looks stunning in her floor-length sky-blue nightdress, and the navy two-piece silk pajamas with pale pink flowers Alex is wearing give her a sweet kind of softness. Sierra looks relaxed and confident in silver. Wearing a short yellow lacy nightie, Kristin actually appears nervous, her eyes darting toward Noah, then Alex and Evie.

I bite back a grin. She *should* be nervous.

Jake walks in, his fingers grazing mine as he moves past to the Christmas tree. I swear, that man just barely touches my hand and I melt.

I clear my throat and call for cameras rolling. "Action!"

Jake winks at me, then offers the camera his million-dollar smile.

"Well, ladies, here we are, down to the final four. This morning, only three of you will be continuing on to vie for Noah's heart. It's been an incredible journey, from twelve girls to three. Santa's Most Eligible has assured me that he already feels himself falling in love, isn't that right, Noah?"

"That's right, Jake," Noah asserts, smiling at the four remaining contestants. "And again, I want to thank each of you for the time you have taken to be here, opening your hearts to me and making me feel...well...feel things I haven't in a very long time."

Jake puts his hand on Noah's shoulder. "Ladies, please step forward to reveal your stocking."

Kristin starts forward before anyone else. Maybe she thinks if she gets to the stockings first, she'll be rewarded with a candy cane. I quickly gesture to Carianne to step in and pretend to check the microphone in the back of her dress off-camera to stall her. As much as I don't like Carianne, she does a pretty good job puttering around the clearly annoyed Kristin.

At my cue, she releases Kristin. Sierra, Alex, and Evie have already revealed their candy canes with gasps and big smiles, but Kristin hasn't noticed. She thrusts her hand in the stocking, then screams when she pulls out the coal.

"No, no, no! This is a mistake. It's a mistake!" she cries out, dropping the coal and darting toward Noah. "You don't understand. I'm here for all the right reasons, unlike these other girls! I'm in love with you!"

How Kristin is actually surprised is beyond me. But her reaction is gold. Alison motions to Bob to stay on her.

Noah gently untangles himself from her grip. "I'm sorry, Kristin."

Jake steps over to wrap an arm around Kristin's shaking shoulders and pull her off Noah. She's sobbing now. Even with all the horrible things she's done, I can't help but feel a little sorry for her.

But not enough to stop rolling.

Jake and Noah walk her to the door. Carianne stays with the giddy girls inside while Bob, Alison, and I head outside to capture Kristin's final moments. Mack starts to follow but stops to answer her phone. She waves us on.

Kristin is quiet now, her eyes downward as she lets Noah wrap a furry coat around her and guide her outside to the waiting van. Alison keeps the cameras rolling the entire time, and I get the feeling she, like the rest of us, are eager to see if Kristin just naturally loses it. Jake stands next to me to watch the drama unfold through Bob's camera display.

"I'm so sorry," Noah tells her as he opens the van door. "I really do hope you find the love you're looking for."

Kristin wraps her arms around his neck and starts sobbing again. He gives her an awkward embrace, then tries to untangle himself from her.

All of a sudden, she glares at me. Alison points frantically to Noah, but Kristin ignores her.

"You helped them set me up, you bitch!" she growls, flinging herself at me.

Jake grabs my waist to pull me back, and Noah steps in front of Kristin to block her.

"Keep rolling," Alison mutters to Bob.

"Stop it," Noah says firmly. "You set yourself up by trying to sabotage those girls. Maybe you'll think twice next time before trying to hurt someone just to win a contest."

She turns her glare on Noah, then with a teary huff gets into the van. I swear I hear her say "Loser" under her breath. Whether she means me or Noah, I have no idea.

"Go, go!" Alison points at the open door to Bob and Charlotte, who both look a little apprehensive about riding along with the angry and erratic Kristin. Still, they climb into the van to get the final interview.

The door closes and away goes Kristin. Good riddance.

"Well, that was a thing," Jake says, shaking his head. I reach out to take his hand but drop it when I hear Mack yelling behind us. She's got her phone up to her ear and is angrier than I've ever seen her. Which is saying a lot.

"You have got to be shitting me!" Mack stops next to me. "No, no, give me a few minutes. I'll call you back."

She presses END and thrusts her phone at me. "That stupid bitch. Just look at this!"

Thinking this has to do with Kristin, I take the phone to see a text with screenshots from a social media post. I read the headline in complete shock: "*Santa's Most Eligible* darling Sierra Rivas is a criminal!" Mack switches to her email and shows me the belated background check that indicates charges against Sierra Rivas had been previously filed for petty theft.

Shit.

Jake leans over my shoulder to look at the display.

"Maybe it's not too bad," he murmurs. "Misdemeanors. Sometimes teenagers do things on a dare..."

"One of these was last year," Mack says. "How did you miss this, Sophie?"

My jaw drops. "Me? I'm not in charge of background checks."

"Well." Mack waves a hand. "It's your problem now. Fix it."

"We clearly can't keep Sierra on the show, so..." I start to say.

"That's obvious, stupid," Mack cuts in. "If I'd seen this a couple hours ago, we could've had Kristin stay longer." She glares at the direction the van went as if she could yank it back.

I catch myself before I can foolishly ask why we'd do that. I know the answer. Keeping Kristin and skipping this morning's elimination would've allowed us to gather additional footage to cover the episodes we have scheduled. Now we have to figure out how to fill time, and just adding some random dates with Noah won't cut it.

"I need ideas, and I need them now," Mack says, poking her finger at my chest.

I swipe her hand away. "Well, clearly we can't have any additional footage of Sierra on the show. We'll have to cut her and issue a statement."

Mack nods absently, her eyes on her phone as she texts someone. "Go get Noah and tell him the situation. We need him to talk to cameras about how he was going to cut Sierra anyway."

Poor Noah. After everything that happened with Bianca,

then Kristin, and now Sierra, I can't imagine asking him to do this. He's already looked like he's regretted signing up for this show. My experience as a contestant has really made me soft, I guess. But more than that, I want Noah to *want* to be here to find love with either Alex or Evie. They deserve it and so does he.

"What about having Jake record the statement?" I glance at Jake and plead with my eyes for him not to disagree.

"Why would he be better than Noah?" Mack asks.

"Because Jake would be the official statement from our program, not just Noah. If Noah does it, it'll look like he made the decision to cut Sierra, when it's our show's responsibility. We don't want to look like we condone theft."

Mack purses her lips to consider that. I know she gets it, though. It will make more sense from the network's perspective to have an official spokesperson show how seriously we're taking this.

"I'm happy to do it," Jake says. "I can portray this as, 'The safety and security of our cast and crew is our top priority,' and that sort of thing."

Mack nods. "You may be right. Fine. Jake, you do it, and get it recorded now. Sophie, go make arrangements with the other hotel and tell them they have to put Sierra up for the night since we can't have her staying here. I'll have Carianne escort her in a bit."

IT TAKES us all day to finish everything. To fill in the moments Noah was going to have with Sierra, we have him take Evie and Alex to a horse farm for a fun day. Carianne goes along to capture footage with a couple cameramen while I stay with Jake. Jake does his recording to camera, which will air tomorrow night after the regular episode. Having both Kristin and Sierra eliminated in one night presents a major challenge, since we will be short an episode. But I'm too exhausted to think about it. Between the additional footage Carianne returned with today and the interview with Jake, we haven't left the editing room. Thankfully, the kind hotel concierge brings us sandwiches, smoked salmon, snacks, and beverages.

Alison, Jake, and I are just finishing the final touches on the piece with our remote editor in LA when Mack joins us, flopping into a nearby chair. I play the footage for her and am completely shocked when she nods and waves a hand. "Fine. Wrap it up." Usually she has a ton of edits in addition to Alison's.

Mack groans as she gets up to leave. "I'm going to go soak in that hot tub, and I don't want to hear any more about this damn show tonight." Then she's gone.

I collapse into Jake's arms. "What a night."

"What a night," he agrees, resting his cheek against my hair.

"A soak in a hot tub sounds good to me. At least, a hot tub that doesn't have Mack in it."

Jake brushes his lips across mine. "My room has one, if you're interested," he says in a low voice.

That's an easy yes for me.

Ten minutes later, my fatigue somehow vanished, I'm in my bathrobe and walking through Jake's door. His bedroom is about twice the size of mine, and the bathroom is huge too. The hot tub is on a slightly elevated platform and filled with steaming water, soft pink bubbles, and Jake. His arms stretch over the sides and he looks completely relaxed.

"How's the water?" I ask, trying to not look as nervous as I feel.

"Great! Hot. But not as hot as you."

He grins as I roll my eyes at his attempt at a cheesy line. I kick off my slippers, then take a breath and drop my robe.

I'm wearing nothing underneath.

Jake's eyes widen, and his grin falters. "My god, woman, how can you be even more beautiful now than when we were together?"

I walk slowly to the hot tub, feeling every inch as beautiful as Jake says. "You bring up a good point," I tell him, dipping a toe into the water. Hot, but perfectly so.

"You *are* beautiful," Jake murmurs as I lower into the tub and glide through the water to him, my breasts pressing against his chest as I wrap my arms around his neck.

"Thank you, but that's not the point I want to discuss." I look at him directly. Judging by his completely bemused expression, I don't think he remembers much of what he said before. "You said 'when we were together.' Are we again? I need to know if we're just having fun here or if this is leading to something more...well, more."

There's a part of me that worries he'll feel put on the spot and just say what he thinks I want to hear, considering we're both naked in the tub. Which is also why I'm giving him an out by offering that we could just be having fun. But Jake gently cups my face with his hands, his warm eyes filled with a deliberate seriousness that makes my breath catch.

"Sophie, after all we've been through, I wouldn't be here with you if I didn't think we had a chance for a future. And no, I'm not just saying that to hook up," he adds as if reading my mind. "I'm falling for you again, so hard that it honestly scares me."

Me too, Jake.

But I don't say it. Instead, I press my lips to his. Our kiss is gentle at first but grows more urgent as we lose ourselves in each other. My body tingles with desire for this man who makes me crazy in every wonderful way.

CHAPTER 22

Snow-laced Kisses

EVIE

I can't believe today has finally arrived. My last date with Noah before he has to make his decision.

I've stripped down to just my bathing suit, which is insanity considering it's twenty-six degrees outside. A soft white robe hangs from a hook, and I wrap it around my body. It's hardly enough material to keep me warm. Inwardly, I laugh. Perhaps this is a sign of true love because I'm willing to do this for Noah.

A deep breath, and then I'm stepping outside of the toasty warm changing room into the wintry cold of Lapland. Noah is waiting for me in a robe of his own.

"You ready for this?" he asks.

The black slippers provided to me don't keep the snow from creeping up the sides of my feet. I shiver from the chill.

"Let's do this," I say, determined to be brave.

Big fluffy snowflakes fall from the sky. They're the kind that tempt you to stick out your tongue and catch a wish. We follow the guide to a rectangular-shaped area of snow-packed walls, lined with doors on either side.

"The walls are two meters of snow thick," our guide explains, opening one of the entrances.

We take off our robes and duck into a narrow ice corridor that opens into a small room of snow. Wooden planks are set on ice blocks, making up a bench on either side. A glow lights up the snow-white walls.

"It's so cold in here," I say, my teeth clattering against each other.

"You're shivering." Noah draws me to him, and I nestle in close to his warm body.

"Do not worry." Our guide chuckles. "It will be around 175 degrees Fahrenheit in here shortly. The walls will melt a few centimeters, creating the sauna experience. This is why a sauna can only be used one hundred times."

"Wow, this sounds very exclusive," I say, a little shocked.

We settle on one of the benches, and the guide shows us how to use the hot water to start the sauna. Then one of the cameramen sets up the camera and starts recording.

"You have ten minutes to enjoy yourself," our guide explains. "Have a good time!"

We thank him, and once the door shuts, it's just the two of us, shivering in the cold.

"Want to do the honors?" Noah asks, handing me the ladle.

"If it means we'll get warm, then yes!"

I open the pot and scoop out a ladle of steaming water, pouring it onto the stones in the pot. Instantly, the snow puffs into a cloud of smoke, filling the space. We're encompassed in a cocoon of steam. A cry of surprise escapes me as the snow room transforms from freezing to hot. Warmth spreads through my body, soaking all the way into my bones.

"Wow." Noah sighs. "My muscles are finally loosening up."

"After feeling cold for days, it's so nice."

Noah pivots and kisses me. I run the pads of my fingers along the lines and indents of his corded muscles, memorizing each part of his body. The scar on his left side, which he tells me was from a ski accident, to the line of freckles along his bicep. Thick mist coats our skin, and complete silence drapes over us like we've entered a world only for the two of us.

Our kisses deepen. His hands skim along my sides, thumbs teasing just at the edge of my bikini line. His breathing is heavy, and his body is tight as if it's taking every ounce of effort to keep himself in check. My back arches as I ache to be closer to him, wishing the cameras were gone and we had all the time in the world.

Finally, our time is up, and though I'm hot and ready to escape the heat, I also don't want to leave the relaxing bubble of our sauna. Our fingers are laced together as we emerge. I blink against the bright light of the day. Cold air nips at my skin once again, waking me up like I've been asleep for a very long time.

"Now this is a shock to the body, but it's invigorating." Noah laughs and throws his arms up with a "woot!"

The camera crew is there, catching every moment. Sophie guides us around the corner to where a frothing hot tub waits for us, along with glasses of champagne.

"That felt amazing, didn't it?" Noah says as we climb into the bubbly water, snowflakes drifting around us like we're in a snow globe.

"It was unlike anything I've ever experienced," I agree as we clink our glasses together and sip our drinks.

Somewhere between heartbeats, Noah has set down his glass and his lips are back on mine. His tongue swoops into my mouth. He tastes like champagne and smells like fresh snow. His hands run along my arms, and I shiver at his touch, not from the cold but from yearning. The memory of our last kiss and how I nearly lost control with him flickers in the back of my mind, but I push those thoughts away, desperate to enjoy this moment together.

His palms cup my face. He drags his lips up to my forehead. Sighing, I shift so I'm straddling him, needing to feel his body against mine. Wanting to be as close to him as I possibly can. I can't quite explain it, but this kiss feels different than the others.

Maybe it's because I don't know if it will be our last or if it's the first of a million.

"KIPPIS TO LOVE," Noah says, beaming at me from across the dinner table.

He raises his glass of glögi—Finnish mulled wine—and we clink our drinks against each other. Sitting here in a private room in the Snow Hotel feels like a dream. Soft Finnish carols play over the speakers, and the ice walls are illuminated in pinks and blues.

After our heated sauna and hot tub experience, we headed to our changing rooms and switched into formal attire. Noah looks drool-worthy in an inky-black tux with his hair combed back and freshly shaven. I changed into a spaghetti-strapped silver sequin dress that hugs my body like a glove. When I picked this out with my book club friends, I had no idea I'd be wearing it in an ice hotel. Thankfully, Sophie rummaged up a wool wrap to chase off the chill.

"This has been an amazing time, but you must be missing your home and lodge," I say as I dunk a chunk of rye bread into my creamy mushroom soup.

"It's been nice to take a break," Noah agrees. "But we're about to enter the lodge's busy season. My family is taking up the slack for me, but it's not easy for my dad after his heart attack. I'll be glad to get back and help him out."

We chat about small trivial things, but soon, Noah moves the conversation into dangerous territory.

"Tell me a little more about your past relationships," Noah says. "You said you went through a tough breakup?"

Suddenly, the bread on my tongue tastes like sandpaper. I know we need to have this conversation, and I can't avoid it forever. I twirl my spoon through my soup.

"It went great until it didn't," I begin. "I met Ted at a fundraiser for my school. He was working for Joe's Carpentry, and they donated some bookshelves for the event. I was in charge of collecting the donations, and we got chatting. He seemed really sweet and attentive. It had been so long since I'd talked to a man who wasn't one of my students' parents or a colleague. As you can guess, I don't get out much. Work sucks away my social life."

Noah chuckles at that. "You and me both."

"Anyway, he asked me out for a drink, and before I knew it, we were dating." I abandon my spoon and start fidgeting with the sprig of holly decorating the table. "It felt so good to have someone, you know? To not come home to an empty house and to share experiences with someone else."

My throat tightens and I glance up at Noah, but he simply remains quiet. He takes my hand in his as if sensing my emotions.

"But then things got busy last Christmas," I bulldoze on, hating the memories but knowing at the same time I need to face them. "I was in charge of the school Christmas play, and then there were report cards and end-of-the-year parties.

There's the shopping for the family and faculty Christmas cookie exchanges. I love Christmas, but sometimes my schedule is a little too full."

He chuckles. "It's not fair. It should be the time we just enjoy family and friends."

"Well, Ted was sure enjoying one of my friends," I snap and then laugh at myself. "Gosh, I don't think I've actually called him by his name since we broke up last January. While I was busy doing all those things, as I mentioned to you before, Ted was also busy cheating on me."

"I'm so sorry, Evie." He squeezes my hand. "The guy is a complete idiot."

"I didn't know it at the time, but all during last year's Christmas season, he had other relationships, including the one I told you about with my coworker. He was so sneaky, or maybe he was right, and I was too busy to notice. If I hadn't caught them, I think I might have still been in that awful relationship, which is pretty depressing now that I think about it."

I shudder. "I'm over him, over it all. But I want to believe that sometimes we have to go through hell to discover that something beautiful is just waiting for us on the other side. As you know, my friends applied for me to be on the show to get over the Cheatster. At first, I didn't really take this seriously. But during this short time we've had, I can already see what an amazing guy you are and also how great we are together. I really want to believe in us."

"I want to believe in us too," he agrees, and he reaches out and skims a finger along my jawline. "After getting cheated on by my ex, I didn't know if love would ever be an option for me again. But you have shown me that I can love again."

My heart stops at his words. Is he saying he loves me?

He blinks and looks around as if suddenly realizing we're

being filmed right now. He clears his throat. "And that reminds me. The hotel has offered us one of their glass dome rooms. You don't have to stay the night, but it would give us more time to spend together in privacy without the mics and cameras."

"I'd love that." My smile spills into every cell in my body.

Alison calls cut and then sets up some shots of us kissing and exiting the restaurant. My heart races at the possibility that the endgame of all this could be us together. It feels too good to be true, and yet, it feels like the truest thing I've ever known.

"I'm glad you said yes to staying," Noah says. "It's a bit of a trek to the glass igloo, but I'm excited to go somewhere where we can have time to talk privately."

The hotel staff brings out a sled for our luggage. Alison makes sure she has the camera crew situated for the best shots. Noah takes my hand and guides me outside toward where our glass igloo is located, hauling the sled with our bags behind us. Wind blows against us, kicking up snow and bending the pines.

"Being out here feels like the wilderness, doesn't it?" I say as we tromp through the snow. I try to ignore the fact that a camera is practically in my face. Oh, the irony of my words.

Unlike other nights that we've been here, the sky is clear and star-studded. It's full of dreams and possibilities. We come up to our pod and step inside, warmth instantly soaking into my skin. As we take off our coats and deposit our bags by the door, the cameraman does a quick sweep of the room to get some footage.

"I think that's a wrap," Alison says, her eyes sweeping the room to make sure they got footage of everything.

Sophie turns to us. "What she means is you can go all the way into the room now."

The foyer has a bathroom and a coat area, but the rest is completely covered with glass on all three walls and the ceiling.

"This is the coolest room I've ever been in." I soak up the view of the forest and the stars twinkling above.

Sophie starts ordering the crew to pack up their gear. Then she gives me a hug, wishing me a good night.

"Have fun," she tells me. "I'm going to boot the camera crew out so you two can have some time together. If you need anything or want to head back to your room, have the hotel call me. I can have a car here in no time, got it? But you can also stay until morning. It's totally up to you."

"You're the best," I tell her.

"I really am," Sophie agrees with a wink. Then she saunters off while ordering the crew to pack up.

Then, just like that, Noah and I are alone once again.

"I kind of feel like we escaped the show," Noah says, "It's been tough being on camera and making sure I'm fair to all the ladies. But this...this is great."

We kick off our boots, and while I collapse on the soft white bed, Noah pours us a glass of wine and lights the candles set up on the perimeter walls before turning the lights off. As we drink our wine and stare at the stars through our glass ceiling, we start talking about hopes and dreams, and even what our lives would look like after this.

"I guess ultimately it comes down to who you choose in the end," I say, not wanting to talk about Alex, but her name is like the elephant in the room.

"I don't look at it like that," Noah says, setting his glass down and shifting to face me. "It takes two people to make a relationship. You have to choose as much as I do."

Confusion mixed with tentative hope swirls through me. "What are you saying?"

"I'm saying you're the one." His fingers tenderly skate down the side of my face. "It's you I want at the end of this. Ever since our first kiss, I knew we had a physical connection, but then after that day at the Christmas market and seeing not just how much fun we have together but also how well we connected, I started falling hard for you."

"Hearing you say that makes me so happy."

"But it was when you left my place upset and confused, I knew I was in trouble." He pulls me to his side, wrapping his arm around me. "I wasn't sure if you'd stay. I was terrified of losing you."

"I was scared of getting hurt. You know that." My heart beats wildly in my chest. "Guess I still am."

"Don't be scared, Evie," he whispers into my ear. "Because you've won my heart. It's you I want. No one else."

"Really?" I shift around so we're facing each other. I need to look into his eyes and see the truth, and as much as I don't want to talk about Alex, I need to. "There's still another person here."

"Alex is a great person and has become a good friend in all of this. She's funny and smart, but we just don't connect romantically, you know? Tomorrow, I'm supposed to go on a date with her, but I'm going to tell her I've made my mind up and I'm choosing you."

All of the emotions I've been bottling up explode out of me. I want to sing and dance and scream, but instead I do what I love doing best. I draw him closer, aching for his lips to be on mine, to feel his hands on my body.

"I love you, Noah," I say. As I utter those words, it's like I've jumped off a cliff. I'm diving headfirst into unknown waters, holding my breath, waiting to hear what he'll say.

"And I love you, Evie. Passionately. Desperately."

A switch flicks between us. The knowing that we're the end game. We're the fated mates from the storybooks. Our lips find each other. Our kisses are heated, chasing away the strongest Arctic winds. My hands tug at his shirt, and he helps me yank it off. Then I'm dragging my sweater over my head, tossing it and my bra across the room.

He gasps at the sight of me, his lids growing heavy as he takes me in. "You are stunning," he whispers, pulling me to him so our bodies are one.

"How far do you want this to go?" I dare ask.

"As far as you want." His lips skate down my throat, hot and sending goosebumps racing along my arms.

I don't question his intentions anymore. My fears of betrayal fall away. Wordlessly, I begin unzipping my jeans. He sucks in a deep breath, and without a single word, the rest of our clothes come off.

"You are like Christmas morning," he says, his voice deep and heavy as his arms wrap around me like he never wants to let go. "There's nothing better in the whole world than you."

His mouth takes mine in a kiss that leaves me breathless. He rolls over so he's hovering over me. I take in the lines of his muscles, hardened from hours skiing the slopes. His hand curls around my breast, his gaze soaking me in like he's memorizing my every curve. Then his mouth is on my breast, teasing and coaxing my nipples until they harden under his touch. Inch by inch, his hand slides down my stomach, further and further. Then along the soft skin between my legs. A desperate need for him screams from my core. He slips his finger inside me. A cry breaks from my lips.

"Being with you is all I could ever want," he says, breathing heavily himself. "I've been dreaming of this moment every night since we met."

I can't answer. I can't even see or think straight. My back arches to his touch. All I can focus on is how I want him. Every inch.

"Now," I manage. "I need you."

Wordlessly, he pulls out a condom from his bag and slips it, and then he's pulling me closer. I slip down on top of him and he groans with pleasure. The moment our bodies collide, I cry out from ecstasy as he fills up every inch of me. His large hands wrap around my waist, and we begin to move together in perfect sync. I'm soaring down the slopes at midnight. Speeding through winter's trees. I close my eyes, savoring each wave, each explosion. Bright sparks illuminate the back of my lids.

"I never want this to end," I whisper breathlessly.

"It doesn't have to," he promises, kissing my breasts.

Finally, we collapse against the sheets. Our bodies are slick with sweat, and the world still spins. My heart is dancing because I know I've finally found my forever person.

"That was the best Christmas present I could've asked for," I tell him and run a finger along his lips, which he quickly kisses. "You make me so happy, Noah. I've never felt this way with anyone before."

He shifts so he's facing me. His eyes take me in, a lazy smile curling on his lips. "I feel exactly the same way. I can't wait to make you happy for the rest of your life."

We lay on our backs again, just as the sky above illuminates into green hues, twisting like ribbons, dancing over us in celebration.

"The aurora borealis," I whisper. "It's so beautiful."

"It really is," Noah agrees. He's not looking at the sky, but at me.

"Let's spend forever together."

"I can't wait," he says, kissing me all over again.

THE NEXT MORNING, it's hard to leave our little love dome. The cold greets us as we step out like a slap back into reality.

"I don't want to leave our cozy escape," I admit as we make our way to the front of the hotel, where a taxi is supposed to meet me. "And I especially don't want to leave you."

"Don't worry," Noah assures me, kissing the top of my head. "I just need to take care of one last thing, and we'll be able to start our lives together."

I must look ridiculous because I literally can't stop smiling. Every step feels like I'm walking on air. But when we round the corner, my feet falter. There before us is the film crew, Cari-anne, and Alison. They're videoing us.

"What's going on?" I ask Noah, stumbling in shock. "I thought they weren't going to film us today."

Before he can answer, the door to the SUV sitting in front of the hotel slides open. Out steps the last person I want to see on the planet.

Ted, the man I despise more than anyone.

"Hello, Evie," Ted says, smiling broadly as he strides to us. "Surprise!"

"What are you doing here?" I sputter.

"Who is this?" Noah asks.

"I'm Ted Wilson. Evie's boyfriend. But I bet she didn't tell you that, did she?"

"What?" Noah stumbles for just a moment. His hand breaks free of mine. "You mean ex-boyfriend."

"No, not ex." Ted presses his lips together and shakes his head as if he's sad to tell Noah the truth.

"Yes, ex," I burst out, suddenly coming to life. "What the hell are you doing here, Ted? And how did you even know where I was?"

"I came to take you back home," Ted says, way too calmly. "I know we agreed for you to do the show to boost your name and brand so you could make some extra cash for our big day, but after watching a few episodes, I just couldn't do it anymore. It was too soul crushing."

"What are you talking about?" Noah croaks.

"She's been lying to you, man." Ted shakes his head sadly. "We're still together."

"That's a lie!" I say.

"You can stop pretending now, baby," Ted tells me. "It's over. I don't want to live this lie anymore. I want us to just leave this all behind and start planning our wedding like we wanted to. Forget the money. We'll bake a cake and get married by the justice of the peace. I don't care."

"I don't understand," Noah half whispers. He's whiter than snow.

"He's a lying dirtbag," I growl. "We are *not* together and haven't been for a very long time thanks to his cheating."

"Hey!" Ted holds up his hands. "I get that you're upset, but you have to understand how I feel too. This has been really hard for me to watch you make out and pretend to like the dude."

"You need to leave." Noah grinds out the words. His fists bunch up.

"Not until I take my girl with me," Ted says. "And if you need proof that we're still dating right up to before you started shooting the show, I have it. Be sure to check the dates on the sign behind us."

He holds up his phone, showing off a picture of Ted and

me kissing passionately at the airport. The schedule of flights is lit up behind us like a confession.

My heart dives. This isn't happening. He must have photoshopped it or used AI. It's utterly fake. Absolute garbage.

The world spins out of control. My tongue feels thick in my mouth. I can't even process words to respond to his accusation.

"You should go," Noah tells me, his tone stiff and colder than winter.

Ted moves to take my hand, but I jerk it away, shoving him backward in the chest. When I turn to explain things to Noah, he's gone.

CHAPTER 23

Pine-scented Problems

ALEX

I don't know how to feel walking into this one-on-one date with Noah. It's the last one we will have before the show takes a weeklong break before the engagement ceremony. After this I won't see Noah again until he potentially proposes. The thought has my stomach doing a series of somersaults. I grip my overnight bag tight and try to steady myself. So much is riding on how tonight goes. Soon I will either be planning a wedding or nursing a pretty intense heartache. I'm hoping with all my heart it's the first one, but a small, fretful voice inside me keeps insisting it's not.

Noah's waiting for me next to a gorgeous matte-black Bentley, his hands tucked inside the pockets of his wool coat, a pensive expression on his face. I wave, but he's so deep in his thoughts that at first, he doesn't notice. I deflate a little.

"Hi," I say loudly enough to nudge his attention back into the present. I don't have to ask why he's so distracted. I know. Even though Evie and I haven't been allowed to talk anymore since our last group date—not until after Noah makes his final choice—Sophie and I had a quick conversation this morning.

She told me what happened with Ted and how she spent half the night consoling Evie.

I still can't quite wrap my head around it.

Evie's boyfriend showing up, claiming they're still dating. Offering up a picture of them kissing at the airport. Everything I know about Evie makes me believe this is ridiculous and that the photo must be faked just like she maintains. It has to be a set up—the same way it was for me with Bianca and Kristin—only it's her ex, probably looking to cash in on Evie's fame as one of the final two. Why else would he wait until now to show up?

However, Noah doesn't seem to see any of this, at least not according to Sophie. And watching him now, I believe her. He looks almost sick. Evie mentioned he'd been cheated on in the past, so this little drama is just playing on all his worst fears. Betrayal is a bitch. I've had my share of experiences with it, even if they weren't romantic. It makes it hard to trust anyone again.

I close the last few feet between us. Noah finally looks up and forces a smile. I hate it. I don't want my last moments with him to be awkward and half-hearted, but he's obviously nursing a pretty big hurt. Wincing, I can't help wondering: did he think she was the one? Is that why he's so distraught? I can't ask him, at least not in front of the cameras, not when I'm not supposed to know what went down. Admitting that I do could put Sophie's job in jeopardy. Besides, the rules of the show forbid us from talking about the specifics of the other girls' dates with Noah. It's so we never really know where we stand with him. It makes for good TV but wreaks havoc on the self-esteem.

"Ready for some fun?" Noah asks, his breath steaming in the icy air as he opens the passenger side door of the Bentley and smiles down at me, this time with more sincerity and warmth. He reaches for my overnight bag and I hand it over, my heart lifting a little. The betrayal has to sting, but if he and I have the connection I keep hoping we do, he isn't completely devastated. He's just upset by the idea of being made a fool of. Because Evie isn't the one. I am. That voice pipes up again.

No, you're not.

I order it to shut up.

"Absolutely!" I say with a bit more brightness to my voice as I hop into the car. Noah gently shuts the door, puts my overnight bag into the back seat, then walks around to the other side and gets in. As usual, a waft of his fresh soap smell fills the car. That scent is becoming very familiar and comforting. My shoulders start to relax.

Alison is crouched by the open driver's side window, ticking off a litany of instructions.

"We're going to hold here and get some footage of the two of you driving away looking happy and excited with a lingering shot on the car to satisfy the Bentley team," she says. "Then we'll follow you to the Christmas market to film your time shopping."

Noah presses his lips together and nods before closing the window. Suddenly, the world goes quiet. We are as alone as we can be in this moment. The camera crew is positioned in front of us, shivering collectively, the world around them quickly darkening as the little bit of sunlight caught in the spindly branches of the trees behind them disappears. I'm still not used to how little daylight there is here. It's late afternoon and it's almost completely dark already.

Alison motions for Noah to start the car and for both of us to smile.

I pull my seatbelt across my lap and grin like I'm the

happiest girl in the world, like I can't wait for tonight. Which isn't really a lie. I am looking forward to it, but there's no way I'll be able to completely enjoy this date until we clear the air.

"Don't react," I say softly between my teeth. "But I know what happened with Evie."

Noah swallows hard, but otherwise manages to do what I've asked.

"I'm so sorry," I say, turning slightly so the camera can't get a clear shot of my face in case the cameraman can read lips. I pretend to be rummaging around in my purse. "And I know we aren't supposed to talk about it on our date and all—and I'm not going to pry, but I just wanted to let you know that it's okay if you're upset." I glance up at him and when I can't decipher his expression, focus back on my purse. "I get it. You don't have to fake that you aren't. Not with me."

Should I reach out and touch his arm or something?

I'm not sure whether he needs or wants me to. I'm so not good at the whole emotional support thing. I mean, I can fake the right words, but I never know when to physically comfort someone. It's probably because I spend so much time alone. Weirdly, I always know what my characters should do in situations like these, but when it's me in them? All that knowledge goes right out the window. I literally freeze up.

Noah starts the Bentley's engine and then grabs my hand and gives me a grateful look. "You have no idea how much I appreciate you saying that," he says. "Last night was hard, but I refuse to let it get in the way of today and ruin our time together, okay?" He leans over and turns on the radio then brushes his lips across my cheek. "So how about you play deejay and pick out some driving tunes for us."

I can't suppress the giddy bubble of hope rising inside me because he sounded so sincere just now. "You got it," I say, pressing buttons...and finding nothing but Finnish music. "Okay, so I guess we won't be singing along," I say.

Noah laughs. "Why not?" He listens to the song for half a second then joins in, his brow furrowing as he tries and fails miserably to mimic the lyrics. His voice isn't half bad and something about his complete commitment to the moment and all its silliness also manages to be the perfect icebreaker. I can feel all my apprehension melting away.

THE CHRISTMAS MARKET is so much better than I imagined it would be. I was picturing a street running down the center of town filled with food and craft stalls, but no. We park along the side of a frozen river flanked by trees draped with Christmas lights. Lining both banks are the stalls I thought we'd see, but there are so many they stretch into the distance and out of sight. And instead of walking from stall to stall, people are skating, pulling little miniature red sleighs meant to carry their purchases. It's like something out of a Christmas card, it's so quaint. I am definitely using it as a setting in one of my future books.

We grab our own skates from the rental hut at the front of the market and head for the ice.

I am wobbly as hell and grab his arm for support. "I haven't skated since I was about seven," I say, my voice as shaky as my legs.

"It's okay." He grins. "I've got you."

He pulls me smoothly along and before I know it, I'm getting the hang of it, matching his rhythm.

"I thought we could get Christmas gifts for our families," he says. "There's lots of cool handmade stuff that you can't get anywhere else." He stops in front of a hut full of wood crafts and picks up a beautifully carved reindeer. "For your dad maybe?"

He's fishing. Up until now I have completely avoided talking about my family. But if we end up getting engaged soon, it's time he knows. "My parents died when I was twelve," I say. "It was a car accident."

He sets the reindeer down. "I'm so sorry," he says softly. "I can't imagine how hard that was—especially at that age. Middle school is hell enough and then to go through it without your family..." His voice trails off.

I pick up a wooden Christmas tree, carved so ornately every pine needle stands out. It's beautiful. "I had my Aunt Sarah. She was my mom's sister. She took me in, but she was only twenty-three and not really ready for the whole kid/responsibility thing. In a way we sort of raised each other."

Noah is looking at me with a mix of pity and admiration. It makes me want to avoid his gaze completely.

"It's okay," I say. "I mean, I turned out fine and it's been years since I lost them. Fourteen to be exact."

"Still," he says. But then he doesn't seem to know what to say next. And of course he wouldn't. He spends all his time with his parents. He's helping run their business enterprises, for god's sake. He's probably never been alone, like really alone...ever. He has no idea what it's like.

But even so, the fact that he doesn't know what to say disappoints me a little. I can't help it. This far into the show and our dating journey together I want him to take me in his arms and kiss the top of my head and tell me that he wants me to become part of his family. That from now on, I'll always have a place to go, and every holiday I'll sit at a table crowded with people I love and who love me, everyone laughing and eating and having fun. It's all I've ever dreamed about and the sort of thing I make sure every one of my heroines gets in the end.

But instead, he takes the Christmas tree from me and hands it to the man running the booth. "We'll take it," he says to him before turning back to me. "A little keepsake for tonight."

It's a sweet gesture. I shake my head. I'm being over-analytical. Real life isn't a novel. Expecting him to read my mind is definitely unrealistic. I pick up the reindeer and hand it to the man. "For him. His keepsake."

As we watch the man wrap up our souvenirs, Noah leans into me and whispers, "They would look good together. On my fireplace mantel back home."

"Yeah?"

He nods then turns toward me. "You're pretty great, you know that? A guy would be crazy not to get what a catch you are."

My heart takes the express elevator to my shoes.

"You're not so bad yourself," I say in the most awkward way possible and inwardly cringe. I am terrible with compliments—both giving and receiving them. My face heats up despite the cold. As comfortable as I've felt around him until now, somehow I still feel strange trying to be romantic and flirty. Curse my introverted nature.

Noah laughs, then gathers our wrapped packages. Together we skate back out onto the ice to explore the rest of the market. It's magical—all the people gliding around in merry little bunches, their laughter ringing through the air, the smell of burning firewood and hot chocolate. The market must go on for several miles. I've never seen anything like it. Even the show's crew is caught up in the moment, the cameraman beside us quietly humming Christmas music between takes. Noah holds my hand the entire way. His grip is strong and reassuring. I like being here with him, the quiet ease between us as we skate. He's one of the nicest guys I've ever met. A girl would be crazy not to see what a catch *he* is. So why am I still hesitating about giving my heart up completely?

Our next stop is a petting zoo filled with snowy rabbits and reindeer. Noah gets some apples and carrots to feed to them. One of the reindeer nearly knocks me over as he pushes past his buddies to get to the apple in my hand.

"Whoa, easy," I say as Noah comes up and stands beside me. His face is next to my ear, close enough that I can feel his breath against my neck. "He likes you," he tells me, tilting his head in the reindeer's direction.

"I think it's the apple, not me," I say as the reindeer polishes the fruit off and then wanders away without so much as a backward glance.

"I'd like to have a lot of them one day," Noah says.

"Apples?" I ask, and he laughs.

"No, animals. And kids. My dream is to expand the lodge and add a working farm, so as much of the food we serve on premises is provided by us as possible. I want to run it with my wife and our family. Create a legacy that enhances my parents', you know?"

This is our last date, so I guess it's time to talk about the future a bit and it does thrill me that he wants to do that. I hope it means he's thinking seriously about a future with me in it. But listening to him also fills me with panic. I'm not sure when or if I want kids. And while I like animals, I worry about having more than one or two. Whenever I work on a new book I get totally immersed. Sometimes I survive on peanut butter and banana sandwiches for days, not bothering to leave the house or keep up with basic chores. How would that work with kids and pets to take care of?

"How many animals?" I ask.

Noah shrugs, a smile playing on his lips, his eyes distant as he pictures the future he wants and has already obviously fallen in love with. "A herd of cattle for sure. Some goats. A couple of dogs. Maybe a cat or two. Definitely several horses. Chickens and pigs."

My panic rises. "And kids?"

"I'd love at least three, but four is what I always picture in my head."

I feel like I might hyperventilate. He must notice because he starts backpedaling quickly. "Of course, nothing's set in stone. I mean, the most important thing for me is finding the exact right person to build my life with. Everything else is negotiable."

But is it? I saw the way his face lit up as he talked. He really wants all of it.

I close my eyes and try to picture myself there—living at the lodge on the adjacent farm raising kids and helping grow crops and take care of animals. There is something a bit appealing about the idea of it. All those little faces around a dinner table. Morning rides on horseback with Noah. Family Christmases at the lodge. It's like something straight out of a Hallmark movie. Loneliness isn't something I would have to experience ever again.

"What do you think?" Noah asks.

I take a deep breath and smile. "I think it sounds pretty amazing."

He pulls me close and kisses my forehead softly. "Good," he says, before pressing his lips to mine, his arms tightening around me. And my panic doesn't go away exactly, but it definitely fades as he gently strokes my cheek with his thumb.

Whenever I've imagined my future, I've always pictured myself in Paris, living in an apartment in the sixth arrondissement writing from an office that overlooks a café, the smell of coffee and fresh baked baguettes lingering in the air. I am a huge literary success, and I travel the world to meet readers and research my next projects. In these fantasies, the people who might be there with me have always been vague—there, but like figures seen through smoked glass. The life he's sketched out couldn't be more different than this one. Can I want what he does?

I think so?

I pull him closer. Noah's special, the type of guy I've always wanted. I can write from a farmhouse just as easily as I can from Paris. Maybe his dream can be my new dream. Our dream. Together.

We skate to the end of the market to a giant Christmas tree. It must be taller than a three-story building. And the ornaments! They're handcrafted and utterly unique, intricate wood-carved scenes of Finnish life. And there are bright red apples and little goat figurines made from straw, even adorable little elves wearing red felt hats. In the distance the Northern lights dance. God, it's so beautiful I can barely breathe.

"This date has been so magical," I say, leaning my head against Noah's shoulder. "Thank you."

He grabs my hand and pulls me toward the tree. "Just wait. It's about to get even better." He leads me to a tiny opening at the back of the tree. Turns out it's a hollow tree frame covered in pine branches. Inside is a small table draped with a red tablecloth and two chairs with furs hanging from the backs. Lanterns made of ice surround it all. Between them and the tree's string lights, the entire space emanates a warm buttery glow.

Once seated, we're served a collection of Finnish foods: sauteed reindeer, Karelian pies filled with mashed potatoes, and the most delicious salmon soup. All the skating has me half starving and I eat more than I mean to. Noah and I are both so focused on the food, Carianne has to remind us to stop and chat for the camera a few times.

I am starting to hate the constant presence of her and the cameras. The "Wait! Do that again. Smile bigger this time!" orders that make my stomach tie itself into knots. It makes being in the moment hard, especially when the server brings one final tray of food: two cups of steaming coffee and the world's largest cinnamon roll for us to split with the words "Read me" written in frosting.

I frown. "I just did?"

Noah's face flushes. I think it means to read what's under the plate. It's adorable how nervous he suddenly is. He clears his throat as he lifts the cinnamon roll plate up. Underneath is a piece of simple cardstock bordered by gingerbread men with gold lettering. I lean in and read what it says aloud—not because I want to, but because Alison hisses at me to.

We've sipped cocoa and skated the market square,
Under twinkle lights and frosty air.
But now the night is starting to slow,
And we two are wrapped in candle glow.
Will you stay with me when the flames go low?
While the snow falls soft, let time move slow?
We could talk till dawn or not at all—
No pressure, just a Christmas wish
That we'll stay snuggled up all night like this.

Judging by the look on Noah's face, someone from the show wrote the poem, not him. I'm guessing that after what happened with Evie they are really trying to make things work between us. He arches an eyebrow and winces as if he suspects the poem's so cheesy I'm bound to say no. It is cheesy and silly...but I also somehow find it desperately romantic. I can't help myself. I am a romance writer, after all.

I sip at my coffee to hide the giddy smile forming on my lips. A whole night with Noah. Alone. No more cameras or crew. Just us.

Noah hands me the card. I tuck it into one of my shopping bags. Definitely keeping it forever.

"Yes, please," I say shyly, grabbing Noah's hand in mine.

Less than an hour later we're nestled into a cozy cabin surrounded by tall pines iced with snow. A fire crackles in the stone fireplace and nearly every flat surface is covered in candles. Christmas garland and wreaths decorate every room, including the bedroom where a large old-fashioned bathtub sits under a picture window with a view of the night sky. Someone's already filled it with water and bubbles. A pair of thick white robes hang from hooks on the wall beside it.

The crew films Noah and me exploring the room. Alison coerces us into doing a little schtick where we push the crew out of the bedroom then kiss as we slowly close the door. It's super awkward.

Once they're gone and it's just Noah and me, the weirdness lingers. It's the first time we've been alone all day, and suddenly I have no idea how to act. We both eye the bath at the same time.

I start to ask him if he wants to get in when he starts talking first, all in a rush. "How about you take a bath and relax a bit? I think I'll go get some more wood for the fire.

It's getting kind of low." He smiles, but it's a nervous sort of grin.

He's already walking out the bedroom door before I can say a word.

My stomach twists a bit. Is he having second thoughts about being here alone with me?

I sink into the bath and stare out the window at the stars as I try to puzzle out how to approach the rest of the night. Do I want something to happen between us tonight? Does he? But before I have much time to think, there's a knock at the door.

"Can I come in?" Noah asks softly.

I gather the bubbles around me. "Sure," I say, feeling suddenly more vulnerable and exposed than I ever have in front of the cameras. He's going to see me. Naked me. I think maybe I want him to, but I'm also scared— the abrupt way he left the room before sort of put a damper on the mood.

Noah sits on the edge of the bed and leans his elbows on his knees. "Sorry about practically running out here before. I think I sort of panicked for a second. It's just strange being here. After the other night with..." He lets his voice trail off. Then he shakes his head and clears his throat. "I'm not really this guy. Someone who dates multiple people at the same time."

"Well, I'm not really the type to date a guy who dates multiple girls at the same time," I say. "I get it." I focus on the bubbles, so I don't have to face him. "I don't like knowing that I'm having to share you. Or that you're kissing someone else... or doing more than that." I swallow hard. I've been trying not to think about him sleeping with Evie. I know their date ended badly, but her ex didn't show up until the morning and she was still with Noah then. They obviously spent the night together. But did they have sex?

I don't want to ask, but I also don't think I can sleep with him if I don't know for sure.

Noah clasps and unclasps his hands. "I really like you, Alex. You're smart and talented and ambitious." He leaves the sofa to come sit beside the tub so his face is parallel with mine. He stares at me, and the expression on his face is so raw, so open.

"And you're so straightforward. I never have to guess whether you're telling me the truth." He reaches up then and tucks a bit of my hair behind my ear. "I don't think you're capable of lying."

I smile. "Um, I basically lie for a living. I'm a storyteller, remember?"

He laughs softly. "On the page yes, but in reality you wear all your emotions on your face. You know that, right? I can always tell exactly what you're thinking."

"Maybe that's not me being a bad liar so much as you being extra observant."

He shakes his head, his hand lingering on my neck, his fingers in my hair. "No, I've trusted the wrong people plenty of times. You want people to see you. The real you."

Do I?

Yes, I realize. He's right. I do want people to see me for who I am—the bad and the good. Because I can't trust that they really like me—or love me, for that matter—until they have.

I meet his gaze and the way he's looking at me, with something close to wonder, has my stomach doing slow somersaults.

"You are something special," he says, and then he leans over and kisses me. It's different from all the others we've shared— deeper, more intense. He cradles my head with his hands and slips his tongue inside my mouth. I close my eyes. Every part of my body comes alive. I pull him closer until he's leaning over me, inches above the water.

He lets one hand travel down my back along my spine to the curve just above my butt, and my skin tingles. But then all at once he's pulling away.

I open my eyes. "What is it?" Heat floods my cheeks.

He shakes his head. "I can't do this. Not tonight. You deserve to have someone's full attention and I just can't give that to you right now." He rakes a hand through his hair. "Even if we make sense. If it's going to happen between us for real, I want the moment to be right, away from this show and all those damn cameras. And with everything that's happened with Evie..." He lets his voice trail off.

"You don't want whatever might be developing between us tarnished in any way?" I ask, guessing what he's getting at.

"Exactly."

And as much as our kisses just now had me ready for more, I think I agree. No, I know I do. When—if—we sleep together, I want it to be private too. Just him and me.

"So what do we do now?" I ask. "Try to get some sleep?" Then I laugh. I'm way too keyed up to sleep.

Noah gets up and paces the room, then stops next to the glass-fronted cabinet near the door. He opens it and pulls out a well-worn game of Clue. "You game?"

I smile. "Only if I get to be Scarlett."

Sophie's Choice

"This has gone far enough!" I yell at Mack after reviewing the dailies. She's spent the last hour giving the production team notes for splicing certain scenes to make Evie look guilty. "You know Evie and Ted broke up a long time ago."

Mack, completely undeterred by my rants, points to the screen and tells Janira, our story editor, "Stop. Right there. Take ten seconds of that clip and put it here, then cut the rest. Evie needs to look embarrassed, not confused." She chews on her pinkie fingernail. "I wonder if we should reshoot Ted's interview in the car. He might not come across as sympathetic as we need him to."

"He's not sympathetic at all. Neither are you," I add spitefully. "And no one will believe this. The viewers like Evie."

"So, what does that matter?" Mack asks without taking her eyes off the screen. "This is television, sweetie. We could put lipstick on a pig and call it a supermodel and they'd believe it. Viewers accept what we show them. That's why we have jobs.

And that's why you're going to help if you want to keep yours."

"That photo had to be doctored. For you to just put it out there for everyone to see before we could even verify the story —that's low, even for you, Mack."

"I don't know that it's doctored, and frankly, I don't care." She pats Janira on the shoulder. "Call me when you have this part edited."

Mack turns to face me. "Listen, Alex is favored by the viewers to win. If we want a season two of the show, we need to give them what they want."

"But you're playing with Noah's heart."

Mack burst into laughter. "Noah's heart? What do you think this is, a Hallmark movie? This is a reality show, girlie, and the truth is what we decide it to be. Right now, we decide Alex is to win, so Alex will win. If you can't handle this, I understand. You know where the door is."

I turn to storm out.

"But, Sophie," Mack calls out, pausing me in my tracks, "remember that the industry is very small, and I have a very long arm. If you choose to do something stupid, you'll find yourself back in your tiny hick town before you can say 'fired.'"

My stomach knots up. Again, it doesn't matter that I'm from Houston, not some tiny hick town, because the point is valid. Mack would fire me, and I'd be blacklisted from working in Hollywood. No way do I want to return home jobless, forced to move in with my overbearing mother who would spend every moment reminding me she told me so while complimenting my smart lawyer sister in the same breath. I'd rather live in a box on the street than give my mother the satisfaction.

I leave the room and head straight to Jake. He's talking

with a couple of the camera guys and laughing. He stops when he sees my face.

"What's wrong?" he asks, following as I walk past him toward the patio. I stop in a quiet corner out of sight from the cameramen and turn to him.

"Just hold me for a while," I whisper as he wraps his arms around me. Remembering my therapist's advice to try mindfulness each day, I close my eyes and push all thoughts of Mack and this cursed show out of my mind and focus on being in Jake's warm embrace. He rests his cheek on the top of my head and gently caresses my back. I inhale the faint but heady scent of his cologne, an intoxicating blend of sandalwood and pepper that I've always found incredibly seductive. He wears just enough to drive me crazy, and I'm pretty sure he knows it.

I reluctantly back away from him. My problem with Mack is very real, and if I'm not careful, I'm going to ignore it for the more tangible option of throwing down with Jake right here, right now.

"Mack is editing the video to show that Evie conspired with that Ted guy. Which is one hundred percent bullshit. Evie didn't do anything. Mack has it in her head that having Alex win will boost ratings and ensure a season two."

"I thought you liked Alex."

"I do! She's one of the nicest people I've ever met. But this should be a real choice between her and Evie. Not a forced one. Noah should have the chance to choose the girl he loves without the show's interference."

Jake laughs. "I'm sorry," he says in response to my confused look. "I thought you were telling me the show shouldn't interfere. What business do you think we're in? The goal of *Santa's Most Eligible* isn't to find Noah true love. The goal is to get enough buzz for the network to agree to a season two. Then a season three, and so on."

"I don't need you to tell me what this business is about," I snap. "I know, and I also know I'm guilty of some shit too. But these are real people with real lives, and we're screwing with them."

"Hey, I don't like it either. But I didn't make the rules. I'm just playing by them because that's my job. It's your job too," he reminds me.

"Not anymore." I turn to walk away. I'm going to go straight to Mack and tell her exactly where she can shove her network buzz.

"Sophie, wait!" he calls out. "Please don't tell me you're actually going to give up your career over this."

I turn to see a sincere look of concern in his eyes. "I can't do this, Jake. Not to them. If I do, I will never be able to live with myself."

He sighs heavily. "Ethics. Something you don't see a lot of in Hollywood. Not surprised at all to find it in you." He takes my hand, his eyes warm and full of resolve. "All right. If you're going down, so am I."

"What do you mean?"

"I mean I'm not going to let the woman I love throw herself under the bus. I've had a good career, but if I let you go this alone, what does that say about me?"

My heart almost stops. Did he say *love*?

When we were dating, we referred to it as "the L Word," and neither of us ever really said it. Does he really love me? As I look into his warm eyes, I can see the sincerity there. I wasn't ready for the L Word then; am I now?

I nod. I know, as I have always known. He pulls me to him,

his lips grazing my brow, fingers sliding down my arm, melting me.

"I love you, Soph," he murmurs into my ear.

"I love you too, Jake."

I wrap my arms around his shoulders as he lifts me, our kisses full of love and promises of a future. The show doesn't matter, the consequences I'll most certainly face don't matter. The only thing that matters is us.

He sets me down but doesn't let go of me. "Let's go face Mack," he says, tucking a wayward strand of hair behind my ear. "Together."

"Wait," I tell him. "What if we play this our way?"

"What do you mean?"

"Why tell Mack at all? She'll just fire one or both of us, then do it her way anyway. Noah, Alex, and Evie will still get hurt. What if we just tell Noah? Give him all the information and let him make an informed choice."

Jake frowned, considering that. "We don't have any proof. What will make him believe us?"

I take out my phone. "It might be a long shot, but it's time to do some digging."

Around twenty minutes and one cup of coffee later, with Jake leaning over my shoulder in the dining room, I come across a photo on one of Ted's friend's Instagram pages—a pretty redhead in a bikini draped around Ted. Searching through the comments I find what I'm looking for: "Isabelle girl you're hottt!"

Five minutes later, I've found Isabelle's page, and five minutes after that I hit the jackpot. A very familiar photo with one difference — *Isabelle* is the girl being kissed by Ted at the airport.

"Bingo," I gleefully say to Jake. "He *did* doctor it, the piece of shit!"

"You're amazing," Jake says. "Let's go show Noah."

"Hang on." I screenshot the post and send it with a few details to one of my closest friends from college who also happens to be an influencer. She'll get the word out there. No need for the world to hate on Evie for something she didn't do.

Take that, Ted. And Mack, I add silently.

Jake pulls me into a hug, kissing me. "Let's go, my love."

CHAPTER 25

Is This Love?

ALEX

My heart is in my throat as I climb into the horse-drawn carriage that's going to take me to Noah. The horses are covered in jingle bells. Every step they take is full of music—and rattles my nerves. This is it: the engagement ceremony. Do I end this day with a fiancé or on my own? Will it be a fairytale Christmas Eve proposal or something closer to a nightmare?

This moment doesn't seem real. *I* don't *feel* real. It's like I'm hovering outside my body or something. I keep replaying the past few weeks with Noah. Every moment. Taken as a whole, are they enough to make an engagement feel like the logical next step?

My gut says no, but the romance writer side of me keeps trying to convince me it's yes. Getting engaged doesn't mean we have to ultimately get married, right? It just means we're committing to continue to get to know each other off-camera. And as my editor has reminded me about a dozen times, it would be great for my books if Noah and I do leave here with a happy ending—so perfectly on brand. I'd be lying if I said that didn't play a small part in the temptation to accept Noah's proposal—should he make one.

The past week has been the craziest of my life. I've spent almost all the time sequestered in a tiny apartment in town to prepare for the final episode of the show. The crew—mainly Sophie—brought me meals because I wasn't allowed to leave since downtown is crawling with papparazzi. Then there were promo segments to film to get viewers pumped up for today's live Christmas Eve proposal event. And formal interviews with half a dozen media outlets. *And* photo shoots for several magazines, including *Vogue*. I got chosen for a feature because according to polls, I am the audience favorite to win Noah's heart. I still can't believe the clothes they put on me—this to-die-for Christian Siriano gown. Then there were the fittings for a dress to wear to the engagement ceremony and the engagement ring Noah might give me tonight.

But maybe the best thing to happen since I last saw Noah is career-related. Because the show's gained so much popularity, my books have seen a massive surge in sales. Three of them hit the New York Times bestseller list at the same time. One even made the top five! So I spent all my time back home signing tip-ins for additional print runs for all three before I was due back here.

Now I'm sitting in the back of a horse-drawn carriage in a gown so pretty I'm afraid to move in case I manage to somehow tear it. It's the most flattering shade of emerald green with a subtly sequined bodice and a form-fitted skirt with a slit that ends mid-thigh. Over that is a fuller second skirt in the same color, which helps the dress be both princessy and sexy at the same time. I touch one of the gorgeous diamond earrings dangling from my ears—on loan from the town's jewelry store, Sparkle and Shine. The earrings are heavy, but they make me feel glamorous in the best way. I'm also wearing the coolest bracelet: a chain of diamond-encrusted Christmas wreaths. No matter what happens next, I get to keep it—which will be amazing if tonight goes the way I hope it does.

I take a deep breath and try to steady myself.

What is going to happen next?

Will Noah actually propose?

I've gone back and forth mentally about what he'll do. Now that I've been away from him and the other girls and the show, I'm not sure what to think. About how he feels. About how I feel.

Am I truly in love or at least at the beginning of it?

I've thought about him nonstop. Dissected every conversation, every kiss and caress. I definitely have feelings for him. But how do I know if they're the kind that last forever? I've heard people say that when you know you know. But I'm still not sure. It was definitely attraction at first sight and more as time went on, but forever love?

Is it fear that's holding me back? Or something else?

I know Evie has really strong feelings for him. And Noah has strong feelings for her. I've seen them together. I would have to be completely dense not to know this. But then Evie's ex showed up and changed everything between them. Sure, Noah was upset at the beginning of our last date together, but by the end he seemed to be considering me more seriously.

Except we didn't have sex, a voice inside me whispers. I wasn't ready to and neither was he. At the time we both agreed it was because we didn't want to taint things between us, but I can't stop thinking that was just an excuse. I don't think I wanted to, period. And I can't help feeling like Noah only considered it because he was in a vulnerable state.

I clasp and unclasp my hands as the carriage winds its way to the lodge. The parking lot is at capacity and several shuttles are lined up along the drive. The entire town will be here for the proposal ceremonies. Because they were so involved with choosing who Noah would marry, he wanted them here. And I get it, but for someone as introverted as me, the thought of standing in front of them for this makes me want to throw up from nerves.

And I get that the townspeople are only one element to worry about, that millions of people will also be watching tonight play out from the comfort of their homes, but I can't see them, so they almost feel imaginary.

Ugh.

I swallow down bile. I really might be sick. The closer I get to the lodge the more nauseous I feel.

The carriage pulls to a stop beside the lodge's entry.

Oh my god.

Oh my god.

OH MY GOD!

I am seriously going to jump out of my skin. That familiar urge to run, the one I had the very first night, rears its head again.

Jake opens my carriage door and offers me his hand. I search his face for some clue about what the next few minutes might hold. Damn. His poker face is on point.

"You look lovely tonight, Alex," he says. "Merry Christmas."

"Merry Christmas to you, Jake," I say, my voice trembling with nerves. "And thank you."

I manage to get out of the carriage without falling on my

face, which is a minor miracle because my legs are actual Jell-O. I glance at the lodge's entry doors. They've been covered with black cloth so I can't see inside. My heart stutters, nearly stopping.

"How are you feeling tonight?" Jake asks. Cameras are trained on me from every possible angle. I search the crews' faces, desperate for some clue as to what is about to happen, but there are so many lights everywhere I can't see anyone clearly besides Jake.

"I'm okay," I say. "Nervous, but okay." This is a bold-faced lie. I am not okay. I am nowhere near okay. I thought I could do this, but now I'm not so sure.

Run, run, RUN!

"Well, you're doing better than us, then," Jake says, winking into the camera as he talks directly to the live audience. "We are on pins and needles to see what Noah decides."

Something about what he says rubs me the wrong way. Why just Noah? Why aren't they wondering what I'll decide? Are they that sure my answer will be yes, even when I'm not?

I lick my lips. The red lipstick the makeup artist applied feels sticky. My mouth is dry. My palms are wet. Despite the cold air, I'm sweating. I am a mess.

Jake squeezes my hand. "Noah is waiting for you inside," he says. "Ready to see him again?"

"Only if he's about to propose," I say before I think better of it, then immediately regret it because I'm pretty sure this isn't true.

My candor surprises a laugh out of Jake. "Good luck, Alex," he says.

I murmur my thanks then turn toward the doors as they open simultaneously, right on cue. Classical Christmas music plays from somewhere inside, but once again, I'm surrounded by bright lights and am mostly blind to what's inside.

I pass the crew and there he is. Noah. Standing near the fireplace, right beside the lodge's grand Christmas tree, exactly where he was that first night we met. His hair is combed neatly so his curls are more like waves. He's wearing a deep green velvet jacket over a black turtleneck and pants. It's a sophisticated look, especially the cut, which is sort of retro mod and very cool and my dream style on a guy—one I've actually written about in my first book. They must've chosen it for him with that in mind. But it's clear he isn't totally comfortable wearing it; I can tell by how stiffly he's standing. He tugs at the collar. This look isn't him at all. The Noah I've come to know would prefer a flannel shirt and jeans.

And this, for whatever reason, is the thing that makes me realize this is not my moment. Noah is not my guy. He never was. To him, I would be just like that velvet jacket, something that doesn't fit right.

He pastes on a smile the second he sees me. Seeing how it doesn't reach his eyes, I let out a sigh. I'm right. He knows it too.

People are seated throughout the lobby, creating an aisle from me to him, all of them dressed in their Christmas best in complementary shades of red and green. I spot Noah's Aunt Julia near the back of the crowd sitting beside the man from the bookstore in town as well as Noah's parents arm in arm in the front row.

The walkway is covered in red rose petals and lined with candles. And the decorations! The lodge was Christmassy before, but now it's like something out of a movie. Garlands are draped on every wall. Dozens of wreaths hang from crimson bows over every pane of glass on the floor-to-ceiling window. Gingerbread cookies decorate the tree: intricately iced hearts, candy canes, and engagement rings. Fake taper candles flicker from every bough, giving the tree a nostalgic look like something out of *A Christmas Carol.*

It is perfectly romantic. I couldn't imagine a scene more ideal for a proposal. I try to absorb it all so I can write about it in my journal later—about the time I took myself out of the running for this show.

"Alex," Noah says.

"Noah," I say back.

I walk toward him, my heart sinking. Now that I'm here, I am more and more confident about what needs to happen next. I am going to bow out of the competition for Noah's heart. I'd be a terrible person not to. He really is the perfect guy —but for Evie, not me. And it's not just because he doesn't like ballet or is more comfortable in flannel than Dior. I don't love him and suddenly I'm pretty sure I never will, not the way I should.

The second I'm up the aisle, Noah grabs both my hands in his.

"From the moment I met you, I knew you were special," he says. "Not because you're beautiful—although you are. Or talented—although you're that too." He takes a deep breath. "It's more that you are one hundred percent yourself all the time. You're never fake or insincere or dishonest. Throughout this entire experience I never wondered where you stood. I always knew you were here for the right reasons."

I stop him there. He hasn't said the word "but" yet, however, I am certain it's coming because what I see in his eyes right now is a perfect reflection of what I'm feeling.

We aren't a match.

I clear my throat. The tension in the air is so thick it's

almost a physical thing—like a storm cloud hovering over our heads, threatening to unleash.

"And you are special too," I say. "One of the nicest, most wonderful men I have ever met. But this isn't love between us."

The crowd gasps.

Noah lets out a breath, clearly relieved to have me say it first. "I know," he says simply, squeezing my hands a little tighter. "And I'm sorry."

I shake my head. "Don't be. I'm not. I'm so glad I mustered the courage to be here. To meet you. To take part in all the competitions and dates. To take a chance on love even if it didn't work out."

For some reason, the second I say the word "love" my throat tightens and my eyes fill with tears. Still I soldier on. "The past few weeks have changed me for the better and for that I will always be grateful for the time I've spent here with you."

This is the right thing to do and I am proud of myself for doing it, yet my heart feels like it's shattering. I'm not the one. This isn't my happily ever after.

"Alex?" Noah says softly.

"It's okay," I finally blurt out as I try desperately to keep the tears pooling in my eyes from falling. "I'm going to be just fine. And so will you. Provided you do the right thing tonight."

Noah wraps me in his arms.

"You are going to make some guy very happy someday," he whispers in my ear.

"And you are going to make Evie very happy tonight. If you follow your heart," I whisper back. "Fairytale endings don't come around every day, you know. You'd be a fool to give up too quickly on yours."

I pull away first, steeling myself as I do. "I wish you the

best, Noah," I say for the audience and the cameras, my voice a bit hoarse and thick with emotion. "Merry Christmas."

He opens his mouth to say the same, but I don't wait to hear it. I turn and walk down the aisle as quickly as I can, then out the door and into the limo that's waiting for me outside, the driver ready at the passenger door to let me in.

When I slip inside the limo I'm fully expecting to be alone, but instead my editor, Owen, is there, holding a bottle of champagne and two glasses. I throw my arms around him.

"You have no idea how happy I am to see you," I say. And it's true. The last thing I wanted to be right now was alone.

"You handled that like a total boss," he says.

I pull away and wipe at my eyes. "Yeah? Well it doesn't feel like I did."

He hands me the glasses and then opens the champagne. "Not the ending either of us were hoping for, but sometimes the universe has other plans. Better plans." His eyes twinkle mischievously as he arches one eyebrow. "Would you like to know what they are?"

I narrow my eyes at him as he pours the champagne. "What are you talking about? What plans?"

Owen clinks his glass to mine. "Your happily ever after is still very much on the table. I've been quite busy securing it for you."

This surprises a laugh out of me. "Oh really? How? Details, please."

Owen nods toward the driver. "Not here. Later. Once we're alone. But I promise you one thing: you are going to forget all about Noah in no time." His excitement is palpable as he instructs the driver to take us to the airport.

And I can't help myself; an ember of hope kindles inside me, intense enough to ward off the emotional chill that had seeped into my heart during my farewell with Noah. I am going to be okay. Just the act of admitting Noah and I weren't the right fit felt like a really big step in that direction. Whatever Owen's got up his sleeve, I think I might be ready for it. Because one thing I know for certain after going through the past few weeks is that real love is possible.

If Evie can find it, well then so can I.

CHAPTER 26

My Christmas Bachelor

EVIE

My stomach twists into knots as I pace the hotel room like a caged animal. I'm a monkey trapped behind bars at the zoo. Mack, the producer, told me I was forbidden to leave the room based on the contract I signed. It's been an hour since the camera crew came in here, taking pictures and video shots of me getting dressed in my fairytale floor-length gown.

They snapped shots from every angle, likely to show off the one-shoulder silver gown with silver beading and embroidery on its fitted bodice. I can't blame them. The dress is stunning, flaring out from the waist with the beads trailing down the dress like falling stars.

Now I'm waiting. Waiting for my heart to be accepted or destroyed. I push back the curtain and look out the hotel window into the town square, quiet except for the falling snow. Everyone must be at the ski lodge to attend the live finale.

After watching the episode where Ted shows up with his fake revelation that I tricked Noah, the odds are in favor for them to vote for Alex as his final pick. She's beautiful, successful, and a great person. What isn't there to love? And she wasn't planning a scheme to get famous with her secret boyfriend like Ted made it look like I was doing.

If only I could talk to Noah about what happened. I don't have his personal number, and I can't get in touch with him through the lodge because his calls are all screened.

What must he think of me? I'm still kicking myself for freezing up that night. Why didn't I say something right away? Why didn't I chase after him?

I'm about to go face Noah for a potential engagement and we haven't talked about Ted showing up with his lies. It's so messed up.

He told you he loved you, my heart reminds me. *And you love him.*

Except sometimes love isn't enough. I clench my fists and kick off my heels in frustration.

A knock on the door jolts me with terror. It's time! Swallowing my fear, I swing open the door to find Candice and Melody, my book club friends.

"Surprise!" Melody exclaims. The pompom on the top of her hat bobs up and down.

"Oh my gosh!" I blink in shock and then give them both a hug. "It's good to see you both. I can't believe the show let you come see me."

I peer over their shoulders. The security guard is gone, and there aren't any camera crews.

"They didn't." Candice pushes herself into my room. "I sent your guard on a little goose chase with a false tip, but he'll be back any second."

Quickly, I step back so they can enter and shut the door. "So what are you doing here in Vermont?"

"We got your message, but you didn't respond," Melody says, wringing her hands. "We got worried."

"So you flew all the way up to Vermont?" I ask, crossing my arms.

"We drove," Melody admits. "Left last night."

"What?" My eyes bug out.

"Stacy is here too," Candice adds. "She's waiting in the car."

"Now I feel terrible. I'm so sorry I didn't respond," I say. "They took my phone away yesterday when I arrived, or I would've told you not to worry."

Candice adjusts her scarf and clears her throat like something is bothering her.

"You look stunning." Melody presses her hand to her chest, but her face is full of sympathy.

"What is it?" I ask. "You both are acting weird."

"Did you get a chance to talk to Noah yet?" Candice asks hopefully.

After the episode of Ted showing up in Finland aired, we had an emergency book club meeting. I told them exactly what happened. Right away, Candice started looking for lawyers on my behalf while the other two tried to think of ways to get in touch with Noah. But the part that touched me the most was that they believed me without question.

"The show won't allow me to see or talk to Noah until the final candy cane ceremony," I explain. "Truth is, everything feels off, you know? I didn't get a chance to explain myself to Noah. Everyone in town must think I'm awful. Honestly, why would they vote for me believing I did what Ted accused me of?"

"Jackass," Melody grumbles, crossing her arms.

"Okay, it's time to confess why we really came," Candice

says and sucks in a big gulp of air like she's about to tell me something awful. "This morning on the Reality Show Secrets Reddit page, someone leaked the news that the townsfolk are voting for Alex."

My heart stops for a moment and then takes off again, racing. "You think it's legit?"

"Don't know." Candice wraps her arm around me. "But we didn't think it would be fair for you to go into that ceremony today without knowing."

"We're the ones that signed you up for this stupid reality show." Melody takes my hands in hers. "We feel awful that you've had to go through all of this. We didn't want your heart to get…"

She presses her lips together as if she can't say the last word.

"Broken?" I finish, choking on the word. The full impact of their news hits me like an avalanche.

Noah doesn't love me.

He isn't going to choose me.

An aching chill seeps through my body. It's too late for my heart. It's already Noah's whether he realizes it or not, and nothing can change that. Somewhere along the way, he pieced my shattered life back together. Like an idiot, I thought I was whole again. I thought I was stronger than ever before.

"I was a fool," I whisper.

"No." Melody hugs me while Candice squeezes my shoulder tighter. "Ted was an asshole. But when you go to talk to Noah—"

"No." My head spins like I'm on a merry-go-round that I can't get off. "I may not be able to control Ted's antics or Noah's love for me or even how the show perceives me to the townsfolk, but I can control myself."

Both women's eyes widen.

"What are you going to do?" Melody asks.

"You said Stacy is in the car below?" I ask. They nod. "Tell her to bring the car around to the window. Meet me outside. We're leaving."

"Like you're going to sneak out?" Melody asks with a gasp.

"Yep." I start gathering my belongings. "Hurry. They'll be here any minute to take me to the ski lodge."

"Are you sure you don't want to talk to Noah?" Candice asks. "It might be good for you to let the cameras hear your side of the story."

"I want out. I want to be free of all of this." My throat is closing up. Tears prick my eyes. "Please do this if you care about me."

"Of course," they say and duck into the hall.

I bolt the door. Outside, the security guard starts yelling at my friends. I'm tossing the last of my items into my suitcase, when someone knocks.

"It's go time, Evie," Carianne calls out through the door.

Crap! I'm out of time!

"I need to go to the bathroom," I yell back "I'll be right there."

"Fine, but open up so we can get the film crew positioned." Carianne rattles the doorknob.

Desperately, I shove open the window. Cold air blows inside, sucking my breath away. I toss my suitcase out the window. It lands in the snowbank below just to the right with a thump.

"Evie!" Carianne calls. "Let us in!"

There isn't time to change out of my dress, so I jam my feet into my boots and climb over the window ledge. My feet dangle below me as I cling to the windowsill, snowflakes dancing around me. The drop is about ten feet, but facing Noah or even the cameras feels a whole lot scarier.

My stomach swoops as I let go of the windowsill. I plummet into the soft snowbank below. Ice cold stabs my body as I sink waist deep into the snow. My teeth start chattering.

Stacy's car screeches around the corner, stopping right before me. Melody and Candice leap out of the car and haul me out of the snowbank while Stacy grabs my suitcase.

"Hi, Evie!" Stacy says as we pile back into the warm car. "Looks like this just became a rescue mission."

Shivering, I nod from the back seat. "Thank you for helping me."

"That's what friends are for," she says, but then frowns. "You're freezing to death. Here, take my coat."

The camera crew come rushing outside and start videoing us.

"No time!" I exclaim. "They spotted us."

"Hurry, Stacy," Candice says from the front passenger seat. "Drive!"

"On it!" Stacy hits the gas and the car screeches out of the parking lot. I sink lower in my seat to avoid the cameras, wishing for the nightmare to end.

"Someone turn on the GPS," Stacy says. "I don't know where I'm going."

As the three argue about which way to go, I sit up from where I've been lowered in my seat to help them, only for my heart to drop.

"We're headed the wrong way!" I exclaim. "This is the road to Noah's ski lodge."

"Shit." Stacy pounds her steering wheel. "Shit, shit, shit!"

Quickly, she slows down, pulls off to the side of the road,

and makes a three-point turn. I grip Melody's hand beside me as the production crew van comes barreling up behind us.

"Do you think they'll follow us the whole way back to Florida?" I ask.

"They'll just stick around for some footage." Melody squeezes my hand, but I don't miss the worry in her eyes.

Stacy veers the car back onto the road and starts heading the way we came when a limo comes flying past us. I lean forward. My chest squeezes.

"That's one of the production company's limos," I say breathlessly. "Don't let them box you in!"

The limo moves in front of Stacy's car. A head pops out from the sunroof.

"Noah?" I lean forward between the two front seats to get a better view. My heart swoops like the evil traitor it is seeing his gorgeous face. He's wearing a black tux. The wind is whipping his hair about as he waves his arms over his head. "What is he doing?"

"Looks like he's trying to get your attention," Melody says. "I think he wants to talk to you."

"He's only making things worse," I grumble.

"Don't worry, I'll take care of him," Candice says smugly. She rolls down her window and flips him off. He ducks back into the limo.

"I'd try to get around him," Stacy grips the steering wheel tighter, "but these roads are so twisty. I'm afraid I might hit someone."

I thought Candice got rid of him, but Noah pops back up. This time, he's holding a piece of paper. It has a bunch of numbers. He makes the gesture of a phone with his hands and pretends to make a call with it, but then the wind rips it from his hands and it flies away.

"He wants to talk." I swallow hard, pain stabbing me all over again. "But I don't want to talk to him."

"But isn't that what you wanted?" Melody reminds me.

She's right. Ever since that morning in Finland, I've been begging and trying to talk to Noah. This is my chance. And that's when the truth hits me. I'm terrified to face rejection from him. I don't want to hear him tell me that he doesn't love me because I don't know if I will ever get over him.

I close my eyes. I can't run forever.

I've been spending so long hiding from love, you'd think I was playing some sort of game of hide and seek. But what if my biggest problem isn't falling for the wrong person. It's that I let Ted convince me I didn't deserve something better. Running sure hasn't made me safer or fixed things. It's just another kind of heartbreak.

This is my chance to be brave. To not run from heartbreak, but embrace it and all the messiness that comes with it.

"Pull over," I tell Stacy, focusing back on the limo. "You're right. We need to talk."

Stacy pulls off to the side. The limo in front also pulls over, and the van following us does too. I open my door and shiver as I step out onto the snow-crusted ground. Vaguely, I notice Stacy putting her coat over my shoulders while the camera crew swarms us like a pack of wolves. But I don't care. My whole focus is on Noah, jumping out of the limo.

He runs toward me like he's worried I might duck back into the car and drive away. It's tempting, but I clench my fists and lift my chin. It's time to face my fears. I walk out to meet him right by the Moose Crossing sign.

"Evie," Noah says, his breath coming out in puffs in the cold. "Please don't leave until we've talked."

"You're right." I cross my arms, terrified I'll throw them

around his neck. Just seeing him standing in front of me is torture. I missed him so much. "I shouldn't have left without talking to you, but I heard the town chose Alex."

"I'm sorry you heard about it that way." He grimaces and rubs the back of his neck. "It's complicated."

So it *was* true. I suck in a deep breath and barrel on. "I respect their decision, and at first I didn't think I could face you and the cameras." I glance around at the crew filming us right now. So much for that. My friends have climbed out of the car, arms crossed like they're ready to join in a fight. "I shouldn't have run. I just couldn't stand being hurt again, and this time on live TV."

"Oh, Evie." His face is contorted like he's being tortured. "I never wanted to hurt you."

"The truth is, Ted is a liar and an asshole for trying to take the most important thing in my life from me. He knew that to really hurt me was to take me from you. Like I told you, I didn't come on this show for love, but to find myself again. Except during the process, I did what I told myself not to do. Fall in love with you like the idiot I am. That's what makes this so hard. Alex is a great person, and I have no hard feelings. I hope you both find happiness together."

Tears trickle down my face because my heart is screaming, wishing he could find happiness with me. Wishing that seeing him again wouldn't make me fall in love with him even more.

Noah steps toward me. I back up. "You have it all wrong, Evie. It's you I love. You are the one I want to be with."

I freeze and blink in confusion. "I don't understand. The rules of the show..."

"Forget the rules," he interrupts, taking my hand. It warms me all the way to my toes even as snowflakes cake my lashes. "And when does love have to follow the rules anyway? You have my heart. That's why, when I heard what Ted said, it terrified me more than anything. If we're being truthful, I was considering a life without love just so I wouldn't be hurt again. Now who's the idiot here? Also, Sophie told me the truth about the doctored photo. Which just proves that I'd let fear take over. I believed a lie when I should've believed in you."

My heart melts. Those words...they're too good to be true. They're what I've been hoping and dreaming of ever since I left Finland.

"Wait." I search his face. "So you're not marrying Alex?"

He grins, and that twinkle is back in his eyes. He bends down on one knee in the snow, reaching into his pocket. He pulls out a ring and holds it up to me.

"I don't want to be afraid to love ever again," he says. "Instead, I want to live my life proving my love to you over and over. I wished for love this Christmas. Will you marry me, Evie Winters?"

I gasp. Behind me I hear my friends cheering. But all I can focus on is him. Joy balloons my chest until it's like I'm going to explode. "Yes, a thousand times, yes."

He slips the diamond on my finger. It glitters brighter than the snow. Then he rises to his feet and wraps his arms around me, kissing me like the world belongs only to us. I melt against those perfect lips.

"You've made me the happiest man," he whispers, trailing a finger along my jawline as he stares at me like I'm the most wonderful thing he's ever seen. "Merry Christmas, my love."

"Merry Christmas," I say, and kiss him all over again.

The cameras zoom in on us, but this time I'm not annoyed or upset. Instead, I turn to them and say, "Please let Santa know that this guy has been taken and is no longer his Most Eligible."

CHAPTER 27
A New Adventure

ALEX

The studio lights are blinding as I step on stage to face the press. My heart is at full sprint, beating so fast I put a hand to my chest to calm it before I pass out. Every major news and entertainment outlet is here. I've never had so many cameras aimed at me, recording my every move, my every breath, not even when I was on *Santa's Most Eligible*. If not for the glass of bourbon I downed in the green room just now I would probably be hyperventilating.

After I left the show alone, the amount of sympathy and love I received from viewers was staggering. I knew I was the audience favorite, but those words held no meaning until I went home and my social media was flooded with hundreds of thousands of messages from fans. Owen keeps telling me I'm the It Girl right now and to celebrate, but it's all so surreal I have no idea how to do that. I went from feeling anonymous to literally being on the cover of magazines overnight.

And the attention isn't going to die down anytime soon. Especially not after today.

Sweet Jesus.

The thought has my heart pounding harder.

What have I gotten myself into?

I force my trembling lips into a smile and head toward Jake, who is already center stage holding his arms out to me, waiting for a hug. He is surrounded by bookshelves filled with artfully arranged romance novels (more than a few of which are mine, strategically placed to catch the eye) and trinkets that hint at the announcement we're about to make. A ceramic castle. A world globe. A statue of a knight. Behind the shelves a giant screen projects a vast forest background with sparkling fairy lights drifting through the air and a sky painted in cotton candy pinks and blues so it appears we're in an open-air library in the middle of the woods.

I have to hand it to the crew. It's absolutely stunning.

I laugh under my breath, shaking my head. It's been exactly one week since I said goodbye to Noah at the lodge and stepped away from the show as the contestant who didn't win his heart. To say that things have changed radically since then would be an understatement. I mean, I'm here at this moment, aren't I?

"Welcome, Alex!' Jake exclaims as if he hasn't seen me since the last episode of *Santa's Most Eligible* was filmed when we've been prepping for this moment for days.

"Thank you, I'm excited to be here," I say, focusing on keeping my hands at my sides instead of crossed over my chest because my new publicist says this stance is more open and accessible. I am acutely aware of how many people are watching me—both in this room and around the world. And I have the same urge I had that first day on the show in the lodge —to run. But I won't. Not this time. Even if I'm scared half to death.

Jake's expression turns sympathetic. "How are you doing? Your final moments on *Santa's Most Eligible* were so heart-breaking. Tell us how you're feeling now that you've had time to process."

I take a deep breath. "I'm good. I mean, that day was tough. I really did like Noah." I turn to face the cameras and smile. "Who wouldn't? He was a great guy." Saying this out loud a twinge of regret creeps into my voice. "I really wanted him to be the one."

The room has suddenly gotten so quiet I can hear myself breathing.

I reflect for a moment, picturing Noah's face. That easy smile of his. "I wanted my happily ever after. And for a while I convinced myself it was him. Because I loved the idea of knowing for the rest of my life who my person is."

There is a collective murmur running through the crowd of reporters, a series of nodding heads that let me know that what I'm saying is resonating. It gives me the courage to continue.

"But if I'm honest, I knew from the start that he wasn't it. We had chemistry, sure, but not the kind that stops you in your tracks."

Jake beams at me. "I love your honesty and vulnerability, Alex. It's what made you such a fan favorite."

I don't know what to say to this. I'm not very good at taking compliments, so I just force a smile and change the subject. "But I am thrilled for Evie that she found true love with him. They are absolutely the perfect fit."

I clear my throat and grin mischievously at Jake. "And I'm happy for you and Sophie too."

This surprises a laugh out of Jake and he actually starts blushing. "Thanks."

Sophie and Jake's relationship was impossible to keep a secret, especially after some behind the scenes footage was "accidentally" leaked to the press by someone on the crew. I'm pretty sure it was Mack and that there was nothing accidental about it. The scandal of there being a supposed mole among the contestants only made the show more popular.

From the wings, Carianne waves at us to move things along.

"Speaking of true love," Jake starts. "I think you deserve to find yours. Which brings us to why we're both here today."

Cue the drumroll...or half a second of silence to build tension. Everyone seems to be holding their breath—me included.

Jake faces the cameras. "This spring the romances Alex writes about will leave the page and become a part of her real life as we go in search of the perfect man to complete her literary lifestyle. Ten lucky guys will be invited to embark on a quest for her heart. Will you be one of them? Alex's journey to find her happily ever after is only just beginning. And we need your help to make it come true on our brand-new show, *The Book Boyfriend*. Applications are now open. Let this new game of love begin!"

As he talks, the title of the show appears in flowery script across the sky in the forest scene behind us. It's official. There's no going back now. My stomach flutters like a thousand tiny birds have been let loose inside it.

All the cameras swivel in my direction and zoom in.

I lick my lips and smile into the lens. Is the man meant for me out there somewhere watching?

God, I hope so.

Thank you for reading! If you enjoyed this story, we'd appreciate it if you'd leave a review and tell us what you loved.

Would you like to read a bonus scene of Evie and Noah's wedding and their romantic wedding night? Go to JuliaSilverwood.com for details.

The fun doesn't have to end. Alex's journey continues in the the next book in the series, *Santa's Next Chapter*. Continue reading for a sneak pick at Chapter 1!

Santa's Next Chapter:
Chapter 1

MAIDEN IN DISTRESS

Alex

I must be out of my mind.

Is the prospect of finding true love and securing a fabulous book career really worth allowing myself to be tied to a pyre in the middle of a medieval village surrounded by torch-carrying extras dressed in period costumes?

I'm starting to think the answer is no. I glance down at the white lace gown I'm wearing. It's more nightgown than ball gown, a full-length shift meant to make me look vulnerable and pure, all maiden-like.

Yeesh.

A camera drone hovers just over my head, capturing all the action. The village square surrounding me is full of people: crowd actors, camera people, and crew. It's the first day of filming for my new reality series, *The Book Boyfriend*, a reality dating show where I'm supposed to find true love with one of twelve dashing dudes. Already, I want to crawl under a rock and die.

What was I thinking agreeing to this?

The short answer: I wasn't.

I was upset and deflated after failing to find true love on *Santa's Most Eligible*, another reality show I should've never signed up for–well, okay, that's not true. I did get two new friends out of the experience. I'm just being salty now because I'm so uncomfortable.

I glare up at the drone, wishing my arms weren't tied behind my back so I could bat it away. Instead I mentally give it the finger, and hope the vibes are clear even if I can't make the actual gesture.

"You're supposed to be having fun, remember?" Owen, my literary agent and best friend, calls from off set. He's sitting next to the director, Alison, with his phone out, documenting all the behind-the-scenes action for my social media.

"This is your moment to shine," she adds, her voice musical and full of nervous energy. "So while we want you to appear as if you really are in distress, we were thinking more fear less anger. You shouldn't look like you're about to kill someone."

She puts her hands together prayer-style and mouths the word "Please."

I close my eyes and take a deep breath. I'm being a brat. Everyone here is counting on me to put my whole heart into this production–literally. Their jobs depend on it. Besides, it isn't like I don't want to find my true love. I do, especially after seeing my fellow *Santa's Most Eligible* contestant, Evie, find hers. I'm not really regretting being here so much as I'm embarrassed. This whole damsel in distress bit is over the top and silly and I'm not good with being silly–probably because to pull it off, I have to be vulnerable. While that's easy for me to do on the page when I'm writing a romance novel, it's much harder to do in real life when I'm not channeling a character.

I give my shoulders a little shake and try to get rid of this epic case of nerves.

"Just remember, your readers will love this," I tell myself.

"What?" Alison pulls her headset away from her ear.

"Roll 'em," I tell her, and get my game face on. *Okay, Alex, let's do this.*

One of the crew rattles off the take number, closing the clapperboard so loudly I jump.

Here we go.

I channel my inner heroine and struggle against my restraints. "Help!"

Cameras in the air and on the ground capture me from every angle. I knit my eyebrows together and really try to ham it up like I'm seriously freaking out, even though every inch of me is cringing inwardly. This is why I'm not an actor.

The "villagers" inch closer to me, waving their torches, several threatening to set the wood at my feet on fire.

What did I do to deserve being fake-burned at the stake?

Not one damned thing.

This whole scenario makes no sense in that there's no real plot arc, but Alison swears it doesn't have to. It's just a romance novel-inspired bit of drama meant to give the show's male contestants an outlandish introduction.

I glance up, past the thatched roofs of the buildings in front of me to the rolling hills behind them, where twelve men on horseback are gathered, bathed in the light of the setting sun, their suits of armor shining. My potential love interests. Ready to save me from the flames.

My heart skips a beat despite how uncomfortable I am. Is

one of them someone I could truly be interested in and maybe one day love?

A second camera crew surrounds them as the one focused on me takes a break.

"They've really managed to make them look heroic, right?"

The show's host, Mia Taylor, comes to stand beside me. She's one of those rare Hollywood glamazons who's even better looking in person than on screen. Her hair is gathered in a complicated updo, and she's wearing an intricately beaded gown with a bodice that makes her waist look minuscule. The full skirt is made of damask and makes swishing sounds every time she moves. She's as regal as a queen, her blue eyes glittering with confidence.

I can only nod because even though we've met briefly once before, I still don't know how to hold a conversation with someone as famous as she is. She's done a series of blockbuster movies and last year was nominated for an Academy Award. Why she took a job hosting a reality show is beyond me. But it's a mystery I'd like to solve if I ever muster the courage to ask her.

Mia adjusts the lace around her wrist and sighs. "Well, I'd better leave you to it." Then she leans over and touches my shoulder lightly. "I'm so excited to be working with you. I love your books and I just know we're going to be great friends."

Does she mean it? Maybe. It's hard to tell with Hollywood people. They lie far more often than they're honest, but I want to believe that she does.

Mia Taylor reading my books and wanting to be my friend. Shaking my head, I watch as she goes to stand by Alison and Owen behind the main cameras. This is all so surreal.

Someone on the hillside crew must give the go-ahead to

start rolling, because suddenly the knights on horseback are galloping this way, the sounds of the horses' hooves loud enough for me to hear them from this far away. They're neck-and-neck at first, but then one horse pulls away from the pack. Its rider is taller than the others, more imposing too. My stomach flutters with nerves.

A camera drone flies over him, capturing every heart-pounding moment of his descent to the village. He lashes the horse with his reins, body bent forward, head low. He is determination personified. It's impressive.

Alison clears her throat. "Okay, Alex, here he comes. Cameras on you again, in three, two, one..."

I start thrashing against my restraints again. "Help me, please!" It's getting a little easier the more I do it.

The lead knight careens into the village square, pulling on his reins hard. The horse comes to stop a few feet away, nostrils flaring, a storm cloud of dust surrounding him. The knight turns his head in my direction, then, helmet over his face. I have no idea what he looks like, and okay, so *that's* incredibly sexy, the not knowing. I shiver–and definitely not because it's cold.

He's watching me so intently.

I shift self-consciously, very aware of how the dress I'm wearing hugs my curves.

The rest of the men slow to a stop beside him a few moments later, knights all of them, similarly disguised. Double sexy. Not gonna lie. All of these mystery men are here for me. I lower my head so no one can see the exhilarated look on my face.

So maybe now I don't regret signing up for this. It's surprising how much I'm liking this all of a sudden, falling for all the drama the same way the viewers will.

The first knight dismounts with the practiced ease of someone who's been on horses before...a lot. As he does, the others follow. They're brandishing swords–the Hollywood kind meant for show, not actual death. The villagers advance on them as if determined not to be swayed from burning me at the stake.

The knights take them as they make their way to me, knocking torches from their hands, causing my captors to surrender. It's all choreographed so well, it almost looks real, even from my vantage point mere feet from them.

My stomach flutters are now a full-on flock of birds. I feel like I might jump out of my own skin.

Here they come.

The first knight climbs the pyre, leaning close to untie me. Even through the armor, I can smell his cologne–a mix of vetiver and leather, the exact combination I always describe my love interests as wearing because it's my favorite. The man's done his homework. He removes his helmet and tosses it to the ground.

I take in his chiseled jaw with a hint of scruff bordering it, twinkling blue-green eyes, and wavy dark hair. He's hot. Very, very hot.

"Hello Alex," he says, his voice low and rugged enough to make my legs get all trembly.

"Hi...whoever you are," I say, swallowing a nervous, schoolgirl giggle because good grief, woman, get a hold of yourself!

"Emmett. It's nice to finally meet you." He lets the last of my restraints fall to the ground, scoops me up, and carries me off the pyre before gently setting me on the ground.

The other knights gather round us, lifting their swords to the sky in triumph.

"Cut!" Alison hollers, her face flush with excitement.

"Knights, you did an excellent job. We got what we needed in one take. Amazing. Now, please head back to the stables for your debrief and tonight's shooting schedule."

"But wait, aren't they all going to take off their helmets first?" I ask. If Emmett is any indication of how the rest of them will look, I'm a very lucky woman.

Alison laughs. "God no! That'll happen when we film them arriving at the castle tonight. This segment is just for the show's intro."

I'm disappointed, and it must show on my face, because Alison gives my shoulder a squeeze. "You've only got a few more hours to wait. And the rest of your afternoon is so full the time will fly by. Trust me, tonight will make it worth the wait. We've got something very special planned."

I make a face. "More uh, special than this?" I gesture at the pyre and village, my nerves ratcheting up again. I'm not sure I'm ready for whatever it is.

But Alison's already walking away, guiding some of the knights toward the stables.

Knight Emmett doesn't follow but instead lingers beside me. When Alison is out of sight, he lifts the visor of his helmet a bit so I can see his eyes. They're a mix of forest hues, dashes of brown, gold, and green.

"Until tonight then." He bows then, and it should be cheesy, but somehow, he makes it work, and I get that trembly-leg feeling all over again.

Damn. All I've seen are his eyes, but it's somehow enough to know he's hot, like Henry Cavill-level handsome. And I'm one hundred percent certain I made the right choice.

This show is going to bring me my happily ever after. I can feel it.

Continue Alex's search for her happily ever in *Santa's Next Chapter*, an exciting new reality series. It's going to be a wild ride of romance, mystery, and pure fun.

About the Authors

Vivi Barnes, Julia Silverwood, and Amy Christine Parker are best friends who bonded over their love of telling stories and going on adventures. They live in sunny Central Florida with their families, where inspiration is just a beach day away.